LITTLE GIRL GONE

"When is the last time you cheered out loud for a character in a novel? That's what I did as I read Drusilla Campbell's LITTLE GIRL GONE. The complex relationships between Campbell's richly drawn characters took me on a psychological roller coaster that tested my expectations, my values, and my heart. This story of tension and triumph is a perfect book club selection. Don't miss it!"

—Diane Chamberlain, bestselling author of
The Secret Life of CeeCee Wilkes

"Nobody gets to the marrow of human flaws and frailties better than Drusilla Campbell. In LITTLE GIRL GONE, you are immersed in the lives of people you think you'll never meet and come to care deeply about what happens to each of them. This is a compelling story that won't leave you alone even after you've turned the last page."

—Judy Reeves, author of *A Writer's Book of Days*

THE GOOD SISTER

"Should be on everyone's book club list."

—*Publishers Weekly*

"A novel about motherhood, sisterhood, and even child-hood...In a novel which examines the sometimes devastating effects of postpartum depression, Campbell has managed to humanize a woman whose actions appear to be those of a monster rather than a mother. Through her sister's eyes, we are able to understand and even empathize with Simone Duran, a woman who has failed as both a wife and mother."

—T. Greenwood, author of *The Hungry Season*

"Can you have sympathy for a woman who attempts to murder her children? The way Drusilla Campbell tells her story, yes, you can. Even more important, in this unflinching look at family relationships, postpartum depression, and the complex lives of the characters, especially the women in this book, you can come to understand how such an unthinkable act can happen. Make no mistake, THE GOOD SISTER is a painful story, but it is also a story that will carve away at your heart."

—Judy Reeves, author of *A Writer's Book of Days*

WILDWOOD

"The pull of family and career, the limits of friendship, and the demands of love all come to vivid life in WILDWOOD."

—Susan Vreeland, *New York Times* bestselling author of *Girl in Hyacinth Blue*

LITTLE
GIRL
GONE

LITTLE
GIRL
GONE

A NOVEL

Drusilla
Campbell

GRAND CENTRAL
PUBLISHING

NEW YORK   BOSTON

Grand Central Publishing
Hachette Book Group
237 Park Avenue
New York, NY 10017
www.HachetteBookGroup.com

Printed in the United States of America

First Edition: January 2012
10 9 8 7 6 5 4 3 2 1

Grand Central Publishing is a division of Hachette Book Group, Inc. The Grand Central Publishing name and logo is a trademark of Hachette Book Group, Inc.

Library of Congress Cataloging-in-Publication Data

Campbell, Drusilla.
  Little girl gone / Drusilla Campbell.—1st ed.
    p. cm.
  ISBN 978-0-446-53579-3
  1. Kidnapping—Fiction.   2. Missing children—Fiction.   I. Title.
  PS3603.A474L58 2012
  813'.6—dc22
                                                    2011015394

For Nikki

Acknowledgments

Family, friends, and colleagues I love and respect: in the end, these are who matter most to me. Without all of you, *Little Girl Gone* would just be a conversation in my head. I am grateful...

...for all the people at Grand Central who make it such a good company to work with: Jamie Raab; Emi Battaglia; Beth de Guzman; Jennifer Reese; Siri Silleck; Liz Connor, who takes so much time and care on my covers; and my editor, Karen Kosztolnyik.

...for my agent, Angela Rinaldi, whose support has made the difference.

...for the distraction of family dinners, birthday parties, and those insane Charger/Steeler Sundays with Isabelle and Matt and Grayson and Nikki and Addy, cupcakes in the oven, dogs running around the backyard digging up the new lawn, and the general happy chaos of real, not fictional, lives.

...for Rocky Campbell, my advisor and media sage and go-to guy for all things electronic.

ACKNOWLEDGMENTS

...for Margaret Ellen, who closed one house and opened another, schlepped and sorted, and stayed happy through the process more or less.

...for Judy Reeves, San Diego Writers Ink, and the Ladies of the Arrowhead Association, who inspired and entertained and kept me on the straight and narrow. And finally,

...for Art, the guy in the kilt, the love of my life and still my hero.

LITTLE
GIRL
GONE

Chapter 1

Madora Welles was twelve when she learned that some girls are lucky in life, others not so much. On the day her father walked into the desert, she learned that luck can run out in a single day. After that, there's no more Daddy telling the whole story of "Jack and the Beanstalk," start to finish, in one minute flat. No more laughing Mommy standing by with a stopwatch to make sure he doesn't cheat. Lucky girls did not have fathers who changed from happy to sad, easy to angry to tears in the space of an hour, locked themselves in the shed and banged on things with a hammer. No lucky girl ever had a father who walked into the desert and put a bullet in his brain.

Yuma, Arizona: the town is laid out like a grid on the desert flats. Single-story buildings, fast-food joints on every corner, dust and heat and wind, lots of military, and a pretty good baseball team. That's about it.

Madora's mother, Rachel, said Yuma killed her husband, said it was killing her too. To save herself she turned on the television, stepped into other people's stories, and got lost. For a long time she forgot to care about her daughter. Failing in school, drinking, and wading into the river of drugs that ran through the middle of Yuma, Madora was seventeen when she met Willis Brock.

Madora's best friend was Kay-Kay, a girl from a family with slightly better luck than her own. Instead of using a gun, Kay-Kay's father had been drinking himself to death for a few years when she and Madora latched onto each other like twins separated at birth. Rachel recognized trouble when she saw it come through the door chewing gum and smelling of tobacco, but Madora had stopped listening to her by then. Rachel fell asleep in front of the television, in the old La-Z-Boy lounger that still smelled like Old Spice.

Madora and Kay-Kay and a boy named Randy who knew someone who knew someone else who had a car drove south of Yuma, into the desert near the border, where they had heard there was a party house and big action. Rachel had told Madora a thousand times to stay away from the border, but in the years after her father's suicide, Madora's life was all about escape and rebellion; and the drugs and remote setting excited her. Until the bikers came she was having a good time drinking bourbon from a bottle and smoking grass, taking her social cues from Kay-Kay. Unconsciously, she copied Kay-Kay's slope-shouldered, world-wary posture, and she was careful not to smile too much or laugh too loudly. Not that there was ever much humor at parties like this; and what passed for conversation was dissing and one-upping, arguments and aimless, convoluted complaints and comparisons of this night to others, this weed to the stuff they smoked the week before.

At seventeen, Madora's thinking was neither introspective nor analytical, but she was conscious of being different from Kay-Kay and the slackers around her and of wishing she were not. She wanted to eradicate the part of herself that was like her father: a dreamer, a hoper, a wisher upon first stars. At the party that night in the desert she kept to herself the resilient romantic notions that floated in the back of her mind. Never mind the odds against it: a handsome boy would come through the door, and he would look at her the way her father once had and she would feel as she once did, like the luckiest girl in the world.

Instead the bikers came. Voices rose and the air snapped; the music got louder and the run-down old house vibrated to the bass beat.

Kay-Kay put her mouth close to Madora's ear, her breath an oily whiskey ribbon. "I'm gonna do it." It was so noisy, she had to say it twice. "Those guys, they brought crank. I'm gonna try it."

Madora had been drinking and toking all night. Kay-Kay's words didn't really sink in, but what her friend did, she wanted to do as well. "Me too."

In a room at the back of the house, they sat on the floor

opposite a bearded man with a gold front tooth who said his name was Jammer. Men and girls—long-haired and skin-head, pierced and tattooed and leather jacketed, all strangers to Madora—leaned against each other, stood or squatted with their backs to the wall. Jammer wore a black tank top so tight it cut into the muscles of his overdeveloped arms and shoulders and chest, and his hands were spotted with burn scabs. He held a six-inch pipe with a bulb at the end and played the flame of a lighter under the glass taking care not to touch it with the fire, rolling the pipe as he did.

Madora watched in fascination as the pale amber cube in the bulb dissolved. Her lip hurt and she realized she was biting down on it. *I shouldn't be here*, she thought, and looked at Kay-Kay. One sign that her friend wanted to leave and Madora would have popped to her feet in an instant. But Kay-Kay was mesmerized by the pipe in Jammer's hand. She leaned forward, watching avidly as he turned and rolled it. A drop of saliva hung suspended from her lower lip.

The others in the room passed a joint and spoke softly; occasionally Madora heard someone laugh. The door to the rest of the house was shut, but beneath her Madora felt the beat of the music. In the smoky room her eyes watered and blurred. A man crouched behind her, pressing his knees into her back. He held her shoulders and urged her to lean back.

"Relax, chicky, you're gonna love this."

Jammer held out the pipe to Madora, and Kay-Kay

elbowed her gently and grinned encouragement. Madora thought of a birthday party, the expectant moment just before the lighted cake and the singing began.

The man behind her stroked her arm, running his fingers along her shoulder and up into her hair. He whispered, "Don't be afraid. I'll take care of you."

She took the pipe between her fingers and put her lips around the tube. She started to inhale, but just as she did, the image of the birthday party came back to her, and she saw her father holding the cake; and she was six again, and no matter what, Daddy would always take care of her. Her throat closed; her hand came up and dashed the pipe onto the floor. Someone yelled and her head exploded in white light and there was no yelling or talking, no music anywhere, just a burning pain as if her head were an egg and someone had thrown it against the wall.

She struggled to her feet, fell to her knees, and stood up again. Someone grabbed her and pushed her against the wall. Hands groped at the front of her T-shirt and she flailed and tried to scream but her throat and her lungs had frozen shut. More hands grabbed her arms and dragged her across the floor; her ballerina slippers came off her feet, and her bare heels tore on the broken linoleum. A door opened and she fell forward into a wall of fresh air. Someone shoved her into a chair and she sat down hard, gagging for air.

A voice growled. "Stay with her."

Kay-Kay's voice came from far away. "Holy shit, are you all right?"

Madora's left cheek jerked as her eye blinked crazily.

"You want me to call your mom? Oh, Jesus, Madora, I can't get her to come out here."

Madora wanted to stop the twitching, but her hand couldn't find her face.

"No one's gonna stop partying to drive you home."

Her hands and feet and head were attached by strings. She bobbled like a puppet.

"Jammer said you only got a whiff. Lucky, huh? Are you listening, Mad? He says like only one in a trillion people react bad like you. It might've killed you. I can't believe how lucky you were."

Someone was stirring her brain with a wooden spoon.

"No one wants to leave yet, and anyway, Jammer says you'll feel better."

Then she was alone on the porch outside the house. A coyote padding across the yard stopped to look at her, moonlight reflected in its yellow eyes. Kay-Kay returned and sat beside her for a few moments, holding her sweating hands, and then she went back in the house.

The desert temperature dropped, and the air, cold and dry, lay over everything. The sweat dried on Madora's body and she shivered, and her teeth rattled like bones in a paper bag. She dragged her feet up onto the chair and wrapped her arms around her knees. She rested her face on her knees and tried to close her eyes, but the lids bounced as if on springs. In the house someone had turned up a CD of an old Doors recording. The keyboard riffs scored her senses and the beat got down inside her, deep. Her muscles ached with it.

Car lights streaked across the cholla and prickly pear. For a moment she was sightless, then bleary-eyed, and the figure coming toward her seemed to emerge out of water like something blessed, a holy vision. Without knowing why, she tried to rise from the chair where she'd been cowering. Her legs wobbled under her and he reached out, helping her to balance.

"Hey, little girl, you better stay down."

She saw two of him, sometimes three, floating like a mirage, but his voice was clear and strong. Under it, the pounding beat and the keyboard riffs grew fainter until they seemed to come from far out in the desert, where she knew there must be a party going on but nothing that concerned her anymore.

"Don't be afraid, little girl. Willis won't let anything bad happen to you."

Chapter 2

Five Years Later

Madora Welles rose from the living room sectional where she had spent the night and drank a cup of instant coffee, standing in the carport outside the kitchen. The cement was cool and slightly damp, and her bare feet stuck to it in a pleasant way. She ran her fingers through her light brown hair, a color her father had long ago described as mouse. Little Mouse had been one of his pet names for her. *Little Mouse, Pug* because her nose was pert, *Runt* because she was short. *Sweetheart Girl.*

How odd that her father's voice, though he had been gone ten years, still came into her mind as if he were sending messages by a circuitry available only to them.

Before six on an early summer morning, as the moon dropped below the western horizon, the sky over the Laguna Mountains was a wash of pale yellow, and the cool air smelled of sage and pepper and damp sand and stone. Rough chaparral covered the bottom and slopes of Evers Canyon, softened by the cream-colored blossoms of the chamise and the curves and hollows of the tumbled, biscuit-colored boulders. The rocks were ancient, Willis said, maybe two hundred million years old.

Madora was twenty-two years old, and two hundred million was a number so big she wasn't even sure how to write it.

From behind the Lagunas, the sun rose and kissed the head of Evers Canyon that loomed directly behind Madora's house. In the nearest town, Arroyo, and in San Diego, thirty miles west, people were just waking up, but Madora was alert as she and the dog walked across the yard and the cul-de-sac to where a weathered sign marked a trailhead into Cleveland National Forest, a vast, barren territory of mountains, rocks, and chaparral. A rock one hundred yards up the trail resembled a chair, and she often went there to sit and think and watch the land as she waited for the sun; but this morning Willis wanted her to stay near the house. She leaned back against the trail sign and swallowed the last of her coffee as she waited for the sun line to slip down from the canyon rim and melt the stiffness in her shoulders and neck. Willis said she'd feel better if she lost twenty pounds.

It was June and the weather had turned the corner, heading into full summer. The balls of sagebrush scattered across the sloping land were already brown. Soon the house would oven up and stay hot day and night until

October. Although Madora opened all the windows to lure the slightest breeze, at the dead end of Evers Canyon the trapped air did not move much. Dust settled on every surface and clung to the curtains' coarse weave. It powdered Madora's skin, got in her eyes and hair and ears; her nose was so dry it sometimes bled. June meant that July was on its way and right behind it August and September, the hottest months of the year. Fire season.

The pit bull Madora had found as a puppy pushed against her leg, wanting attention. Though Foo was only a few months old, his personality had begun to organize itself into a mixture of aggression and timidity, curiosity, loyalty, and affection. During the previous night the cries coming from the woman in the trailer behind the house seemed to frighten him. He whimpered until Madora drew him against the curve of her body where she lay on the sectional.

There had been five cabbage-sized pups in the box at the side of the road, only Foo left alive and him just barely. Brown and white and squint-eyed, he had felt in her hands like a small warm loaf of bread. Coyotes would have gotten him if Madora had not seen the box. Coyotes and hawks. Spiders and snakes. The world was full of danger. In Cleveland National Forest even the plants had spikes and thorns.

She buried the puppies in the sand along the dry stream at the back of the house and gathered stones for a cairn. She gave Foo water and then evaporated milk from an eyedropper and put a hot water bottle and a scrap of blanket in a box for him to snuggle up to. Willis said they couldn't afford a dog, but Madora convinced him otherwise, pointing out that a pit bull would be a good watchdog. He needed shots and a tag with his name: Foo. Madora wanted him to have a proper license from the county, but Willis didn't like signing forms that required his name and address.

Foo had become part of Madora's nursery of injured animals and struggling plants. But he was more than that. His companionable presence made the long days less monotonous. She talked to him about the things that mattered to her; and as he listened, his small bright eyes never left her face, as if he believed she had all the answers, if only he could figure out what the questions were.

Under the carport there were pots and planters and whiskey barrels full of zinnias and cosmos and petunias, flowers that endured the heat as long as they were watered. On a shelf made of bricks and boards, a homemade cage held a rabbit with one ear ripped by a hawk. After six weeks it still cowered at the back of the cage. In another cage, she kept a coyote pup she'd raised from skin and bones, wild and mean. She had found him on the far side of the truck trailer where the girl was.

As Madora walked back across the road, back to the house, a stranger, a hiker or a boy riding a mountain bike, would have seen a fair-skinned girl made beautiful by innocence, candid green eyes, and skin turned to gold by the sun. But almost no one ever came this far up Evers Canyon; there were much easier trails into the Cleveland.

Madora and Willis had lived in the three-room house at the end of Red Rock Road for almost four years, renting from a man they had never met who kept the rent low as long as they paid on time and asked no favors or improvements. In Madora's memory the months and seasons blurred; one summer was as hot as another, one winter as dry as the next. Country life suited her, but nature's ruthlessness was frightening. On a walk with Willis she had stepped into a spider's net cast between two trees on opposite sides of the trail. As she pulled the sticky webbing from her hair and face, a butterfly came away in her hand, its wings as dull and dry as paper. Madora wanted to destroy the web, but Willis admired the intricacy of the silken weave. He said there was a circle of life and coyotes and spiders as much as girls and butterflies were part of it.

Madora didn't believe that life was a circle. Tending her damaged animals, she saw that it was more like a canyon back, where some got trapped and only a few rescued.

In the truck trailer up on cement blocks, the girl named Linda had screamed through the small hours of the night. Willis worked as a home health care provider and before that he had been a medic in the Marine Corps. He promised that compared to fixing men torn up by IEDs and land mines, delivering a baby was nothing. But still she screamed. Willis had given her pills, but Madora guessed from the cries that they had not been sufficient to ease her labor pains. Anyone walking by could have heard the noise

12

she made, but the house was at the end of the road, almost a mile from its nearest neighbor, and the residents of Evers Canyon kept to their own business.

In the kitchen Madora followed the directions Willis had made her repeat back to him a half dozen times. She put a clean plastic tub in the sink with an old towel folded on the bottom. Another towel she folded in half and laid out on the counter beside the sink. On the other side she put a clean sponge and a bottle of lemon-colored extra-gentle bath soap and a third towel. The day before she had scoured every surface in the kitchen with Clorox, making her eyes burn and water. On her hands and knees she scrubbed the kitchen floor until she thought she would wear through the old vinyl to the gappy floorboards beneath. Afterwards she wouldn't let Willis wear his shoes indoors until he pointed out that if Foo could run in and out, he should be able to as well. Madora could not ban Foo. He would be hurt and confused. She gave him a bath and washed the floor again.

She heard Willis come around the corner of the carport, his boots crunching in the gravel. He opened the screen door and let it slam behind him. He carried a bundle in his arms, wrapped in a flannel blanket.

"Do you remember what I told you?"

She nodded, taking the baby from him.

"When you're done, put him in that nightgown thing with the cord at the bottom." Willis's black hair had come out of its ponytail and hung down thick and straight on either side of his handsome face, casting shadows and deepening the lines of exhaustion that accentuated the slant of his cheekbones. He looked like John the Baptist in a picture on the wall of the Sunday school Madora attended as a child.

In Madora's arms, the newborn was light, a feather in a balloon wrapped in tissue.

"He's so small."

"Around six pounds, I'd guess. Not bad, considering."

"How's Linda?"

"Passed out, but she'll be okay. She tore bad, so I had to give her more pills than I wanted. I stitched her, though. *No problemo*." He walked out of the tiny kitchen toward the back of the house, his voice muffled through his sweat-stained shirt as he pulled it over his head. "While I'm gone I want you to go in there and give her a good wash and change the sheets. I bought some of them female napkin things. She'll need those."

"How long will you be gone?"

He didn't answer.

The baby in Madora's arms did not feel as she remembered her baby dolls had, the snug way their rubber bottoms had rested in the curve of her arm when she was seven years old. Her grip on this shapeless mass was uncertain, and it was a relief to lay him on the towel beside the sink. She pulled back an edge of the thin blanket so she could see his face. She was sorry to think he was ugly, but it was the truth. His low forehead was covered with black hair, his

14

nose squashy, and his skin as red and scratched as if he'd been in a playground fight. She laid her index finger on his cheek and his puffy eyelids fluttered—such thick black lashes!—and opened just enough so that Madora could see that his eyes were the color of deep water.

"You had a rough time, didn't you, little guy?" Her voice appeared to startle him. He jerked his arms and legs and made Madora laugh. At the sound, his eyes widened. She smiled at him and put her face close, wanting him to see her smile, as if this might go some way toward assuring him a happy life.

Be lucky, she thought.

As Willis had instructed, she ran a few inches of warm water into the plastic tub in the sink and unwrapped the blanket from around the baby's body. She stifled a wash of disgust at the sight of his flesh painted with a sticky slime of blood and a white, almost cheesy substance. An inch of tied-off umbilicus hung from his stomach. Madora wished she knew if all babies looked this awful in the first moments of life. It would be a disaster and ruin all Willis's plans if he tried to give the baby boy to the lawyer and he was rejected. Willis was in a saving frenzy, talking about medical school and how much he needed the lawyer's twenty-five thousand in cash.

When the water touched the boy, he went rigid and yelped—a cracking huff of surprise that subsided when his chest and arms and legs submerged. After a moment, he seemed to like the water, and Madora wondered if it reminded him of the time before he was born. Did a baby in the womb feel imprisoned or safely cared for? It seemed like the older she got, the more often such crazy and unanswerable questions popped into her mind.

She poured a minute drop of liquid soap into the palm of her hand and smoothed it over his saggy mottled skin. His eyes stayed locked on hers, hardly blinking. She was not sure if he actually saw her; still his fixed, deepwater stare had an absorbing intensity and she believed that he was memorizing her. A year from now, if she saw him in a stroller in a supermarket, he would look up at her, lock eyes, and know her.

From the bathroom Madora heard the sound of shower water hitting the metal wall of the stall. Normally she didn't like it when Willis used too much water, but this morning she would not mind if he took one of his long scalding showers and drained the tank.

The slippery baby bundle rested on her forearm and she ran her fingers between each digit of his feet and hands. She lathered the thicket of black hair and felt the pulse beneath the softness at the back of his head. Willis had told her what this tender spot was called and warned her to be careful of it. She trembled with the fragility of his body, and her tears salted the warm water. Cradling his buttocks in her palm, she smoothed away the sticky residue of the birth canal, moving her fingers up under his chin and beneath his arms. From between his legs, a cloud of bubbles popped to the surface of the bath and Madora laughed.

She lifted him from the water, long and limp and skinny; and as she did he cried again, a piercing sound Madora understood immediately as surprise and cold. She quickly wrapped him in a fresh towel and held him against her heart, patting and crooning soft assurances that he would soon be warm.

No one needed to tell her how to hold him and pat him dry. The skill was born in her, an instinct. Since she held her first baby doll, she had wanted to be a mother. In high school, career day never interested her. Kay-Kay had talked about joining the army and called Madora a wuss because the idea did not appeal to her.

The water sounds from the bathroom stopped, and the shower's plastic door banged against the outside of the stall.

"We have to hurry now," she whispered, fiddling with the disposable diaper, determining front from back. "We don't want to make Willis cross, do we?" In the dry air of the June morning, his hair was a dark nimbus, floating like the tag ends of sweet dreams from before he was born. Madora slipped the cotton gown over his head and tied it at the bottom with a drawstring, enclosing his feet. The gown was blue for a boy, though they had not known what the sex of the baby would be.

It would have been dangerous to take Linda to a doctor, and so Willis had handled everything. From the perfection of this little boy, it seemed he'd been right when he said a doctor was not necessary. *All over the world women have babies without the help of doctors.*

During her five months in the trailer Linda had never spoken about the baby's father, even when Madora asked directly. Whoever he was, Madora knew he didn't deserve anything as precious as the lamb in her arms. Nor did Linda. Willis had arranged for him to be adopted through an attorney who specialized in such matters, a friend of the nephew of one of Willis's clients. The adoption attorney did not ask many questions and told Willis it would not be necessary for Linda to sign any papers. He would deliver the baby to his new parents. There would be a birth certificate with their names on it.

He would not need to be fed immediately, according to Willis, but she hoped the lawyer had made arrangements just in case. There should be another person with him to hold this small creature and prepare a bottle when he cried. A pain cut through Madora when she imagined him strapped into a cold car seat, hungry and suffering and only hours old, just new in the world and passed from hand to hand like something bought in a store.

Willis came into the kitchen wearing the Levi's she'd pressed for him and the heavy denim shirt that was as dark as the baby's eyes. He had combed back his hair and twisted it up on his head. He looked from the baby to her and smiled and lifted his soft, felt cowboy hat off a hook and put it on.

In Madora's experience even the most attractive people had imperfections—a bump on the bridge of the nose or one eyelid a little droopy—but Willis's face had no such irregularities. The two sides matched exactly, and this balance gave his face not only beauty but also an appealing serenity because there was nothing about it that needed to be adjusted. The first time she saw him, he was standing in front of her on the porch of the old house in the desert. So beautiful and calm. She thought he must be an angel.

She said, "I'm worried about him."

"The lawyer? He'll be there."

"The baby."

"I checked him over. He's fine."

"What if he gets hungry?"

"The lawyer'll take care of that. We're going to meet up in Carlsbad."

"Let me come with you."

"I'm tired, Madora. I want to get rid of this—"

"He's not a *this*. He's a boy."

Willis's expression said that he had heard enough. "Give him to me."

She pulled back, ducking her head.

"You ought to try being a little sympathetic, Madora. I've been up all night. Linda just had a baby and she's pretty knocked out, but she'll come to soon, and when she does, she'll need you."

The baby arched his back and twisted his mouth, making sucking sounds as Willis took him from Madora. She opened the screen door.

"Willis?"

He stopped under the carport and scowled at her.

She said, "I want to have a baby."

"Is that was this is all about?" His chuckle was softly derisive. "You got bit by the baby bug?"

"I'd be a good mother." She knew this. "Please?"

"Don't push me, Madora."

Chapter 3

The Great Dane truck trailer where Linda had spent almost five months of her pregnancy was eight feet wide and twenty-seven feet long. Up on blocks, the trailer had been on the property when Madora and Willis moved in. An eyesore, but too big to move.

Like many neglected rural properties, this one had for some time been a dumping ground for derelict machinery and equipment, but Madora disregarded the trash when she saw the little house. Stepping across the threshold for the first time four years ago, she had been afraid to hope that Willis would finally want to settle down, marry her, and have a family. A weight dropped from her shoulders when he said the spot suited him fine. She disregarded the cracked and bumpy orange and brown linoleum, the oven that did not work, the stained sink. These were temporary eyesores and inconveniences. All that mattered was that the gypsy months of wandering the West were over and her real life had begun. As if to prove he felt the same, Willis had taken the time to paint the house a deep, forest green and trimmed the windows in white. Working as a team all one weekend, they had dragged the rusty backhoes and graders, the carcass of a refrigerator, the flat tires and corroded tanks and coils of wire, and dumped them behind a mound of boulders, where they still lay like the skeletal remains of the property's history. The Great Dane trailer could not be moved without a tow truck, so they stippled its battered aluminum exterior in camouflage shades of gray and green and tan that blended with the sycamores and dusty cottonwoods along the dry creek bed at the back of the property.

Initially, Willis had been fascinated by the trailer, but then he forgot about it and more than three years passed. Eight months ago, he had cut a window-sized hole up high on one side and installed an air-conditioning unit and an electric generator to power it and a few lights. Madora assumed he was making a room for himself, a place to study when he went back to school.

He never mentioned Linda. He just brought her home and put her in the trailer one rainy night.

He had brought her into the kitchen, water dripping off his ankle-length plastic raincoat, his black hair plastered and shining against his head. Behind him, had stood a girl with straggly hair in frayed-out Levi's and a yellow T-shirt, hip shot out, staring down at her bare feet.

Madora remembered thinking that Linda looked like a Tinkertoy, round in the middle with sticks for arms and legs.

"She's pregnant, Willis."

"You think I'm blind?"

"You've got to take her to a doctor."

"Pregnancy isn't a disease, Madora. Besides, I'm a Marine Corps medic. I can manage a pregnancy. It's not brain surgery."

At that moment, Madora was juggling four or five thoughts at the same time, and it was hard to know what to say first. She didn't mind helping this pregnant teen with nowhere to go, and she admired Willis for his generosity and didn't want him to think she was stingy. But they were always short of money by the end of the month, and feeding one more was going to be a stretch.

"And where's she going to sleep, Willis? We've only got the one bedroom."

"I fixed up the Dane."

"The trailer? But it's freezing out there." All the blankets they owned were on Madora and Willis's bed, plus an old sleeping bag. And still they were cold at night.

"I put a mattress down and a couple of blankets and she can wear those flannel pajamas."

The ones he had given Madora. A gift of soft, blue flannel pajamas at the start of the cold weather, a surprise. She loved his occasional and unexpected bursts of generosity, and she knew it was small of her to begrudge this girl the comfort of warm pajamas.

"What's she going to eat?"

"I stopped on the way home and got a couple of burritos."

"Where'd the mattress come from? And the blankets? We don't have any extra blankets." If she asked too many questions Willis would become defensive and then angry and accusing. He would say she did not believe in him and lacked commitment to their shared life, the terms of which he set without consulting her. And that was all right. She was by nature a follower. He was smarter than she and far more worldly. But she needed to know the truth. "Did you plan this ahead, Willis?"

"I'm going to take her over to the trailer now." He opened a kitchen drawer where this and that collected and pulled out a padlock.

"What do you need that for?" *Another question.*

"She's been on the street, Madora." His tone implied Madora was a stupid girl, perhaps a little retarded. "Do I have to tell you what that means? She's probably got drugs in her system and she could start hallucinating and walk right out the door. Believe me, Madora, I know about this kind of thing. The lock's for her own good." He paused. "Get it?"

All Madora knew of the world was what she'd seen from behind Willis, on tiptoes, looking over his shoulder. What he said made perfect sense.

"She needs a hot drink," he said. "Make a thermos of tea and put a lot of sugar in it. I'll come back and get it." Before he left he smiled at Madora. "I don't want you getting wet, catching a chill. It's pretty bad out there. I'll come back for the tea. Don't trouble yourself."

"Just tell me first. Did you plan this out ahead of time?"

He had never hit her, never even threatened her, but sometimes Madora felt the possibility of violence flow between them like an electric current.

"I'll tell you the truth, and will you then be satisfied or will I have to keep explaining myself?" He sighed like a porter putting down his load after a long day. "I'm not going to lie, Madora, about how much this hurts me, your doubt. After all we've been through and all we've been to each other, you still don't trust me. When the person I love most in the world doesn't trust me or believe in me, do you know the pain, Madora? Trust and love, they're almost the same thing. If you don't trust me, it means you don't love me. You *can't* love me."

The wind rose, whining up Evers Canyon and moaning in the eaves of the house, driving the rain hard against the windows. A draft came in at the floorboards and ran like a spider up the back of Madora's leg. Along the creek somewhere a branch broke off a cottonwood, sounding like a pistol crack.

Willis sat, resting his elbows on his knees. "Maybe I should have told you before, but it happened too fast. I didn't do a lot of thinking or planning."

And yet he had a mattress and blankets in the trailer, waiting. Madora let the thought slide away, out of her mind forever.

"I admit, I've been watching Linda for a couple of days. Every time I went into Arroyo she'd be standing by the long stoplight near the freeway, holding up this feeble little sign saying she's pregnant and hungry, and today when I saw her, in the pouring rain, I knew I had to bring her home." His dark eyes looked into Madora's, and she read in his expression a deep and inexpressible longing to be understood. "And I knew—I *thought* I knew—you'd want to help her too. I guess I just totally misunderstood." He stood up. "If you really want me to, Madora, I'll take her back to town. But is it okay if she eats? First? She needs *something*."

Awash with shame, Madora laid her hand against his cheek. The goodness of the man brought tears into her eyes. "You're right; you did the right thing. We'll make the trailer comfortable for her." Madora would not think about the mattress and blankets laid out in advance or consider the implications of the padlock. "You go along and get her settled. When you come back I'll have her tea ready."

And the flannel pajamas.

Chapter 4

A few miles away, in the town of Arroyo, Django Jones dreamed of his mother. She was wearing her favorite red dress with the pleats that flipped out around her knees, and her hair shimmered with lights of silver, copper, and gold. Django had a green garden hose in his hand and he was spraying her and she was laughing. Her laugh was like light, like rain, like water splashing over rocks.

The room in which he awoke—it was the third morning now—was a quarter the size of his bedroom at home, and he could tell from the boxes shoved into the closet and corners that it had been a kind of utility room before his arrival. Across the room on a beat-up old dining room table, Django's backpack reminded him that he was going to school that day whether he wanted to or not. He tried to imagine Arroyo Elementary School, K through eight, and he knew he wasn't going to like it.

He fished his laptop off the floor beside the bed, powered on, and checked the time against the clock on the table. He had half an hour before he needed to get up. As he logged on, his hands trembled with hope.

First he Googled *Jacky Jones*, his father, and there were many new entries: bios and obits and memorials, a lot of people writing about how they knew him when he was the hottest guitarist out of England in the early seventies. He scanned these quickly. A woman wrote about having sex with him after a concert and making a plaster cast of his penis.

Gross.

He went to Facebook and did a quick scroll, not paying much attention to the entries, looking for a clue that his parents were alive. He was sure they would find a way to send him a message. He went to his e-mail, saw nothing interesting. If the story of the accident was part of a top secret government thing, a message from his parents verifying this would be in code, of course. Django was smart; he would figure it out. Or, if they were being held for ransom, the note would come by mail or maybe a telephone call. Django's father was super rich and famous, and his half brother, Huck, was probably a billionaire. The kidnappers would want a lot of money, but Django had made up his mind that he wouldn't call the FBI when he heard from them. The feds would tell him to be cagey, not to pay the demand, but he was willing to pay any amount to rescue his mother and father.

There was nada from his homies on Facebook or e-mail or Twitter despite his having written them a couple of times every day since he got to his aunt's house. Plus texting and tweeting and leaving messages on their cells. He looked up at the ceiling and opened his eyes wide to dry up the tears he felt coming. He blinked hard but it didn't help. He was twelve and everyone said his parents were dead so it was normal to cry; but Django had never wanted to be normal.

Jacky and Caro Jones had driven to Reno over the Memorial Day weekend because Jacky wanted to try out his new black Ferrari on Interstate 395, the sweeping stretches of highway and long sight lines north of Bishop. If they had left Reno a half hour later or stopped in Bishop for coffee, if they'd gotten sleepy and decided to risk the bedbugs in a roadside motel. If they hadn't been driving back to Beverly Hills late Monday night along the dark, deserted highway through the Rand Mountains, the hilly, twisty section between Johannesburg and Randsburg. If a drunk in a pickup had not shot out of an unmarked side road: no lights, ninety miles an hour.

Django wanted to jam a pencil through his ear, kill his imagination and obliterate the screams and the sound of metal slamming into metal.

The morning after the accident when Django came into the kitchen, rubbing the sleep out of his eyes, it had not seemed unusual to see his father's manager, Ira, leaning against the kitchen counter, drinking coffee. Ira had been his father's manager since the seventies, and they often had morning meetings at the house in Beverly Hills.

It was Ira who had broken the news and swore to

Django that his parents had not suffered. Death had come instantly, he said. The news charred Django like a sapling struck by lightning. It burned a hollow space inside him that now, two weeks later, he knew nothing would ever fill. That first morning, Mrs. Hancock, the housekeeper, put her arms around him, and they sat beside each other on the double chair on the kitchen porch. As Django recalled— his memory of those first days had big holes in it—they sat there all day as the sun moved across the wide planks of the whitewashed floor; but it couldn't have been that long because his parent's lawyer came, Mr. Guerin; and he and Ira closed themselves in Jacky's office. While they talked Django went outside and sat by the swimming pool. His father said that exercise was the best thing when a person was upset so he tried to swim laps, but he only got to the middle of the pool before he couldn't be bothered. He lay on his back and floated, staring up at the gray sky. Typical June gloom.

The truth was, when Ira told him his parents were dead, Django had not felt much of anything except stunned. And later, when he started to think about what *automobile accident* and *dead* really meant—what Ira and Mr. Guerin would call *the long-term ramifications*—he mostly felt scared because no one seemed to know what was going to happen to him. He thought he was probably too rich to go to an orphanage, but he had seen the musical *Oliver!* when the senior students at Beverly Country Day presented it at Christmas. After the performance he had asked his mother what gruel was and she said oatmeal, and his father said it was oatmeal mixed with sand and lint and dirt and dog hair swept up off the floor. Django knew he would never have to eat anything so awful, but he remembered the song the orphans sang about *food, glorious food* and it looped through his brain. He went to sleep thinking/singing it and woke up with it still going round and round.

The first day was the longest day in the history of the world. Then, near dinnertime, Huck, his older half brother, turboed through the front door with his bodyguard behind him, talking fast like always. Then Django heard the bawling sounds come out of his mouth and there was no way he could stop them. Huck was almost thirty, the son of Django's father by his first marriage. He had his San Francisco Giants baseball hat on backwards, and he was crying too.

Time and memory got tricky again after that. Mrs. Hancock packed a bag for him and he loaded his laptop and iPad into his backpack. He hunted all over for his phone, and then he found it, in plain sight, right where it was supposed to be. Ira had driven them to a small airport in the valley where Huck's plane was parked. Ira told Django, "Your dad was a great guy and you're his boy all the way." That was when Ira's saggy-baggy face drooped even further and he began crying; and seeing an old guy cry embarrassed Django, but he cried too. Junior, one of the buffed-up bodyguards who always traveled with Huck, picked Django up and carried him over his shoulder and onto the plane like he was two years old.

31

The chopper they took from the San Jose airport landed on the helipad in Huck's backyard. Huck disappeared into his office, and Junior handed Django over to a girl who said she was his brother's personal assistant. Time passed and Django ate a lot and watched television and played video games, and every day people came and went and looked at him and there were more phone calls and quiet voices behind closed doors.

Huck's girlfriend, Cassandra, walked around the house in a bikini, and when she hugged him her boobs weren't soft like they looked. Django smelled marijuana in her hair, same as in his mother's after a party. Cassandra brought him cocoa and popcorn and cinnamon toast and asked him how he felt, trying to be motherly.

Once, when they were playing gin rummy, he asked her, "Are you going to marry my brother?" He had been thinking about what it would be like to live in this house with her until he grew up.

She thought he was joking. "My parents'll kill me if I don't finish college."

Huck had given Django some games his company was developing and asked him to test them out, but Django couldn't take the task seriously. So what if his score went backwards and his avatar got pounded? In real life—every minute—the living, breathing Django was fighting to outrun his misery and the awful sounds and images in his head.

He thought he was going to stay with Huck; but after

almost two weeks and lots more murmuring behind closed doors, there was another flight in a small plane, only this time Huck stayed behind because of business. Junior kept Django company and turned him over to Ira and Mr. Guerin at Montgomery Field in San Diego. They drove for an hour to his aunt Robin's house in a town called Arroyo.

Mr. Guerin told him he was going to live in Arroyo now. "Your mother's sister, your aunt Robin, will be your guardian."

"But I don't even know her. I never met her in my life."

"I know, Django, I know. But your parents wanted it this way. They rewrote their wills last year for that particular reason."

"Does she have kids?"

"No. She's never been married. She's a spinster."

Old maid, Django thought. Was anyone, ever, going to tell him some good news?

"I want to stay with Huck."

"I'm sorry, Django," Mr. Guerin said, blinking hard. "I'm terribly sorry."

Not only were Django's mom and dad gone forever; the Django who lived in Beverly Hills was gone too. The person who woke up in his aunt Robin's house looked like Django Jones—same straight blond hair and brown eyes, five feet four inches tall, one hundred and ten pounds—but he was just a shadow.

He had been with Aunt Robin since Tuesday. Today was Thursday, which was a stupid-ass day to start going to a new school, but nobody had asked him his opinion. Around here he just got told.

His aunt had been kind to him, but she was a chilly kind of person, a perpetual-motion robot who never stopped moving for long enough to really look at him. She was constantly off to do something or go somewhere. She was an accountant with a lot of clients. Around the house she was always cleaning and cooking and sorting through papers and drawers and cupboards, carrying laundry up and down stairs and ironing. Robin had a vegetable garden big enough to feed every kid at Beverly Country Day, and when she wasn't working in the house she was outside in a big hat pulling weeds and watering each plant by hand to conserve H_2O.

No matter what she was doing, there was a subzero negative force field around her like the one that protected Jett Jones when he liberated the children held captive on Planet Chiron in the second *Jett Jones Boy of the Future* novel.

At BCD Django had a great sixth-grade teacher, Mr. Cody, who told him he should write a science fiction novel because he needed somewhere constructive to put his imagination before it got him into trouble. At first Django thought it would be hard to make up a story with a plot and outer-space scenery, but pretty soon he got the hang of it. His father had started calling him Mr. Spielberg *Sir* and bought him a new laptop.

Django had called his teacher from Huck's, but he realized when Mr. Cody's voice got thick and gravelly that his call had upset him. It was the same when he phoned his homies, Lenny and Roid. They talked, but it was freaky, not like it had been.

Django put aside his laptop and closed his eyes.

Life would not be so demented if his friends would just *communicate*.

Django had never had a lot of friends, but Lenny and Roid were a couple of weirdos like him and they were tight. They were math geniuses, but Django was the more creative type, although he aced math and science. Django and his friends were a posse, Mr. Cody said. Something else he said: "*Give you dudes time, you're gonna rule the world.*" Django wondered if this was still true, now that everything in the world had changed.

Django's mom said he was like the empath on *Star Trek*. Often he could sense what people thought and felt just by watching and listening for the words under their words, the words they didn't say. In this way, he knew without being told that Aunt Robin was sending him to school to get rid of him for a few hours.

Django got out of bed and stood at the window. In whichever direction he looked he saw hills and scrub and rocks. Except for the radio he heard playing down in the kitchen, the quiet was so intense it made him think of church and funerals and death.

A memorial service had been held at Forest Lawn. A *grown-up kind of thing*. Django didn't attend but he read about it online and knew that hundreds of famous people were there, including all the members of his dad's old band. Huck faxed Django articles from the *Los Angeles Times* and *Variety*, and he said there was going to be a story in *Rolling Stone*. Someone would call him for an interview but he didn't have to talk if he didn't want to. All the articles said the same thing, that Jacky Jones was one of the great rock guitarists and composers of the twentieth century. There had been music and speeches at the funeral. Paparazzi. Django was glad to stay away. He didn't want to be photographed and stared at. The poor little orphan kid.

He dropped to the floor and lay on his back, staring at the cracks in the ceiling, trying not to remember the time *before*. After a while he rolled onto his stomach and began, slowly, to hit his forehead against the wood. He would keep it up until something good happened.

Chapter 5

Willis left to deliver the baby to the attorney, and Madora walked across the dusty yard back to the trailer. On top of a plastic basket full of clean sheets, blankets, and towels, she carried a thermos of chicken noodle soup. At the curbside door of the trailer she put the basket down and returned to the house for soap and a bucket of warm water. Back and forth, Foo tagged along behind her, his stubby tail aquiver with interest. The curbside door was padlocked and Madora's hands were sweaty with frustration before she got the combination right; it broke apart, and she opened the narrow door to a rush of close, unpleasant air. She jammed the door wide with a stick and brought everything in and set it on the table where Linda ate her meals. Foo watched outside, longing to be invited in, though he never had been.

Madora looked at the girl in the bed, at the mess of bloody sheets and towels Willis had left to be cleaned up. She had an impulse to turn around and walk out the door, lock up, and pretend there had never been a girl named Linda, no baby boy with deepwater blue eyes.

Madora had begged Willis to take Linda to the hospital, reminding him that she was only sixteen, a teenager with slim hips and a flat, boyish figure; but he had been confident, even cocky, about how easy it would be to deliver the baby in the trailer. To everything she said, he had the same reply: *"Childbirth is easy. If it was hard, the human race would have died out by now."*

Perfectly still, Linda rested on her side facing the interior side of the trailer's roll-up door. Her pale hair, darkened by sweat, lay against her neck and shoulders as if painted on. For a moment, Madora wondered if Willis had taken the baby and left her with a dead girl.

"Linda? You okay?" She was afraid to touch her.

Linda turned her head on the pillow. Purple shadows encircled her eyes, making her milk-white face look almost clownish. A pulse ticked in one lid of her half-shut eyes, rimmed red-orange. She tried to speak, but her words were barely discernable, a groggy, undifferentiated burr. It didn't matter what she meant to say. Madora took the meaning. The girl's pain and grief and fear, her shame, and even her rage came into Madora's consciousness like the shock of a gunshot fired close to her head. She dropped to her knees beside the bed, trembling, and spoke without thinking.

"He's beautiful."

"A . . . boy?"

"Oh, God, Linda, I'm so sorry." Willis had not even shown her the child. "He should have..."

Madora stopped herself from saying more. It felt dangerous to criticize Willis.

Linda gripped Madora's wrist, digging her bitten nails between the tendons.

"It's too late." Madora shook her head. "He's gone. Willis took him an hour ago."

Linda's eyes widened, as if it wasn't enough to hear the words; she needed more light to see the truth on Madora's face.

"I couldn't stop him." And she had not tried because she believed that the baby was better off with the lawyer's clients than with Linda, a homeless girl, a panhandler.

Madora wouldn't bother washing the sheets, just bundle them and put them in the trash; and if Willis said that was wasteful, he could try himself to get the blood out. She imagined how it would feel to speak so boldly to him. Then stopped herself. Even imagining was dangerous, for she might become so comfortable in her own opinions that one day she would forget and speak them aloud.

"I hurt..."

"You'll be okay. When Willis gets back he'll give you some more pain meds. And then you just have to heal."

Linda dug into her wrist again. "Shower..."

Linda was never supposed to leave the trailer without Willis. He told Madora that a pregnant girl needed exercise, so he occasionally took Linda for walks up to the ridge overlooking Evers Canyon. Sometimes they even went for drives: Madora behind the wheel of the big Chevy Tahoe; and Linda, blindfolded for the first ten or fifteen miles, leaning against Willis in the backseat, her arm through his and her head on his shoulder. Willis toyed with Linda's fair hair, twisting it around his index finger. Seeing them paired this way, Madora felt a stab of jealousy, though she knew there was nothing sexual between them. The single time she had let jealousy get the better of her good sense and mentioned sex, Willis was appalled and withdrew from her as if she had struck him. Later, when he could talk about his feelings, he told Madora that he was attached to Linda as a brother would be, and she believed him.

On the hikes and car trips that were Linda's reward for being cooperative, she only once made trouble.

They had driven over the mountains into the Anza-Borrego Desert to see the wildflowers that were bountiful after a wet winter and spring. Near the poppy preserve they had turned off the road and driven a few hundred feet to a roundabout where there were no other cars. Where a trail followed a wash, acres of orange-gold poppies bloomed on either side, interrupted here and there by pools of blue lupine. The air buzzed with the business of bees. Madora had thought for an instant of her father and the care with which he and Rachel had tended the gardens behind the house in Yuma, vegetables in the middle and flowers on all four sides. Lost for a moment in her memory, she had relaxed her grip on Linda's hand; and when she did, the girl broke away from her and ran back toward the road, yelling for help, though the desert was as empty as a scoured pan. She was seven months pregnant then and unsteady on her feet, a toddler easy to catch; and Willis had laughed at her clumsy effort and let her get as far as the road before he ambled after her. But back in the car he was ominously silent as he bound her feet and hands with plastic zip ties.

"I'm not an unkind man, Linda." In the rearview mirror Madora saw his dark eyes, drooping with grief. "I thought you'd like a little trip, a chance to see something beautiful. I guess I was wrong. I guess I don't know you at all, Linda."

Through the Tahoe's tinted windows he stared out at the barren mountains as Madora drove up the Montezuma Grade.

"I took you off the streets. You were pregnant, hungry—"

Madora saw such pain and disappointment in his expression that she almost stopped the car. She wanted to slap Linda silly for making this good man unhappy, for being too stupid to realize that without him she would be lying dead somewhere.

Although it was against Willis's rules, Madora knew it would be safe to take Linda into the house for a shower. She was too weak to run away. Willis had said he'd be working an extra shift at Shady Hills Retirement Home when he finished his business with the attorney and not to expect him before six or seven that night.

Madora handed her a clean sheet. "Wrap this around yourself and then stand next to me. I'll help you walk." She folded a cotton dish towel and tied it as a blindfold.

By the time they reached the house, Linda was bleeding. Maybe from inside, maybe the stitches. Madora didn't know about such things. A trail of blood followed them into the bathroom.

"Stand in the shower, lean against the side, but don't turn on the water."

It might not be safe for her to shower if she was bleeding. Possibly she shouldn't even be standing.

"You're not going to pass out, are you? I can't carry you back to the trailer, and if Willis—"

"I . . . can . . . Okay."

Once upon a time in another life Madora had fallen out of a tree and torn a gash in her forearm. A doctor with a tiny anchor tattooed between his index and middle fingers had stitched it up and told her to keep it dry. That night her mother had covered it with a plastic bag so she could take a shower. A plastic bag didn't seem feasible under the circumstances, but Linda had to be cleaned up; Madora knew that. And the stitches should probably be kept dry. She was in the realm of guesswork now, going on instinct enhanced by her desire—her need—to help Linda because she owed it to the baby to care for his mother. She felt connected to the girl now, as if through the boy they were related.

She ran back to the trailer and got one of the sanitary napkins Willis had left there. In the kitchen she tore a clean plastic bag from a roll and cut two long strips about ten inches wide, not an easy thing to do until she figured out a way to pull the plastic against the sharp edge of the scissors. In the bathroom Linda stood in the shower stall, resting her forehead against one metal side. Madora handed her the napkin.

"Put this between your legs," she said and then helped Linda cover the pad with the plastic strip and tie it to another strip that went around her waist. "Now put your hand over the pad and don't let it move. You gotta keep the stitches dry."

Showering was a slow process, turning the water on and off, filling the bucket, gently soaping the girl's long legs and rinsing away the blood and sweat and other fluids from her thighs, sponging beneath her arms and under her small breasts.

"Can you bend over a little? I'll wash your hair."

Linda was fair-haired but her baby was dark. His hair might fall out and grow back blond. Somewhere Madora had learned this often happened. His new parents might not want a blond baby. They would be disappointed. Her stomach tightened. She could not bear that his new parents—whoever they were—would be anything but thrilled by him. She wanted them to love him in the way she wanted to be loved herself. Completely, without qualifications, forever and ever.

She dried Linda carefully and gave her another napkin to stanch the blood and a pair of her own panties, which hung on the girl like bloomers. She hoped the stitches were still good, prayed the bleeding would not go on and on. She could clean up the blood on the floor and shower stall, but

Willis would be suspicious if he saw torn stitches. He would guess that Linda had been out of the trailer. She hadn't seen much, just the inside of the shower. Not enough to identify where she was being held.

That evening while Willis showered and changed, Madora stood at the stove stirring the Dennison's chili, listening to the drum of water against the sides of the shower, dreading that Willis would see a drop of blood she'd missed or a long silver-blond hair caught in the drain. The shower sounds stopped and she heard the whir of the hair dryer. A few minutes later Willis came into the kitchen wearing a pale blue shirt that looked beautiful against his olive skin. He wore his hair long and loose, held back by a bandana around his forehead. After five years, his beauty still struck her as hard as it had that first night. He was a buzz-cut Marine back then, a Marine medic she mistook for her guardian angel. When he took her hand, she had asked him, *"Did Daddy send you?"* And he answered that he had, though later he said it didn't happen that way.

"You were so out of it, Madora. You couldn't put two words together."

"I like that shirt," she said, handing him a beer from the refrigerator. She waited for him to tell her where he'd bought it, but he didn't want to talk, and as always, she took her cues from him. She laid a spoon and paper napkin on a plastic mat, a souvenir of Arizona with a photograph of a lightning storm over the Grand Canyon. He sat down and crumbled a handful of saltine crackers into the chili bowl.

"Some avocado or something'd be nice here. You got any cheese?"

"We're out of everything. I can go to the market tonight." There was a used-book store in Arroyo that stayed open until ten. On the rare occasions when she went into town alone, she liked to stop there and browse through old magazines; but it had been many weeks since Willis let her use the car alone, and she was not sure how to approach the subject with him.

He said, "I'll bring stuff home tomorrow. Make me a list but not too long. I'm running short."

"Did the lawyer pay you?"

"You think I drove all the way to Carlsbad for my health?"

She ducked her head.

"I'm going to medical school. You forget that? It's going to cost plenty. We need to save every penny."

"I know that, Willis."

"Sure you do. You're a good girl, Madora." He pushed his chair back and pulled her down onto his lap. "You took care of things for me. I knew I could trust you."

She laid her head against his shoulder and inhaled the musky scent of his aftershave.

"I couldn't get along without you, Madora. You know that, don't you? You're like the air I breathe."

The scent and the caress of his voice spread a soft warmth through her.

"Let's go in the other room, okay?" He lifted her into

45

his arms. She waited for him to say something about the weight she'd gained, but he held her as easily as he would a child. "I don't think I can go another minute without a piece of you, little girl."

"What about—?"

"Her? Forget about her. That one's not going anywhere."

It was almost midnight when Madora slipped from bed and pulled on a cotton shift. Holding her sandals, she closed the bedroom door against the sound of Willis's soft snores and went into the kitchen. As she passed through the living room, Foo jumped off the couch and romped toward her, one ear flopping lopsidedly, his backend twisting in anticipation of his delayed dinner. Madora poured kibble into his bowl and put it down for him. She turned on the carport light and went outside to check on the animals in the menagerie. When she reached in to give the hawk-shocked rabbit a handful of pellets, the terrorized creature cringed against the far end of the cage.

She walked behind the house and let herself into the trailer. Foo obediently lay on the ground by the cinder-block steps. The interior of the trailer was inky, and Madora used a flashlight to see her way to Linda's bedside.

The girl lay on her back, her clean hair tangled on the pillow. Sleeping soundly thanks to the pills Willis had given her when he got home from work. Faint lines etched her forehead, and Madora was touched by a wistful sadness. A girl of sixteen should have a silky, unfurrowed brow. As she slept, she seemed to chew on something and dreams danced beneath her swollen eyelids. Imagining that she dreamed of pain and of the baby she had never seen, Madora's sorrow grew to an ache that spread through her body.

Poor unlucky girl. Madora knew what it meant to be young and lost, frightened of everything and pretending to fear nothing.

She filled a plastic water bottle from the jug on the table and placed it where Linda could reach it. She locked the trailer again and walked back to the house, meaning to return to bed; but she was wide-awake and taut with emotion. At such a time she would have liked to have a TV, but theirs had stopped working months ago; and though Willis said he would fix it or buy a new one, he did not like to be reminded. A radio would have been company, but reception at the head of Evers Canyon was all static.

The night was long, the day ahead even longer.

She looked in on Willis. He slept soundly, needing his sleep more than she did. He had another full day ahead of him, a few hours at Shady Hills Retirement and then visits to the private clients who doted on him and told him he had a healer's touch and should be a doctor, not simply a home care provider.

The house smelled of the day's heat and chili and dog. She couldn't draw a full breath and went back outside. Overhead, the moon was only a sliver; but far from city lights, stars illuminated the landscape enough to see by.

Madora walked around the front of the house and leaned against the Tahoe, thinking of nothing much. Her mind was empty, a bucket under a spigot waiting to be filled.

Red Rock Road came to a dead end marked by a pair of posts and a reflecting sign of a vehicle with a red line drawn through it. Starlight dusted the miles of wilderness that lay beyond, turning rock and soil and scrub to pewter. Madora made a soft kissing sound, and Foo followed her up the trail to the rock that water and erosion had carved a seat in. Standing on his hind legs, Foo pestered to be lifted, and she arranged herself so she could hold him on her lap.

Behind the trailer, an owl lifted out of a sycamore near the creek and cast a shadow along the trail as it flew silently into a scrub oak near Madora. The night was full of hunters.

Linda was sixteen, younger than Madora had been when Willis rescued her. She was seventeen when she left Yuma with him; and if he was sometimes strange, if there were parts of him as tightly padlocked as the trailer, she accepted these things because his quirks and eccentricities were the price she paid for being loved and for being sure that at the end of the day he would always come home to her. He needed her as much as she did him; he had made that clear on a day she tried not to remember but could not forget.

In a motel in Yreka, he sat on the edge of the bed and pressed a pistol against his ear, a pistol she did not know he owned. There had been a job he wanted, orderly in a hospital, good pay and more responsibility than an aide; but something went wrong and he got drunk and came home raving and crying. He made her swear she would never leave him, and she had done so willingly. How could he doubt her? He said he'd die without her; without her he wouldn't want to live. And in response she said that she was nothing without him either. He had rescued her.

Since that night nothing had changed until today when she held Linda's small boy, and they looked into each other's eyes. She had seen all that he was meant to be and do, the wealth of opportunities that lay before him; and he had looked into her heart brimming with love and known her in a way no one else ever had, not even Willis. There had been a click of recognition between them; and because of it, she was different than she had been twenty-four hours ago.

Chapter 6

Django finally dragged himself up off the floor, dressed for school, and went downstairs to the kitchen, where Aunt Robin ate meals so she could use the dining room as her office.

"I didn't know what you usually ate before school," she said, sounding nervous. "Eggs? Or I could make pancakes." She peered into a cupboard next to the refrigerator. "Oops, sorry, no pancake mix."

Eggs. Pancakes. He didn't care.

She broke three brown eggs into a bowl and beat them with a fork. "I'll drive you this morning, but you'll have to come home on the school bus. One of the home health care providers from Shady Hills is meeting me here to talk about taking care of Grannie after her back surgery."

Django had never met his grandmother before yesterday. His mother had almost never mentioned her.

"How come we never see her?" He was seven or eight when he asked the question. His friends often talked

about visiting grandmothers and grandfathers and aunts and cousins. These proofs of an extended family had been absent from Django's life.

"We didn't get along."

"How come?"

She tapped her index finger on the tip of her nose and he knew she was deciding to tell him the truth or not.

"Doesn't matter, Django, and it's way too complicated to talk about on a hot day. Ask me again in the wintertime."

But he forgot.

Aunt Robin served his eggs, and as he ate, he watched her wiping down the counter and putting the timer, the salt and pepper shakers, and a carafe of olive oil in a straight line along the top of the stove. She had a bookcase full of cookbooks. The only thing Django's mother ever cooked was pasta and grilled cheese sandwiches. The rest of the time they ate in restaurants or either Mrs. Hancock or someone else—a caterer or a hired chef who made great food with low calories—fixed their meals. In the house where Django had grown up, the kitchen was large and brightly lit, shiny with stainless steel. Aunt Robin's was dinky and dark and the appliances did not match. There was one window over the sink and old-fashioned track lights overhead. If Django had not known Robin Howard was his aunt, he never would have guessed it. She was like the kitchen. Something about her made him think of tight corners and not enough air. She wore her shoulder-length brown hair pulled back and tied with a black velvet bow, old-fashioned and boring. His mother had favored earrings that swung a little when she moved her head and sparkled in the light as her eyes did. He looked at his aunt's earlobes and saw that they were not pierced. No rings on her fingers or bracelets.

"Don't you ever wear jewelry?" he asked. "Your ears aren't pierced."

"Well, they used to be but they closed over." She fingered her earlobe. "I've got a box full of earrings I never wear."

"How come?" Django could not believe he was talking about earrings!

"Not my style, I guess." She rinsed his plate and put it in the dishwasher.

"My mom had three hundred and ten pairs. I counted 'em once."

His aunt nodded, some opinion apparently confirmed.

"Sometimes she'd get the Monopoly money and we'd play store with them." He had been a little kid then, just six or seven.

"Hurry now. I've got a busy day."

If he told her his mother had three heads and pointed ears, would she pay attention to him?

"How come I have to go to school? I won't know anybody, and besides, it's June already. No one learns anything this close to vacation."

"I have things to do, Django. I can't leave you here in the house alone."

"Why not? I'm twelve years old."

She smiled a little, and for a second he saw his mother in his aunt's expression, and inside him something began to tear apart, a slow ripping pain in his chest.

"I don't need a babysitter." He managed to get the words out, although he was coming apart inside.

"I think I should be the judge of that, Django. Your mother was smoking in the toolshed behind the house when she was your age."

"I don't smoke."

"She almost burned the place down. If you're anything like her, you're better off in school, where someone can keep an eye on you."

Django stood up and pushed his chair into the table. The suggestion that he might be dumb enough to smoke had offended him; and even though he would have liked to know more about what happened to his mother on that occasion, he wanted to be anywhere but in the kitchen with his aunt. Even school in Arroyo would be better than this.

She touched his shoulder, stopping him. "I'm sorry, Django. That sounded mean, didn't it? Really, I didn't mean to be unkind." She turned away, adding, "You'll just have to be patient with me."

Robin turned on the car radio to discourage conversation with her nephew. Though what she and Django would talk about, she had no idea. All they had in common was Caro, and barely that.

53

After graduating from San Diego State, Robin never had any doubt about what she wanted; and at that time, almost twenty years earlier, Arroyo was a perfect fit. It had been a small town on the move with a forward-looking city council and a town plan that assured her there would always be plenty of affluent residents in need of a good accountant. Like most things Robin did, the move was a measured decision based on research and facts. At the time, her mother still lived in Morro Bay, where she and Caro had grown up, and for a time she had thought she should go back there. But in the end, climate made the decision for her. Arroyo was inland, thirty miles from San Diego, and its warm, dry climate agreed with her.

Caro had always wanted something that was *out there*, and right after high school she went looking for it while Robin put down roots in Arroyo and established her business. Caro and Jacky married on a beach somewhere in Australia and, of course, Robin was invited; but it was coming up on tax season and not a good time for her to be away. She sent her regrets and a small gift. She had no idea what to give a couple whose wedding was written up in *People* magazine.

Sometimes she wished she had rearranged her schedule and gone to Australia. Maybe then she and Caro would have kept their relationship alive. She might have met the man of her dreams in Australia. Maybe, but not likely. There had been men, some lovers, but no one she wanted to spend her life with. She had stopped looking years ago, stopped hoping too. She was resigned to her single life and contented in it. And why wouldn't she be, when she had challenging and absorbing work, enough money, and a small circle of good friends? Her life was good. She didn't let herself wonder why she and Caro had stopped being true sisters. It was something she would never understand. Caro had taken her secrets to the grave.

As she drove Django to school that morning, Robin did a mental scan of the busy day ahead. As an accountant she had several clients, including a firm of lawyers, Conway, Carroll, and Hyde, she would be visiting that morning. For some reason CC&H could not keep a bookkeeper more than a few months, and as a result their accounts were always a jumble. Her ability to make sense of them impressed the partners. They were opening a branch in Tampa and had asked her to go there for six months to organize the office. They didn't seem to care that she was an accountant and what they needed was an office manager. Mr. Conway, the senior partner, insisted she was perfect for the job. She insisted right back that she was not, but he told her not to make a rash decision. *"Think about it, think about it."* Well, she had thought about it for the last month and was no closer to saying she would go.

After a few hours with the lawyers' accounts, she would run some personal errands and then spend the rest of the day in the office at Shady Hills Retirement Home, which was one of several retirement facilities in Southern California for which she kept the corporate books from her office at Shady Hills. She had to be home by three to interview the home health care provider, Willis Brock.

"What do you like to eat for dinner?" she asked Django. He murmured something that sounded like *whatever*, which was one of the obnoxious responses her friends with teenagers complained about. But Django wasn't obnoxious. Robin had little experience with children, but she knew sweetness when she met it. And confusion and sorrow, such deep sorrow that if it were a lake it would be bottomless. "Shall I get pizza?"

"I'm not hungry."

"Well, of course not. You just had breakfast. But you'll want dinner, I know."

He sighed and slumped deeper in the car seat.

She almost stopped the car right then—her impulse to comfort Django was that strong. But as quickly as it came to her, it passed with the assumption that he would not want her comfort. If she tried to hug him he would probably push her away and then they would both be embarrassed. Pausing at a stoplight, she lifted her hands from the steering wheel and saw that they had left moist smudge marks on the dark plastic.

One good thing about Django's appearance in her life was that the lawyers at CC&H would stop pestering her to go to Tampa. They were family men and would understand that she could not traipse across the country with a grieving twelve-year-old orphan in tow.

The three signal lights on Arroyo's main street were out

of synch. She had to stop at every one. At a few minutes before eight in the morning, the little town was just waking up. The Starbucks across from the Catholic church was already crowded, but in the next block most of the shops were still dark.

Django sat slumped, looking out the window. At the back his hair was a tangled mess. She had not realized that twelve-year-old boys had to be reminded to use a comb. He probably hadn't brushed his teeth either.

"It's going to seem pretty quiet in Arroyo. After living in Beverly Hills." He grunted something. "I beg your pardon, Django? You'll have to speak up so I can hear you." She heard herself sounding prissy, like the maiden aunt she was. "Never mind. Maybe I need a hearing aid." It was a joke but he did not laugh.

She thought about the Tampa job and wanted to be there or anywhere far from this sad, lost boy for whom she could not say or do anything right.

Tampa. She wished Mr. Conway would stop nagging her.

A month earlier Robin and her mother had been having lunch in La Jolla, at a new restaurant Robin had read about online. Over a shared crème brûlée, she had mentioned the Tampa offer. Her mother jumped on the idea as if she'd won the lottery. Robin's cool response prompted her to ask if she was afraid to leave Arroyo. Robin laughed at that, of course. There were many things she knew she would not like about Florida—humidity and reptiles were two that figured prominently—but it was the inconvenience that put her off going, the disruption of her comfortable and efficient routine. All very good reasons, but her mother said they weren't reasons; they were excuses.

Django said, "You sigh a lot."

"Really? I wasn't aware of that."

"Are you tired?"

"I always sleep soundly."

"My mom took Ambien."

"Did she?"

Robin caught herself in midsigh.

She supposed that before her time with this boy ended, whenever that was, she would learn a great deal about her sister. Earrings, sleeping pills: these were things she would have known if they had been close or even if they had seen each other just occasionally. But it had been many years since she had done more than speak to Caro briefly on the phone, and those conversations had always been awkward. It was as if Caro was afraid of what she would say if she didn't hang up fast.

But Robin had never thought that Caro was angry with her. There was something unspoken between them that had nothing to do with Robin's failure to attend the big wedding or even the marked differences in their personalities. After Caro and Jacky settled down in Beverly Hills, the time between phone calls had lengthened. In the last five years they'd spoken three or four times, no more.

And now she was gone and Robin was left with regret, a puzzle without a solution. And Django.

Aunt Robin dropped Django off in front of the school ten minutes before the first bell. Arroyo Elementary didn't look any better or worse than he had expected. It was like all the public schools he had ever seen: flat roof, asphalt, cement, chain-link fencing, and stucco painted a color that wanted to be green.

"After school there'll be someone, a bus monitor, I guess. She'll tell you which bus goes by the house. Do you remember the address?"

His aunt was trying so hard to be nice. It would be easier if she just didn't say or do anything.

"I'll walk home after." He wanted to explore Arroyo's small downtown on the remote chance that he would find something interesting. Driving down the main street a few minutes ago, he'd seen a game store, and that might be worth investigating. He held up his phone. "I've got a GPS app. I won't get lost."

"Well, don't dawdle around or I'll worry."

Django wondered if she really *was* concerned about him or if her face was made with a little knot between the eyebrows.

"I'll be home after three. A man's coming by for an interview, a home health care nurse. Grannie's going to need some special help after her back surgery."

He did not care the first time she told him and he still didn't care.

"Django, don't be too quick to criticize the children you meet at this school. You know what I mean? I know they won't be like your friends from before, but maybe you'll be surprised."

She sounded hopeful and Django realized she had no clue what it was like to walk into a new classroom, come face-to-face with thirty strangers, every one defending some small bit of turf, every one looking for something wrong with him, something to laugh at, to judge. He might as well be a creature from Planet X. He had a sudden prick of sympathy for his aunt in her ignorance and felt an impulse to be kind.

"Don't worry about me," he said. "I'll be cool."

The sixth-grade teacher, Mrs. Costello, a pretty, dark little woman, had been in the classroom for fourteen years and had met all kinds of children with every variety of name and attitude.

"Boys and girls," she said, clapping her hands together, "we have a new student today. Will you stand up D-jango? Tell us something about yourself."

D-jango.

He knew she was being nice, but he didn't want to stand up. He slid down into the seat and fiddled with his pencil. Behind him, someone snorted. Mrs. Costello didn't force the issue.

"Well, maybe you'd tell us about your interesting name. I've never had a student named D-jango."

He thought about what his father would say.

Django Reinhardt was a great jazz guitarist. He was Hungarian, and Django's a gypsy name. Django and Stéphane Grappelli played at the Hot Club of Paris.

Instead, he told the teacher, "You're not saying it right. You don't say the *D*. It's just Jango."

He heard a girl's voice whisper, "Jinglejanglejingle bells." Laughter.

Mrs. Costello said, "Well, I'll be sure I get it right next time." She picked up her roll book and began to call out the names of students.

A boy whispered behind Django—"*Hey, Jinglebells*"—and something hit him in the back of the head. An eraser.

Django knew Arroyo Elementary School was going to be just as bad as he'd feared.

At lunchtime Mrs. Costello appointed a short, stocky boy to be Django's "buddy," an honor the boy—Billy—didn't seem to appreciate. His friends, Halby and Danny, thought it was hilarious when he and Django walked out of the classroom together. On the way to the lunchroom Billy pointed out the boys' bathroom.

"If you're smart, you'll never go in there without protection. I know a kid went in to take a leak, lost all his teeth, and he's still in the hospital." He lowered his voice. "Coma."

In the lunchroom Billy pointed Django toward the food line and then disappeared. Django chose a container of macaroni and cheese and one of chocolate pudding. He looked around the crowded and noisy room for somewhere to sit and saw Billy standing in a knot of boys. He recognized Halby and Danny but none of the others. Judging from their expressions and laughter, they knew him, however. Django could tell that they wanted him to walk over, giving them an opportunity to say or do something mean; but he wasn't that stupid. He sat in a corner by himself, took one bite of the mac and cheese, and pushed it away. He wasn't sure what it tasted like, but it sure wasn't cheese. At least the pudding was sweet, but that was all it was.

At Country Day the cafeteria sold things like tuna subs and roast beef sandwiches and hamburgers and all-beef franks cooked on a grill right there where you could smell how good they were. And salads. Django figured he was probably the only boy at Arroyo Elementary who had ever eaten a salad for lunch.

Back in class he went to his desk and sat without first looking down and knew immediately that someone had put something on the seat. He acted like nothing had happened, though, not wanting to give Billy and his mutant friends the satisfaction of upsetting him. He smelled chocolate pudding.

Mrs. Costello announced a spelling bee and divided the class into ones and twos. The ones stood up by the blackboard and the twos were down at the other end of the room. Django was a two and had to walk past everyone. He knew what he must look like from the back with gluey, gummy brown pudding on the seat of his pants. He tried to act like it didn't bother him, but everyone laughed when they saw the mess, and he heard one of the mutants say, "Jinglebells pooped his pants."

At Country Day the teacher would have had the brains to figure out who put the pudding on Django's chair and sent him to the headmaster; but all Mrs. Costello did was sigh and tell Django to go to the boys' bathroom and clean himself up. He stood outside the room after she closed the door, remembering Billy's warning words. Maybe Billy was lying to scare him, but after just a half day at Arroyo Elementary the story sounded plausible, except maybe the part about the coma. He thought about going into the teachers' bathroom, but being found there would be an additional humiliation. The more he thought about it, the more certain he was that Billy, Halby, and Danny wanted him to go into the bathroom; and in a moment at least one of them would show up. Django would end up getting dunked. Or worse.

There had been mean kids at Beverly Hills Country Day. Nasty kids, even boys and girls who cheated on tests and stole from the little kids just because they could get away with it. Django had stayed away from them and they had never shown any interest in him. The worst name anyone had ever called him was "brainiac," and he didn't really mind that because everyone knew he was the smartest kid

Drusilla Campbell

in the class. He had never been afraid of getting beaten up and put in a coma.

His imagination told him just what would happen if he went into the boys' bathroom. One of the mutants—probably his "buddy," Billy—would follow him in, and then it would get nasty. Although this scared Django, at the same time he realized something that surprised him. Part of him *wanted* to fight with Billy, *wanted* a chance to punch him, and then when he was down, kick him in the balls. Of course, the other half of Django knew he'd be the one getting punched and kicked.

Instead of going to the bathroom nearest his classroom, Django walked down to the end of the long open corridor—Mrs. Costello had called it the breezeway—with classrooms and sorry-ass, dried-out landscaping on either side, until he got to an area where he could tell by the decorations on the doors that the first- and second-grade classrooms were located. In the little boys' bathroom the sinks were so low he could pee in them if he wanted to and it smelled really bad, like one of the public bathrooms in Griffith Park where the pervs hung out and his dad had told him never to go alone. He held his breath and grabbed wads of paper towels and rubbed the backside of his jeans until the pudding seemed to be gone. He went back to class.

Mrs. Costello looked at him accusingly when he stepped through the door. "Where were you, D-jango? You've been gone ten minutes."

64

Django looked at the three snickering mutants, and he tried not to smile as he said, "Billy told me never to use the big boys' bathroom." It was sort of embarrassing to talk about bathroom stuff in front of everybody, but he didn't care. He was enjoying himself for the first time all day. "He told me a boy got beat up in there and had to go to the hospital with a coma and he's probably gonna die. Billy said I should go down to the little kids' bathroom."

"I never!" Billy cried.

Django widened his eyes and made a cross on his chest. "I didn't want to get beat up, Mrs. Costello."

"Sit down, D-jango. Django, I mean. And you, Billy, I'll talk to you after school."

As he walked to his place in the line of spelling-bee twos, Django flipped the mutants the bird. He didn't look at them as he waited for his turn to spell, his heart beating like crazy. He'd have to be careful they didn't catch him after school, but the risk was worth it. Besides, Django had decided, he was never coming back to Arroyo Elementary.

Chapter 7

During the school day Django lost the little interest in exploring Arroyo that he'd had in the morning. When the closing bell rang at last, all he wanted was to get back to Aunt Robin's house, scoot upstairs, and close the bedroom door behind him.

He gave his name and address to the woman with a *Bus Monitor* sign on her back, and she pointed him toward the yellow school bus No. 3. He was first in and nabbed the front-row seat almost opposite the driver. If any of his new buddies, Billy, Halby, or Danny, got on this bus and tried to give him a hard time, the driver would see it happen and be a witness at the inquest. Ha-ha.

The bus pulled out of the school parking lot, third in a line of nine. From the window he saw Hal and Danny shambling up the street. They looked up as the bus passed, and Django grinned and gave them the one-finger salute again.

So long, suckers, he thought with a shot of elation that

lasted only a second before he realized that Arroyo was a small town and sooner or later the hole-heads would catch up to him, and it would be ugly. He was not going to stick around all summer, asking to get pulverized. But there was no point calling Huck again. It was too easy for him to say no on the phone. If Django had some money, he would hire a limo and get the driver to take him up to Los Gatos. If he showed up on Huck's doorstep, fell on the ground, and begged him, his brother was one of the good guys and would never send him away twice. But Django needed money to hire a car or even to buy an el cheapo bus ticket, and apart from straight-out theft, he didn't know where he'd get it. He might be a rich orphan, but until he grew up he'd never see any cash. His thoughts got gloomier as the bus ride seemed to take the longest route to his aunt's house. By the time he got out and swung his backpack over his shoulder, he didn't think his life could get any crappier.

He walked along the shoulder of the county road, staring at his shoes, watching the dust color them from white to tannish pink, like the powder in Mrs. Hancock's compact. At some time during the jacked-up school day and without quite realizing it, he had accepted that what he was going through was the real thing, not part of a kidnapping plot or a secret government something-or-other. His mother and father really had died that night on Highway 395, and they were as gone as it was possible to be gone. Forever.

He turned off the county road and walked up the steep

hill to his aunt's house. When the road leveled off, he stopped in the middle and closed his eyes and made a last-chance deal with God. If he wanted Django to believe in him, he would have to prove he was real. Django would shut his eyes and take twenty steps along the road without opening them. Even if he heard a car coming, he would keep his eyes shut because the bargain he was making with the Almighty required that he be brave under all circumstances. At the end of twenty steps, he figured he'd be right around the base of his aunt's driveway. He would open his eyes then and if God was paying any attention at all and if he cared anything about Django, Django would see one of his mom and dad's cars parked in front of Robin's house.

He scuffed forward twenty steps, opened his eyes, and saw a black SUV in front of the garage. Hope lifted his feet, and he ran up the steep driveway, never touching the asphalt. On the flat he stopped and his feet and legs turned to lead. This car had nothing to do with his mother and father. No one he or they knew drove a dusty old Chevy Tahoe with a license plate so bent it could hardly be read. He remembered that Aunt Robin was interviewing someone to help his grandmother. He sagged against the far side of the SUV and laid his forehead on the window. He gave up everything and wept with resignation. His funny, interesting, glamorous, and loving parents were truly dead, and he was on his own.

Gradually, he became aware that there was something or someone in the Tahoe, right on the other side of the glass, looking at him. He cupped his hands around his streaming eyes and peered into the vehicle's interior. A few inches away, a dog with a distinctive pit-bull face stared at him, his pointed ears pinned against the side of his head, his nose almost touching the window glass. He wasn't barking, but his upper lip was curled back, revealing his pointed incisors. If Django tried, he knew he would hear the dog growling.

Coming through town, the bus had stopped for a red light next to a bank building that had a digital clock and thermometer on its sign. It said the temperature on that June day was eighty-six degrees. At the same time that the dog was getting ready to attack Django through the glass, he was panting, his long tongue coming out every now and then, hanging like a limp pink flag.

The rage that came over Django was so quick and powerful that when he thought about it later, he knew it was something out of the ordinary, as much about his grief and his frustration at school as about the dog trapped in a hot car. He charged around the front of the Tahoe and across the driveway, taking the steps up to the house two at a time. He shoved through the porch door with his shoulder and was talking, loudly, before he stepped into the kitchen.

"That dog's gonna die out there. It's eighty-six fucking degrees outside."

"Django!"

"And the sun's hammering down on it. A black car might as well be a fucking coffin! It's probably over a hundred degrees inside."

He stopped.

Aunt Robin and a man were at the kitchen table, both staring at him. She had stopped in the act of tearing apart a form and giving him a copy.

"Watch your language, Django!"

"Is that your car?"

The man talking to his aunt stood up. He was big and broad shouldered and wore his hair in a thick braid down his back. He looked like a cross between a Sioux warrior and an old-time saint, but Django was too angry to be intimidated.

"It's against the law to leave a dog in a car like that."

Red faced, his aunt began apologizing to the man.

Bust an artery. I don't care.

Caro and Jacky were dead, and next to that fact, there were no consequences that mattered to Django.

"You can't leave a dog in a closed car, a black car. In hot weather. He's dying in there."

"Don't tell me what I can't do, kid." The man smiled when he said it, but behind that smile Django saw straight into his heart, and what he saw made him take a breath and then a second one. The boys at Arroyo Elementary didn't like Django, and that was okay. Their right. But this man hated him. "Your aunt and me are finished here. I'm heading home." He smiled at Robin, a different kind of smile. Django called it a man-woman smile. "It's my girlfriend's dog. He got the last of his shots today."

"Django, this is Willis Brock. I told you he's going to help Grannie after her surgery."

Django had a whole-body, bad feeling about Willis Brock.

"He works at Shady Hills sometimes," she said. "That's how we know each other."

It was like she was pretending to be a hostess. But Django read her anxiety as clearly as he did Willis's hostility. She was worried that he would take offense and cancel whatever contract they had made.

"Dogs die in cars closed up like that," Django said again.

"I'll remember that," Willis said.

A dog would freeze solid closed in a car with that voice.

Django watched his aunt walk Willis out to the car and knew from the way she shook her head and shrugged that she was apologizing. Probably explaining that he was a poor little orphan boy and would Willis cut him some slack. Willis opened the car door, and the pit bull jumped out and began to run around in circles.

After the Michael Vick scandal, Django had gone online and read all about the pit bulls that had been rescued. Most of those dogs had been rehabilitated and gone to live with families that understood their special needs. Willis Brock and his girlfriend probably did not know that pit bulls were high-strung and needed consistency and firm, loving control. To Django it was obvious that Willis Brock might know how to be firm but he would be clueless about love. Django almost started crying again, he so much wanted to rescue that dog for himself.

His aunt came back into the kitchen with steam coming out of her ears, and for the next ten minutes she gave him a scolding that burned him up one side and then the other. Django tuned her out until she was finished.

"I don't like him," he said. "I don't think he should take care of Grannie."

"You don't even know him! He's very popular with the old people at Shady Hills."

"I bet he steals from them."

"Django! You have no reason to say that."

It was no good telling her that he was an empath. She probably didn't know what the word meant. "There's something creepy about him. And he's mean."

"Django, the dog was closed in the car for twenty minutes. Less than half an hour."

"It was more than one hundred degrees inside."

"You don't know that." She leaned back against the sink and folded her arms over her chest. She stared at her sandals for a moment. "Well, you're right. The windows should have been open. But that's no excuse for insolence..." She stared at her shoes for so long that Django wondered if he could leave and go upstairs.

She looked up. "Is this the way you were...before?"

"What do you mean?"

"Were you always a knight on a white horse?"

She was being kind. It would be better if she ignored him. He didn't want to care about her.

"If you want a dog, I'm afraid you're going to be disappointed. They're dirty and they require a lot of care, and I just don't have the time for that."

Her voice reminded him of a girl at Beverly Country Day who walked around on tiptoes all the time and never spoke above a whisper.

"Willis has been working at Shady Hills for six months and he's just what Grannie needs."

"If that dog died, he wouldn't care."

"That's an awful accusation."

"But I'm right. Don't ask me how I know. I just do. Okay?"

"No, it's not okay. You were rude to him and he was a guest. You can't do that, Django. There are rules in this house."

As if there had been no rules in the house in Beverly Hills. There had been plenty, and sometimes Django broke them; but mostly he didn't because they made sense. Letting a dog die in a car made no sense at all.

She sighed again and opened the refrigerator. "I don't want to hear any more about this." She started taking things out—cheese and lettuce and salad dressing. "Do you like Caesar salad?"

He did, but probably not her version.

She shook a couple of aspirin out of a bottle and swallowed them down with water from the tap, cupped in her palm. "How was school?"

He popped the top of a soda can. "Great."

"Well, that's good." Her smile made him feel guilty. "I knew you'd get along."

He left the kitchen and went up to his room, closed the

door, and turned on his iPad. He pressed the GPS app and entered the address he had read off Willis Brock's contract. It was on Red Rock Road, out in the country but not far away. First chance he got he was going to ride his bike over there to check on that dog, and if he didn't like what he found, he was going to kidnap him.

As she made dinner, Robin thought about the offer made her that morning in the lawyers' office. Mr. Conway was delighted when he heard Django was living with her.

"Under the circumstances, a change of scene would do you both good."

Though Robin had promised to think about it, she didn't really intend to do so. But that afternoon as she tried to settle into her work at Shady Hills, she had found herself recalculating the same set of numbers two and three times. In the end she left work early and stopped in at a coffeehouse just off the highway. She ordered an iced mango tea and took it back to the car, where she sat, staring into the parking lot.

Mr. Conway had spent twenty minutes singing the praises of Tampa, Florida. The beaches, the weather, the cultural life. He even told her that his wife's best friend from college lived there, someone named Pansy, who would make sure Robin had a wonderful time. He even tried to make her believe she could keep working for Shady Hills and her other clients, communicating by cell phone and e-mail. She had been amused by the way he amassed his arguments until what he said at the end. *That* riled her.

"This is an opportunity for you, Robin. You're too young and smart to get stuck."

What was it about people fond of travel that gave them such an attitude of superiority? Her mother was just as bad.

It had taken all Robin's self-control to get out of the office without giving Mr. Conway a piece of her mind. For one thing, she wasn't young; she was almost forty-three. For another, what he called *stuck* was to her mind a comfortable and productive life. She had a successful business, a nice enough house with a reasonable mortgage, a smart car, and a small circle of friends who cared for each other. Every fall she flew to Hawaii for a week. If, as Conway had said, she was in a *rut*, it was one she liked.

She wondered if she might have to quit her job with Conway, Carroll, and Hyde just to end the argument once and for all.

But Mr. Conway had raised three sons, and Robin thought that when it came to Django, he might know what he was talking about. She wondered what he would think of the scene earlier with Willis Brock. Django had embarrassed Robin, but at the same time she was proud of him for having the nerve to confront Willis, who was, she thought, a rather intimidating man. Caro had been a fighter too. It was one of many things Robin had admired about her.

Maybe their father had also liked this in his younger daughter. Robin wondered for the first time if, in comparison, she might have seemed dull to him. That could explain why, after he and their mother separated, he had stayed in contact with Caro but ignored Robin completely. Nola said he had abandoned Robin, but that was such a loaded word and implied intentionality. She didn't like to use it. Maybe he just found her so uninteresting compared to Caro that he forgot about her.

She was positive that Django thought she was as dull as dishwater. He would hate being stuck with her in Arroyo, unhappy and bored; adding that to adolescence seemed like a blueprint for trouble, and she didn't need Mr. Conway to tell her that. He would be better off with Huck, regardless of his unorthodox lifestyle. They would travel together to places a lot more exciting than Florida and Hawaii, and Django would meet the sort of vital young men and women who would interest him. There would be glamour and adventure and the stimulation a bright boy needed to keep him out of trouble. She resolved to call Huck Jones and use Mr. Conway's persuasive technique, keep him on the phone until he got tired of saying no and agreed to take his brother.

Chapter 8

Despite his run-in with Django, Willis was in good spirits when he got home after his interview with Robin Howard. He kept Madora company in the kitchen as she made dinner and did not mention Linda even once. At such times Madora could pretend that the girl in the trailer did not exist. She and Willis were an ordinary couple, living a commonplace life like the one she remembered in the years before her father walked into the desert.

After his death she had turned to her mother for comfort, but Rachel had nothing to give and Madora was left on her own. The only person who ever tried to explain the suicide was a cousin who came to the funeral and said that Wayne had been a sad sack on and off, all his life. *Sad sack.* Madora hated her cousin for dismissing her father's pain that way. Rachel never talked about him or the suicide at all. And Madora hated *her* for *that*. When she met Willis it seemed like she hated almost everyone, most of all herself.

When she told Willis about her father, he attended to

every word. Her heart swelled with his obvious concern. He urged the whole story out of her without saying much, asking a question every now and then. Afterwards, he talked about her father as if he knew him well, and he explained his death in a way that made sense.

"Men like your dad and me, it's in our nature to love and trust one special woman. You might say, we give away our hearts. And if we get let down, if we get disappointed—"

"I'll never let you down," Madora swore.

She remembered how he held her face between his hands and looked at her with such tender sadness that she felt she might break at any moment. "I hope you mean that, little girl. I pray to God you mean that."

Something about Willis had roused Madora's mother from her stupor of grief. When Rachel turned off the television and started to pay attention, she became aware of Madora's short shorts and bikini tops, the glitter on her toes, and earrings that dangled almost to her shoulders, her failing grades and the complaint calls from teachers. Madora said *"fuck you"* when her mother said she could not see him anymore. *"I'll do what I want."* Day and night they fought until Willis told Madora to stop. *"Just pretend to go along with her. What she doesn't know won't hurt her."* Several nights a week Madora said she was going to Kay-Kay's house to study, and her mother never doubted her. Or maybe she knew the truth all along, but for her, too, it was easier to pretend.

And without her mother doing anything at all, Madora

had begun to change. Willis admired intelligence and self-discipline and insisted that she go to school and do her homework. He told her not to dress trampy, and if she wore too much makeup he scrubbed it off her face himself. He would never touch a girl who used drugs and drank too much, so she cleaned up her life in that way too. Though they made out in the backseat of his SUV until they were both hot and breathless, Willis never touched her intimately, had not even slipped his hand under her T-shirt, which she so much wanted him to. She believed that he held back out of respect, thinking she was a virgin. It was the kind of honorable behavior she expected from him.

On a hot night smelling of carne asada and green water, they took a blanket to the river. In the semidarkness she whispered to him about the two boys she'd had sex with the summer before.

"We only did it a couple of times," she explained, surprised to feel shy when she said it. One of the boys had brought a bottle of tequila and she'd been lying on her back on the blanket between them when one put his hand on her leg and the other touched her breast. She couldn't remember now if she had liked either one of them very much. Or if she had experienced any real pleasure, traded off between two friends on a vacation. In the middle of her story she cried, humiliated. Willis held her close and said that he forgave her.

"It's hard to be a woman," he said. No one had ever called her a woman before, and because he did, she believed he understood her better than anyone ever had before. "You're like a little soft creature in a world full of predators."

That night at the river she had hoped Willis would take her in his arms and do what those two boys had done except with the care and tenderness with which he did everything. She kissed him and ran her tongue along the inside of his lips, pressed her hips and breasts against him. He pushed her away.

"I know what you want, little girl, but I got to tell you, it's not going to happen. Not here on this crap-ass river; that's for sure."

"I thought you liked me."

"I love you, Madora. You've heard me say it, and I think you know I don't lie."

"I could go on the pill."

"Madora, I want you to listen real carefully. Then you tell me if I'm right or not, okay?" He sat cross-legged on the blanket facing her, holding her hands and looking right into her eyes. It was almost dark at the river, but the light of the nearby bonfire flickered across the planes of his perfectly symmetrical face.

"I'm not going to make love to you until you're eighteen. One reason is, it's against the law and I don't want to get thrown in the brig. That'd screw me with the Corps and I'd never be able to go to medical school."

"I wouldn't tell anyone."

He laughed and his warm breath stirred the air between them.

"The second reason we won't do it is even more important. The kind of man I am, I want you to be a virgin for me."

"But how can I—? I thought you said it didn't matter."

"Just listen to me, Madora. If you can stay pure for me until you're eighteen, it'll be the same as if you've been made a virgin all over again. It'll prove that first time was an innocent mistake. You'll be purified and the nasty things those boys did to you, they won't matter. All the parts of you they touched will have disappeared and been replaced with new cells. You know about cells?"

"What if you get shipped out? You might go to Iraq or that other place where they hate women."

He tilted her chin with his index finger. "And if that happens, could you be faithful to me?" He pressed the tip of his finger to her lips. "This is all up to you, Madora. If you don't control yourself, if you tempt me, I'll likely give in, just get carried away. I wouldn't be able to help myself. That's the power a woman has. So I don't want you to say anything right off. Take a minute to think about it, Madora, because this means something. This minute, right now, is the most important moment of your life. Are you mine forever? Can I trust you, Madora? Think hard before you answer."

She didn't want to think, nor was it necessary.

"You can trust me. Forever."

Madora's mother announced that she and Peter Brooks, the man she had been dating, were getting married. It was more than two years since the suicide, and this was a new start for her.

"You too, Madora."

Peter Brooks lived in Sacramento and they would be moving there.

"I don't want to go."

"Who doesn't want to get out of Yuma? Sacramento's a beautiful city. It's green there and Lake Tahoe's only four hours away and Peter's got a nice little house. No more stinky-dinky apartments, Madora."

"What about Willis?" It came out like a wail of pain. "Mom, I love him."

"You'll look back in a year and thank me for getting you away from him."

"Is that why you're marrying Peter? To get me away from Willis?"

"No, but it'd be a damn good reason."

Madora had stopped pretending she was not seeing Willis. He knocked on the door of the apartment now and politely sat in the living room when he came by to take her out. Madora's mother was cool but polite, and she grudgingly admitted that though it defied the logic of what she knew about men, he seemed to have been a good influence on Madora, who had made the honor roll two quarters in a row.

"But there's something wrong with him, Madora. I know he's smooth and handsome but there's something...off."

"You don't know him."

"And I don't want to, honey."

"I'll go live with Kay-Kay." Her best friend had twin beds in her room. "Her mom likes me."

"That doesn't mean she wants you living with her. Someone has to pay for your food and the utilities you use." She was always after Madora for letting lights burn all night and taking too many baths. "I don't have any money of my own. I can't give you an allowance or anything."

"If Peter thinks you're so great he wants to marry you, ask him for money. Are you going to work? Won't that be your money?"

"Don't change the subject, Madora." She opened the closet and pulled out a roller bag. "Put what you need for a week or so in this, and the rest can go in boxes. A couple of guys from the hotel will come by on Saturday and help us load."

"I'm staying with Kay-Kay. And if she won't let me, I'll move in with Willis. He's got an apartment off base."

"Absolutely not."

"He says I should get emancipated so you won't be able to tell me what to do."

"I'm sure he'd like that."

"You can't make me—"

"Madora, emancipation takes time, and right now, legally, you're a child. My child."

Something with claws was trying to climb up Madora's throat. "Don't make me leave him, Mama. Please."

"Honey, it's for your own good." Her mother sat beside

her on the bed. "If you move in with him, you'll end up pregnant in no time and what'll you do then?"

"Mom, we don't even have sex."

Her mother blinked several times.

"Do you think Willis is stupid or something? He knows I'm jailbait. And besides, he says it's good for us to wait and I agree with him. I'm making myself pure for him. It shows I'm committed."

"You're telling me you and Willis are just holding hands?"

"We kiss, but that's all. He honors me." Madora added more softly, "And I honor him." The words were beautiful to her ears, holy in a way she could not explain. "Willis has standards, Mom."

In the end an arrangement was made with Kay-Kay's family, and her mother and Peter left for Sacramento. Madora thought her mother was relieved to get the parting over with. Over spring break Madora took a Greyhound bus to Sacramento, but the visit didn't go well. Peter was pleasant, and his house, while not a mansion, was definitely an improvement over the apartment in Yuma. Madora did not feel safe away from Willis, and she worried about him because two weeks earlier something had occurred between him and another Marine, a woman, and now he was in trouble. He had not been forthcoming with details, but from what Madora gathered, he had tried to help this woman and she misunderstood. She had accused him of hitting on her. Out of nowhere, two other complainants had appeared, ganging up on him. He was going to have to leave the Corps he loved so much; and lacking an honorable discharge, it would be hard for him to get into medical school.

In May he was discharged and couldn't stand being in Yuma another minute. It was a bad-luck town, he said. Terrified of being abandoned, Madora said good-bye to high school six weeks before graduation.

They had spent most of the next year traveling through the West, settling in some places for a few weeks and then moving on. Madora turned eighteen in Susanville and when Willis made love to her for the first time, she felt not simply virginal, but prized. Anticipating life from what she'd seen in movies and on television, she expected passion every night after that, but soon realized that Willis was not much interested in sex; and he became offended if she brought the subject up. Better to say nothing, she decided. When he did make love to her she searched her memory afterwards for what she had done to make it happen and cultivated that behavior: compliant, responsible, just sassy enough to make him smile.

They rarely disagreed; Madora made sure of that. Disputes between them stirred to life demons that frightened her, for though her father had been gone many years, she still remembered the arguments between him and her mother and the pall his inky silences cast over their lives. Whether it was true or because Willis had put the idea in her mind, she believed her mother could have saved him if she'd been more understanding.

Outside Arroyo in Southern California, they found the house on Red Rock Road, and Willis said it was perfect.

"Kinda lonely," Madora said. "I like the canyon, though."

"Sure you do," he said. "We don't want to be around too many people, do we? I'm like your dad. I like the desert."

For the next three years Willis worked odd jobs and Madora waited tables at a diner next door to the Indian casino ten miles up Interstate 8. She loved the work and was good at it. Between them, they made enough money to get by. Willis attended night classes that he said insulted his training as a Marine Corps medic, but he became a licensed home health care provider and soon had a full schedule of private clients. A few days a week he worked at Shady Hills. Wherever he worked, he was popular with his clients. Often he came home with cash bonuses, a bundle of fives and ones, once a jar of coins; occasionally the very old men and women gave him personal gifts, some quite valuable.

Madora asked Willis if they could get married and he told her that would happen when he became a doctor.

"I want you to be proud of me," he said.

One day Madora's 1982 Honda Civic stopped dead and refused to start again. Willis looked at the engine and decided that this was a good time for her to quit working at the diner. A few weeks later he brought Linda home and locked her in the Great Dane trailer.

Chapter 9

A few days after giving birth, Linda lay in bed wearing a red terry-cloth shift and watching a tape on the old VCR Willis had brought from the home of a private client.

"He's an old guy and doesn't watch movies anymore."

Willis had reattached her leash, a wire rope with one end padlocked around her right ankle and the other hooked to an eyebolt set high up in a corner of the trailer. She could move around the trailer far enough to reach the water, the toilet, the table; and her wrists were bound in front of her with plastic cuffs, which gave her limited use of her hands but not enough to do more than relieve herself or get a drink from the bottle Madora refilled every morning.

Madora had been up since just after dawn, busy with chores, and Linda's slovenly ways made her impatient.

"Willis says you have to move around some."

"Tell Willis to go fuck himself."

"You better not let him hear you talk like that. He doesn't like it when girls swear."

"What's he going to do? Lock me up?" Linda barked a laugh and looked back at the movie. It was one of those with shooting and car chases that Madora did not care for.

"Stand up, Linda. I can't wash you—"

"Don't put your hands on me!"

"If you're not clean you might get an infection." *And it would serve you right*, Madora thought and immediately heard Willis's voice in her head telling her to be patient.

"You like this part, don't you?" Linda's punky face pinched toward the center. "You and your boyfriend— you're both perverts."

Madora yanked the plug to the VCR. "Stand up."

If they had been in school together, Madora would have been afraid of Linda. Her personality swung between extremes of violent and docile, and from day to day, morning to evening, Madora didn't know which would dominate. She was smart-ass angry now, but by this afternoon she could be placidly agreeable, begging Madora to play gin rummy with her to pass the time.

During the first days in the trailer, more than five months ago, Linda's tantrums had been fierce. She screamed and sobbed and pleaded to be set free, becoming silent only when she grew too hoarse to speak. Willis had rewarded her improved disposition with a better mattress and a longer leash; eventually he brought a proper bed into the trailer. Over the months he had acknowledged her cooperation with an iPod loaded with music, the VCR, and occasional rides in the car, and he had made the trailer homey with books and magazines and a circle of carpet. If she turned on him, swearing and casting accusations, he took back the VCR or the iPod. Once he took the bed away and made her sleep on the floor. Rewards, punishments, consequences: with these Willis had trained Linda to be cooperative.

Today was the first bad day in a long time.

"What did you do with my baby?"

"He went to a good home." The now familiar warmth spread beneath Madora's rib cage as if her heart were melting. "You've got a lot to be grateful for."

"Omigod, you're kidding me. You are so fucking stupid. I'm a prisoner, Madora, a goddamn prisoner." She held up her cuffed wrists as if to prove it. "And you want me to be grateful? Cut me out of these. Tell me where my baby is. You can't just steal a baby. There's laws against that."

"You ought to be thanking God that Willis saved you." *And thank me too. I'm the one who makes your meals and empties your toilet.* "He gave you a place to live and got a good home for your baby. Without him you'd be dead or a drug addict—"

Linda screamed at her to shut up. She struggled to her feet and stepped toward the table, looked around and grabbed a coffee mug, and with her cuffed hands swept it off the table in Madora's direction. It broke in half.

Madora said what she knew Willis would: "You break stuff, you won't get any more for a while."

Linda screamed more and louder, but at the end of Red

Rock Road there was no one to hear her as Madora closed and padlocked the door.

She returned to the trailer an hour later. Linda was at the table, turning the pages of an old *InStyle* magazine. Her tantrum appeared to have blown over.

"So when do you think he'll let me go? Now that the baby's born there's no reason for me to stay. Right? Madora, are you listening to me?"

"It's not safe on the streets."

"He said he'd give me money for a fresh start."

Madora had heard nothing about money.

"He promised."

"A girl alone is like a rabbit."

"What do you mean, a rabbit?"

"I saved one from a hawk."

"You are weird, Madora." Linda shook her head. "How can you stand it when he touches you, knowing what a creep he is?"

"You don't know anything about Willis."

"I know you're almost as much a prisoner as me."

Madora swept the shadowed corners of the trailer.

"When was the last time you ever left this place?"

The dust seeped up from between the trailer's plank flooring, a never-ending supply. Lizards found their way into the trailer and couldn't get out.

"What if I want to go back to my folks? He's gotta let me do that, right?"

"Ask him."

"I did. Last night. All he'd say was I should relax. He said I'm not ready yet."

"Willis knows best."

"Jesus, forget about the rabbit. You sound like a parrot." Linda leaned forward. Her small mouth twisted, and she held out her hand as if she had something grasped between her fingers, "Madora want a cracker?"

Madora pretended not to hear.

"You're like a little puppet, aren't you, Madora, doing everything Willis wants you to?"

She was not a parrot or a puppet. "I was like you. I was wild too."

"So you know how I feel? Right? You could get me out of here right now, Madora. I'd get as far away from Arroyo as I could and I'd never tell anyone. Cross my heart."

"Willis saved me, Linda. And he wants to save you too. It doesn't seem like it now, I know, but—"

"I would absolutely not go to the police." She tried to cross her heart with her bound hands. "And if I did? What would I tell them? I don't even know where the hell we are." Speaking in a dry tone as though disinterested, Linda laid out a reasonable argument. "I never hear any traffic, not trucks or nothing. But there's gotta be a big road somewhere, so just put a bag on my head and walk me there. I could never find my way back to this place in a million years. Why would I want to?" Tears came into her eyes. "I swear on my baby's life, Madora. I won't go to the cops."

Later, Madora sat on her boulder and Foo nosed around

after ground squirrels. She thought of policemen poking into every corner of the property, using a crowbar to open locked doors and closets, checking for fingerprints and DNA. Madora knew nothing about forensics, but she suspected that she might break her back scrubbing the trailer and still not eliminate evidence that Linda had lived there.

Foo barked and ran a few yards down the trail and then back to sit by Madora, trembling. Barked and ran again. Came back. In the dirt by the turnaround Madora saw a mountain bicycle on its side, its wheels spinning.

"Hey!" she yelled, jumping up. "Hey, I see your bike!"

Madora ran down the trail and when she was near the bike a skinny boy stood up from behind a tumble of boulders a few yards away. He was medium height and his hair was as yellow as margarine.

"Who are you? What are you doing here?" She huffed a little from exertion. "You were watching me."

"It's a public road. I could lie down and take a nap here if I wanted to."

"You try and you'll be sorry."

The boy crouched and gave Foo's head a rough pat, pulled his floppy ears, and then ran his hand down the puppy's muscular shoulders. "This is a great-looking dog. Purebred. See this big chest he's got?"

"You better be careful," Madora said. "He's a pit bull. If I was you I'd get outta here."

The kid laughed.

"You know a guy drives a big black SUV?"

"What about him?"

"Is this his dog?"

"What're you asking me for? It's none of your business."

"If the dog died, it'd be my business."

"What do you mean? He's not gonna die."

"The guy that drives the SUV? He was at my aunt's house and left him in the car with all the windows rolled up. He coulda died from heat."

"I don't know what you're talking about."

"You're gonna have to be careful how you raise him." The boy went on talking about Foo as if Madora hadn't spoken. "I read this thing online about those pit bulls who got rescued from dog fighting? You remember that? Well, some of them had to be put down because they were ruined."

"He's mine. No one's gonna fight him."

"All I'm saying is, you don't want to bend this little guy the wrong way."

"I'm not going to bend him at all."

"He sure is sweet." Foo lay on his back with his four short legs in the air, wriggling with pleasure as the boy scratched his stomach. "I'll buy him from you."

Madora stared at him, incredulous. "Money?"

"Sure. How much do you want for him?"

She had no idea how to respond. She did not want to sell Foo, but she had never considered that he might be worth something to anyone but her.

"Get out of here. He's my dog. Come here, Foo." The dog

jumped up obediently, came to her, and sat on her foot. "See? He does what I tell him. You're lucky I don't sic him on you."

The boy looked surprised. For the first time he seemed to understand that Madora was trying to frighten him away. He paused a minute as if taking in details of the situation. He still did not appear to be afraid.

"Can I have a drink of water first?"

"Why aren't you in school?"

"I ditched. I ditch every day. I wanted to see whose dog this is." Foo walked over and licked his face.

Madora felt a little jealous.

"What's his name?"

"Foo."

"Cool name. Like phooey." The boy roughed Foo's head. "Phooey Louie."

Madora remembered Linda screaming in the trailer only a few hours earlier.

"You shouldn't be hangin' around here. Folks up the canyon like being private."

"Can't I have a drink?"

"No."

"Just outta your hose. I don't want to go in your house or anything."

He looked at the house and Madora saw it as it was. In places the coat of green paint Willis had put down years earlier had weathered through to the gray boards and the trim that had been so crisp and neat when fresh had peeled under the fierce sun.

"I don't want to steal anything."

"Why would you want to go inside?" Madora wondered if he might have been spying around before this day. "What're you looking for?"

"I just told you I don't want to go inside."

"Get out. And don't come back."

"I forgot to bring water. It's hot out here."

Madora guessed that if she told him to leave again he would repeat his request for water; and they would go on like this, back and forth; and the longer they argued, the longer he would stay around and the more nervous and foolish she would feel. She thought of Linda sleeping or watching a video. Something, anything, might set off this odd-speaking boy, and if Linda heard him she would make her own noise to get his attention.

"I don't really live in Arroyo," the boy said as if she were interested. "I'm only staying with my aunt. My real house is in Beverly Hills."

"That's where the movie stars live." In spite of herself, Madora was curious. "You're not a movie star."

"My dad was Jacky Jones. You know him? He was a rock star back in the day."

"Not my day," Madora said.

"How old are you?"

"None of your beeswax."

"I'm twelve."

Madora remembered being twelve and still a little girl playing with dolls, though she had kept this a secret from most of her friends, who had moved on to idolizing television and music stars.

"How come you got a trailer in your backyard?"

"It's not against the law to have a trailer, you know." She started to walk away from him but stopped, afraid he would follow. "Go back to Beverly Hills or wherever you live."

The boy scuffed the dust with the toe of what Madora could see were expensive sneakers.

She asked, "Does your aunt know you're out here?"

"Let me have some water first."

He was not going to leave until he had his water—that was obvious—so she gestured for him to follow her. In the carport a length of hose lay curled on the warm cement. The boy found the end and held it up. Madora turned the handle on the spigot.

"Shit!" The boy dropped the hose and leaped back from it. "That's hot!"

"What do you expect? It's a hot day." She grabbed the hose and without thinking, out of pure ornery inspiration, she forgot about Linda and noise and pointed the business end of the hose straight at him, drenching his shirt and pants. He stood still, his mouth wide open and his arms spread wide while Foo danced around his feet, leaping and barking at the splashing water. The boy looked so surprised, like he'd been struck by lightning, and Madora laughed out loud.

"You'll be sorry!" The boy wrenched the hose away and pointed the water at her. She kept on laughing until she was wet through and her shirt and shorts stuck to her skin. She dropped onto the stoop in front of the kitchen door and laughed until her side hurt and even then she couldn't stop. The laughter came out of her as if it had been boxed down hard, like a spring toy.

On a hard hot day, the water was a benediction.

"You laugh like my mom," the boy said. "She used to laugh a lot."

"Where'd she go?"

"I don't know. I guess she's dead. They both are. Her and my dad."

Madora wondered if her own mother was still alive. She hadn't spoken to her since she worked at the diner up Interstate 8, and then she had done it on a whim and never wanted Willis to know. There had not been much to say in that conversation. Rachel didn't want to hear about Willis's job or about the house on Red Rock Road. Madora did not want to call her mother again after that. She was afraid of the wrenching pull her mother's voice had, tugging her in a direction she didn't want to go.

The boy said, "I guess I'm an orphan. Like Oliver."

"Oliver who?"

"But I'm gonna go up north soon and live with my brother. My half brother. He's really rich."

Madora did not want to hear about the choices this boy had, his dead or alive parents and rich half brother. At the same time, she wanted to hear all about Beverly Hills, and maybe this guy Oliver was someone famous.

"I gotta go," he said. The day was so hot, his pants and shirt were almost dry already. "I'll come back and see you tomorrow."

"You better stay away. My boyfriend doesn't like kids."

"I don't think he likes Foo either." He started off in the direction of his mountain bike. "I won't come if his car's here."

Chapter 10

Robin parked her car in a visitor's space and pressed the keypad on the security gate. Her mother's condo was on the second floor overlooking the Sycuan golf course and casino development that ran along the bottom of a narrow valley ten miles from Arroyo. She was on the balcony sweeping, wearing a pair of pajama bottoms and an old T-shirt.

"You're a vision. I wish I'd brought my camera."

"I could be nude out here and who'd notice?"

"Sit. You're going to make yourself a cripple." Robin took the broom from her and leaned it against the wall. "I interviewed that home nurse guy I told you about. He'll be calling you."

"I had to cancel my trip to Peru because of this wretched back, and now I can't get Caro out of my mind for more than three minutes." Groaning, her mother dropped onto a white plastic chair. "At least on a trip there would have been things to distract me." She used her straw hat as a fan.

Drusilla Campbell

"I tell you, Robin, if that drunk hadn't died in the accident I'd go out and find him and kill him myself, and don't look so shocked. I'd be doing the Lord's work." She squirmed in the chair, trying to find a comfortable position. "My sweet baby...Sometimes I just don't understand God at all." Her eyes filled with tears and she crossed herself, then fanned herself more furiously. "I've been trying to remember the last time she came here to visit, and do you know, I'm not sure she ever did. Is that right or am I losing my mind?"

"Your mind's fine, Mam. She was never here."

"Why not? She and I were never close, and believe me, I regret that. If there was something I could have done. But you two used to get along fine. Something must have happened between you, but it's nothing I ever understood."

"It doesn't matter. She's gone now."

"Gone? I'll say she's gone!" The tears started again. "Your only sister couldn't be bothered visiting you? And you never got out of your own road for long enough to visit her either, did you? I don't understand, Robin." She sat up straight, stretching her back. "You girls were close as children."

Robin let her mother talk on, knowing it was one of the ways she made peace with whatever troubled her.

"We weren't sophisticated enough for her. After she married the guitar player."

Robin laughed. "Mam, you're a stitch. Jacky wasn't just a guitar player. He was one of the greats."

"So you say."

"But you're right. I never made the effort to see her and I should have." Robin did not want to talk about Caro, but by visiting her mother she had virtually guaranteed she would have to. Over the last two or three days she had been troubled by an amorphous regret for something she had overlooked and could not name. Being with her mother only made it worse.

Robin had been fourteen and Caro nine when their parents were legally separated, divorce being out of the question for Nola. Frank Howard left Morro Bay and moved to Los Angeles, and though Caro occasionally visited him there, for some unexplained reason, Robin was never invited to go along. She complained once, and her mother responded by saying that her father was not a nice man and Robin was lucky to have a mother who loved her and not to forget it. She had known better than to ask why, if he was not a nice man, Caro was trusted to his care on weekends.

And Robin *had* been loved; she would not deny or discount that. Her mother had made sure she finished high school at Holy Rosary Academy in Morro Bay and went on to college in Santa Barbara. Robin would have been happy to go to Cal Poly just up the road, save money and live at home, but her mother did not want that.

"You need to get out, get some independence."

"I'm driving up to Beverly Hills in a couple of days," Robin told her. "Caro's lawyer wants me to go through the house. I'm not sure exactly why, but I thought I'd better go. I'm taking Django with me."

"I'd go too if the devil would stop stabbing me in the back with his pitchfork. I'd like to see the inside of that house. Caro sent me photos but I was never invited. Maybe your sister was ashamed of me."

"You know that's not true."

"She held it against me when your father left home."

"She was a little girl, Mam. She was confused. We both were."

"They must have been made of money to buy a lot in Beverly Hills and build a house from scratch. How did she ever get so peculiar, so set off by herself, I'd like to know. I suppose she thought she was better than us because she got rich all of a sudden."

Her mother said such outrageous things sometimes, Robin had to laugh out loud. "You know that's not true. Caro never thought she was better than us. She wasn't that kind of person."

"Then explain to me what happened, why she left us high and dry."

"She didn't leave us. She just went on with her life. And I could have gone up there. I should have. I wish I had."

If she had walked into Caro's house and asked her straight out why they weren't true sisters anymore, not even friends, Caro would have told her. *She knew.* But for a long time, Robin had believed she didn't care that she had no relationship with her sister and father. Now she knew that wasn't true, but it was too late for her to do anything about it.

Her mother talked on about Caro, saying that she had

always craved excitement, taken risks, stepped out to the end of the plank and been unafraid of the deep water.

"She was never scared of anything."

Yet again Robin heard the story of the time Caro was found, aged two (she got younger every time the story was told), atop the old upright piano.

"She was the bravest little girl and you were the complete opposite. But she spent too much time with your father. I'm afraid it ruined her." She patted Robin's forearm. "I know you think you never got a fair shake with him, but you're better off. Trust me; I know. He was not a nice man."

"Has anyone told him about the accident? Do you know where he is, Mam?"

Nola sighed.

"You're still legally married, aren't you?"

"Separated. We're legally *separated*."

"You should tell him."

"I'd rather not, Robin."

"When did you see him last?"

"Years ago." Nola flipped her fingertips, dismissing the matter of where and when. "Do you remember how he smoked? He was a chimney, let me tell you. When he left me he was good for two packs a day. I aired the house for a month and the stink didn't go away."

"You should have gotten a divorce. You could have married again and had a life."

"You forget your catechism, Robin. If we had divorced, I would have lost the church."

"No one cares anymore. You could divorce him tomorrow if you wanted to."

"You toss that word around like it's nothing."

"Divorce isn't the end of the world, Mam."

"Don't lecture me, Robin. You've never been married. You don't understand what it means to make an eternal vow before God."

Judgments came to Robin's mother in the air she breathed and she saw no reason for not expressing them.

"The Catholic Church is different now," Robin said.

"Alas. But my church has never changed and never will."

"You don't even go to Mass anymore."

"Well, look who's talking. The point is, I could go if I wanted to. But I don't care for all that touchy-feely stuff. I liked the way it was when I was a kid. The way God meant it to be."

The clock on the mantel inside chimed. Her mother got up from her chair slowly, her hand on the small of her back. Holding the doorjamb for balance, she went inside and turned on the television. "Do you want to watch Ellen's show with me?"

"I've got stuff to do."

"The boy's a big responsibility."

"Less than you might expect. You know, Mam, I think Caro and Jacky must have been very good parents. He's a nice boy. Beautiful manners."

"Well, that's something."

"And he's so smart. Omigod, he knows all kinds of things."

"Your sister was smart. She could have gone to college if she'd wanted to. She must have gotten her love of travel from me. Your father wouldn't budge from the front yard without a shove."

"The lawyers think I should take him to Tampa. Mr. Conway thinks it would be good for both of us."

"I couldn't agree more. It would get you out of your own way while you're still young enough to enjoy a change of scene. You're timid, Robin. I never raised you to be timid."

"It's not a good time."

"Nonsense. It's a perfect time. Take a risk for once, Robin. Though God knows, Florida isn't much of one, but it's better than not going anywhere except Hawaii. If you don't do it now, I promise you'll regret it. One day you'll have a back like mine, and then you'll wish you'd gone out and enjoyed life."

Chapter 11

Django said, "Are those sandwiches for me?"

Madora literally jumped when he spoke, and the sandwiches she was taking to Linda bounced on the plate.

He had ridden his bike out to see Madora three times since his first visit. At some point during every conversation she told him to go away and not come back; but they both knew she didn't mean it.

"Don't do that," she said, gasping. "Don't ever surprise me like that."

"Are you having a picnic?"

"What are you doing here? Don't you have anywhere else to go?"

Actually, though his timing was bad, she was glad to see him. Until Django started showing up, Madora had not realized how lonely she was. Each time, after he left, she scolded herself for the terrible chance she was taking. A smart, curious boy, how long would it be before he asked too many questions about the trailer? Or Linda heard his voice? Django had brought the world, framed in his quirky personality, into her narrow life. His famous parents and his woo-woo school and the exotic countries he had visited: Madora didn't know how much of it was true, how much fantasy. Nor did she care. He was welcome entertainment.

"You going to eat those sandwiches all by yourself?"

She had made them for Linda, but Madora would rather feed Django, who at least said thank you. Since seven that morning, she had been fetching and carrying for Linda, following Willis's instructions. For breakfast she made her scrambled eggs with toast and a thick slice of fried ham. Madora never got ham for breakfast, but Willis said that after giving birth a girl needed lots of protein to help her regain her strength. Besides breakfast, lunch, and dinner, he also wanted Madora to make her a midafternoon snack. Madora was back and forth to the trailer all day: dusting, sweeping, emptying the portable toilet, even washing Linda, who seemed to have no natural instinct for cleanliness and needed to be coaxed into brushing her teeth and splashing water on herself.

She asked, "Do you like bologna?"

"I don't know." Django peered at the sandwiches on the plate. "What's it taste like?"

Madora wondered how anyone in America could grow up without eating bologna; but Django was strange in many ways. She liked that about him. He used words she'd never heard spoken and talked about dinosaurs and stars and planets with the confidence of a scientist, but at the same time he was ignorant of really ordinary things like bologna. And the stories he told! He was absolutely the biggest liar she had ever met, and that included Kay-Kay, who had told some whoppers.

She set the plate on the stoop in the carport shade. "Go ahead. Try it."

"We never had plain white bread at our house," he said, sitting on the step.

Now she knew he was a liar.

"My mom said it wasn't nourishing."

"Well, pardon me." Madora tried to grab the sandwich back, but Django had already taken a big bite. He took another, chewing with his mouth open, the sandwich going around like clothes in the washing machine. His grin said thanks for lunch and dared her to get after him for bad manners. A bicolor blob of mustard and mayo squatted on his lower lip.

"You are disgusting," she said and sat on the cement step beside him. Across the cul-de-sac a roadrunner scampered up the trail. Even if Django was the king of the liars, he was better company than Linda, who was getting meaner every day. But having him around was dangerous and she could not completely relax. Willis wasn't expected home for hours, but still, if there was an emergency and he showed up unexpectedly... As she and Django bantered back and forth, she was always listening for the sound of the Tahoe on the gravel road.

Madora had seen Willis lose his temper once when they lived a couple of months in Great Falls, Oregon, just a wide spot in the road, really, but greener than anywhere she had lived before. He worked as a mechanic until he was falsely accused of harassing the owner's daughter. Willis told the boss to go fuck himself and his bitch daughter too; and on the way out of town before sunup, he threw a wrench through one of the garage windows. His rage lasted all day and he drove like a crazy man, twenty miles over the speed limit down twisting mountain roads. If he knew about Django, Willis would tear into both of them.

"You shouldn't be here. Willis wouldn't like it."

He shrugged. "My mom and dad are dead. Their car got hit."

He had told her this before. She wondered if he had to keep saying it to convince himself.

She said, "My dad's dead too."

"Did it happen in his car?"

"He shot himself."

"How come?"

"It was my mom's fault," she said. "She didn't keep him happy."

Django stopped chewing and gaped at her with a look of disgust. "That's cracked."

"But it's true."

"Get out. He's the one who pulled the trigger." Django put two fingers to his temple and made a click sound. "No one made him do it."

"He loved her and he trusted her and she let him down."

"How?"

"How should I know? She just did. And when that happens it's the same as putting a bullet to a man's head."

"Who told you that shit? Willis?"

"Don't cuss."

"He doesn't know everything."

"And you do?"

"I have a genius IQ. I took a test."

"So does Willis, probably. He's really smart. Not with books, like you, but he knows stuff."

"Have you got any Coke?"

"Willis says it's not healthy."

"It's okay if you don't drink, like, a gallon a day."

He ate a second sandwich and fed a crust to Foo. "I like this bologna. Thanks. Were you going to eat all these yourself?"

"No, I made 'em for the dog." She flipped him the bird.

He laughed and gave it right back to her. "How old are you anyway?"

"Old enough to know better."

"Better than what?"

"Better than let you hang around here all day." She picked a bit of lettuce out from between her teeth. "If Willis finds out—"

"How come you're scared of him?"

"I'm not."

"Liar."

"He doesn't like strangers."

"He knows me."

"You met him one time. That's not the same as knowing someone."

"If he knew me better, I wouldn't be a stranger."

Talking to Django could be exhausting.

"When's he coming home?"

She shrugged. He had told her that after work he was going to the university for his interview to become a doctor. She had no idea how long such things took.

"What's your favorite TV show?" Django asked. "Did you ever watch *Lost*?"

"We don't have a TV anymore."

"Oh, yeah. I forgot. Weird."

This boy with all his questions was trouble waiting to happen. The truth of that was written in his bright and inquisitive expression. Madora knew what she had to do: tell him to go away and never come back; and somehow she had to sound like she meant it. That was the hard part, because he was just a kid but already she thought of him as her friend; and she'd had precious few of those, even back in Yuma.

Her life would be more interesting if she could go back to waiting tables at the diner up Interstate 8. She had tried to persuade Willis to let her do this, telling him she missed the friendly, hurry-up atmosphere of the diner, where she had been good at making customers feel welcome. Murray, the manager, said she was a natural. She had been proud and eager to tell Willis how she had been praised, but he wasn't impressed. He said all you needed to serve food was two legs, two hands, and a brain the size of a Brussels sprout. At the same time, it was dangerous work; oddballs wandered in and out and got crazy ideas about girls who made them feel at home. Willis wanted her to talk to Linda, make friends with her; and for a time she had tried, but Linda didn't like her and was not interested in friendship unless it meant Madora would open the door of the trailer and let her walk out.

Linda had no time for Madora, but she liked Willis, though not in the beginning when her tantrums had been fierce. She'd twice bitten him, once on the pad of his thumb and again on his forearm. To punish her after the second incident, he told Madora not to feed her and turned off the lights in the trailer. One day in the dark without food and Linda had begged to be forgiven. In the months before her baby was born, after the tantrums stopped and she seemed finally reconciled to her captivity, she had become more docile. She never had much to say to Madora, but when Willis was around she bubbled up, joked, and flirted.

Freedom had returned to the front of Linda's mind since the baby was born. For the last few days she had nagged Madora with questions designed to elicit information about where they lived and how far they were from the nearest town. When she was not asking questions, she was swearing never to tell a soul that she had been held captive. Linda was getting to be a pain in the butt. Willis, unperturbed, said to give her time; she'd settle down again.

Madora asked him how much longer Linda would be in the trailer and his answer made no sense.

"As long as necessary."

Django said, "Got any cookies?"

"Go home and eat your own."

"Willis doesn't like 'em, huh?"

"Willis is none of your business."

"Are you married to him?"

"Not yet."

"My dad was married before he met my mom. He loved her too, but she got sick. Huck was only a baby when she died."

Django talked about his rich half brother nonstop once he got started. He described his mansion with a landing pad for a helicopter, his airplane, and the bodyguards who spent their spare time lifting weights. As he spun his tale Madora imagined a movie about rich people and didn't believe a word of it. It was easier for her to accept him as crazy and a world-class liar than believe a boy with a life right out of the movies, the son of a rock star, was riding his bike around the back roads of San Diego County.

"If he's your brother, how come you hang out here?"

"Just getting things fixed up. My aunt's gonna call him up pretty soon. Why? Don't you want me around?"

"Evers Canyon isn't like Beverly Hills. Once Foo and me were taking a walk and minding our own business and this guy comes out and sits on his front steps and he had this big old rifle on his knees, kind of like it was just

113

resting there, but I knew if Foo or me took one step on his property, he'd prob'ly shoot our heads off." She could tell a tall tale as convincingly as Django.

"A trailer like that one?" Django nodded his head toward the backyard.

"Dummy. A *mobile home.*"

"Does somebody live in *your* trailer?"

"Why would anyone live in that old thing?" The pulse beating at the corner of Madora's eyelid felt as obvious as an earthquake, and she put her hand up to cover it. "There aren't any windows."

"Where's that whirring sound come from? Like an air conditioner?"

It was true. Even from the carport where they sat, she heard the purr of the air conditioner Willis had installed in the trailer. "We have a generator. Sometimes the electricity goes off in the house."

Django finished his third sandwich. "I never heard of a generator going all the time."

"So?" Madora rubbed her eye. "Shows you don't know everything, I guess."

Django burped and laughed.

"You are so gross."

"Me and my friends used to have burping contests."

"You have to go."

Madora picked up the empty sandwich plate and stood. Foo danced around her ankles in expectation of a few crumbs. Django kept talking.

"Willis told my aunt he's going into med school. Is that true? Is he going to be a doctor?"

That morning, talking about his upcoming interview, Willis had been as nervous as the feral cats that shivered around her legs when she laid out a plate of dinner scraps. Madora couldn't do anything right. He called her stupid because his only tie had a spot on it. As if Madora was supposed to know that and clean it ahead of time when she did not think she had ever seen him wear a tie before.

Django said, "He'll have to cut his hair before they let him work in a hospital."

"You don't know about hospitals."

"I don't think anyone wants a doctor with a braid."

"Shut up!"

"What kind of doctor does he want to be?"

"None of your business."

"He looks kinda creepy with all that hair."

"I told you to shut up!"

His face bore its bright and questioning expression, as if he had the right to go where he wanted, open any door, ask any question that popped into his mind. She wondered at this peculiar boy who never stopped asking questions.

"Who are you anyway?"

"Django Jackson Jones."

"You're the weirdest boy I ever met."

"Ditto for you," Django said.

"Me?"

"You remind me of Rapunzel."

"Is that a girl?"

"In the fairy tale. She was a prisoner in a tower waiting for her prince to come along."

Madora laughed. "Willis is my prince."

"Charming," said Django.

"Willis has a gun. If you don't get outta here, I'm gonna go get it and shoot you."

"Have you ever been to Beverly Hills?"

"Are you deaf *and* retarded?"

"I'm going up there with my aunt, so I won't be around for a couple of days."

"That's the best news yet."

"I could bring you back a TV. If you wanted. There's a bunch at the house."

"Leave me alone."

"Okay," he said, walking off toward his bike.

"And don't come back."

"See you in a couple of days."

Chapter 12

Madora watched Django ride off, and when she was sure he would not return to ask another intrusive question or tell her what he thought about something, she went into the kitchen and used up the last of the bologna and lettuce to make Linda a sandwich, which she carried back to the trailer.

The girl was in a foul mood. "It's about goddamn time, Madora. I heard you yucking it up while I was starving in here."

Though it was midafternoon, Linda still wore the shorty pajamas Willis had bought her when the weather grew too warm for flannel. She had rucked her blond hair back in a ponytail and put on lipstick, but there was a sour smell about her, as if she hadn't washed in some time, although Madora brought her a bucket of fresh water and a clean towel and washcloth every morning. It did no good to nag her about cleanliness. Living on the streets as she had, she must have grown accustomed to unsanitary living.

"Who were you talking to?" Linda spoke in a voice that reminded Madora of her own when she was training Foo. "You can trust me. I won't tell Willis."

"I wasn't talking to anyone. You're hearing things."

Linda shrugged and opened the sandwich and lifted out the bologna slice. Tipping her head back, she fed the whole thing into her little mouth, then closed the sandwich and ate the bread and lettuce slathered in mustard and mayonnaise.

"I like you, Madora. I don't want you to get in trouble."

"What kind of trouble?"

"Willis'd be way pissed if he knew you had someone around here. A boyfriend maybe?" She stuck her index finger in her mouth and scraped the food stuck to her gums. "You're my friend. I'd never tell on you."

Madora did not for the smallest sliver of a second believe that she and Linda were friends.

"Boy or girl?"

"Who?"

"Your friend. Outside."

"I don't have any friends."

Linda considered this, and something that had been avid in her manner faded away. Dispirited, she lay back on the bed, licking the tips of her fingers, rubbing them on her bare thighs. She expelled a long breath and absently scratched at the eruptions of pimples along her jaw line.

Madora looked away and swept the trailer as she did every day.

After a while, Linda said, "I wonder what my sisters are doing right now."

"You have sisters?"

"Three, and one brother. Saint Phillip. He had his own room because he was a boy. BFD. I was the oldest. I should have had my own fucking room, but I had to share with three little brats. God, I hated them."

"Is that why you ran away?"

"It's none of your business why I ran away."

"I would have been glad to have a sister. If I had one I'd never run off and leave her."

"You don't know anything. You're just a stupid fat girl."

"I'm not stupid."

Linda looked surprised. "Well, fuck me straight! The parrot can speak for herself."

The sun had just dropped behind the canyon wall when Madora heard the squeal of the Tahoe's brakes and the sound of the SUV's big tires digging a trench in the gravel. Willis slammed the driver's side door. She took a deep breath and leaned against the sink, her arms across her chest, her hands shoved up under her arms.

"What's the matter with you?" he said when he saw her. "You look like an ice cream cone in that pink thing."

She had taken a shower and washed her hair. The pink and white shift was the only thing in her closet that wasn't wrinkled, and the color made her happy, bringing to her mind the smell and taste of a strawberry smoothie. Willis opened the refrigerator door, took out a beer, and slammed the door shut, shaking the boxes of cereal that stood on top like books on a shelf.

He dragged a chair out from the table, opened the beer can, and drank. His Adam's apple moved up and down as he chugged the whole thing without pausing for breath.

"Aren't you going to ask me how it went?"

She didn't have to. She had known as soon as he braked the Tahoe that whatever had happened during his interview, it wasn't what Willis had hoped for.

"The counselor was a piece-of-shit twenty-year-old girl." He leaned over the table and his brown eyes, darkening to near black around the pupils, were unfocused. He had been drinking before he came home. "She told me to go to community college, something about fulfilling requirements."

"You told her you graduated from high school, didn't you?"

"Of course I did, Madora. You think I'm an idiot? She said my grades were borderline and I'd have to make 'em up before the college would let me in."

"But then it'll be okay? Premed?"

"Oh, yeah, yeah. And then when I'm about forty years old I have to take some test, the MCAT."

"That's the name?"

"It'll say if I'm"—he made quotes with his fingers—"med school material."

"Did you tell her you were a Marine medic? And about being a home health care provider?"

"They don't care about any of that."

"But it's not fair. You'll be a wonderful doctor. You should get letters from your clients. Like references."

"Shut up, Madora, you don't know what you're talking about."

He could say all the awful things he wanted. Her love was like a shield; the words bounced off without hurting her. She could not think about herself when he was obviously in pain, so angry and depressed. It was her job to lift his spirits when he couldn't do it himself.

"I know you. I know how good you are."

He set his elbows on the table and looked at her. Beneath their drooping lids, his eyes were almost crossed.

"You've had a lot to drink," she said. "Do you want to lie down?"

He shook his head.

"It's not the worst news in the world, Willis. I mean, it might mean you'll spend more time in school, but in the end you'll still be a doctor, right? And that's what you want."

"Just get me another beer and quit tryin' to be a nurse."

"Maybe that's the answer, Willis."

"What?"

"Wouldn't it be a lot easier to be a nurse than a doctor?"

"You want me to clean up after some bozo no better'n me 'cept he's got an MD after his name? My father was a doctor, Madora, and if he could do it, I sure as hell can too."

"You'll be a wonderful doctor." She knew this with all her heart.

"You bet I will."

"You'll show them."

"I figured it out, drivin' home. I'm not going to let some twenty-year-old college brat tell me what I can do. I'm going to the Caribbean. They got medical schools." He straightened up, belched. "I'll get into one of them, easy."

She hesitated and then asked the obvious question. "Won't that cost a lot? Where would we get the money to move there?"

"Let me worry about that," he said and finished off his beer.

This new plan would involve airplane trips, and she could not guess what other expenses when she considered that on a Caribbean island a foreign language might be spoken and the laws would be different. In some foreign places Americans were not liked. She thought about living at the end of a road in a foreign country, stuck in some kind of hut, unable even to say good morning to her neighbors in words they would understand.

Willis mumbled something about going back to the trailer to watch a movie with Linda.

"Stay with me, Willis." Madora was patient by nature and not given to jealousy, but tonight she did not want him to traipse back to the trailer for consolation. It was her job to make him feel better, but how could she do that if he passed out on Linda's bed? She hated that he sometimes seemed to prefer Linda's company to hers. Maybe if she were thinner, more like the girl she was when Willis found her on the porch at that party in Yuma...

She said, "Linda wants us to let her go."

"I'm calling the shots, not her. Or you either."

"Yes, but maybe we should be thinking—"

"I don't want you thinking at all, Madora."

The disastrous interview had been a heavy blow. If it helped him to be mean to her, she could take it. Although Willis still saw her as the same girl he'd rescued, Madora was not a fragile teenager anymore. Years with him had toughened her. She had grown a skin that did not bleed as easily as it once had.

Django's questions about the trailer had been plaguing her all afternoon. She had something to say and it did not matter if Willis wanted to hear. And if he became angry, at least that would take his mind off medical school for a while.

"I'm worried someone might get curious about the trailer."

His eyes snapped into focus. "Has someone been hanging around?"

"I'm just saying, what if a hiker or a mountain biker—"

He looked at her.

"We'd be in trouble, wouldn't we?"

"If you keep your mouth shut, no one's gonna get curious about a piece-of-shit trailer in the backyard. This place is a dump, Madora. Look around you. The trailer fits right in."

He called their home a dump. She wanted to defend the little house, but when she opened her mouth, nothing came out.

He shoved past her and made his way to the back door, running his hand along the countertop to maintain balance. He pulled the door open, and Foo, who had been outside on the cement, nosing the door, rushed in and darted between his legs. Willis staggered and kicked out, cursing at the dog as he fell against the doorjamb, missed the outside step, and stumbled into the brick-and-board shelf in the carport. He tipped sideways and fell on the hawk-scarred rabbit's cage, stabbing his hip on the pointed corner. With a yell of rage, he whirled and in one movement grabbed the cage between his hands and threw it hard into the cement floor.

Madora knelt beside the wire pen. She opened the door and lifted out the rabbit. Its torn ear had almost healed. The little creature might one day have been confident enough to leave the cage. But Willis had finished what the hawk could not. Madora looked at the rabbit's open eyes and knew that it had died in fear.

Chapter 13

The next morning, Madora cocooned the dead rabbit in a faded blue T-shirt, soft from many washings, and buried it under a cairn of river rocks in the trees behind the trailer. Afterwards she went about her chores in a plodding and dutiful way, trying not to let her mind wander back to the events of the night before. Her silence seemed to irritate Linda.

"What's biting you? Did your boyfriend dump you?"

Madora stopped sweeping and stared at her.

"I *know* I heard you talking to him. Yesterday."

"I wasn't talking to anyone."

"Cut the crap, Madora. The walls of this box are like paper." She stretched languidly and then examined her feet. "Paint my toes today, okay? Willis brought me some pink polish. Kinda pretty."

"I'm busy."

"Willis says you have to do things for me. You're supposed to keep me happy."

"I don't care if you're happy or not."

"Wow. What got into you? The little mouse got fangs all of a sudden."

Madora tried not to respond to the baiting. She knew better than to do so, but Linda was clever. Even silent on her bed, she provoked Madora with a cheesy, knowing smile twitching the corner of her mouth. Madora jerked the table and chairs away from the wall and swept away the dust and hair and crumbs of food. She forced her movements into slow motion and hummed a tune in her head as if nothing troubled her, least of all Linda's goading. It was not easy to do. As she worked she felt Linda watching her, reading her, looking for a weakness to exploit. Madora remembered that in school, girls like Linda were never popular, but they always had a parade of fawning acolytes who stayed on their good side out of fear.

"I hear when Willis yells at you. I hear you outside, walking around at night like a ghost or something." Linda laughed. "You don't have any secrets around me, Madora."

"You're a liar. I don't believe anything you say."

Linda retreated into silence for a few more minutes. Then, "Paint my toenails and I won't tell him you've got a boyfriend."

Madora weighed the bargain, the chance that Linda was telling the truth. Not that she had a boyfriend, but she might have heard Django's voice. If Linda was as knowing as she claimed, it was unlikely she would have kept her secrets. It would have been irresistible to blow the whistle on Madora.

"Tell him anything you want. I'm not your maid."

"More like a slave."

"Look who's talking, Linda." Madora's cheeks burned and she felt her blood pumping in her neck. "I'm the one who's gonna walk out of the trailer in a minute. I'm the one who knows the combination lock."

"So? How come you don't leave him, then? If you're so free, why don't you get a life?"

"I have a life and I don't want to leave."

"Sure you do, Madora." For a change, Linda spoke without malice. "You just don't know it yet."

Madora did not know how to reply. She turned her back on Linda and wet a rag from a water bottle to wipe down the sticky tabletop.

"You were laughing yesterday. I don't hear you laugh hardly at all."

"I talk to myself. I talk to Foo. He makes me laugh."

"Maybe." Linda chewed on her fingernails. "Just so you know, I'm listening."

Madora dropped the rag into a plastic bag and tied off the top. "You'll be gone soon."

The mood in the trailer sparked. Linda shifted on the bed, sitting straighter.

"Did Willis say that?" It gratified Madora to hear Linda's voice break with uncertainty. "Has he told you when?"

"Of course. He tells me everything."

Linda dropped back on the pillows. "You are such a bullshitter." She made a burbling, insulting sound with her lips, but her laugh was unconvincing.

Some days Madora's chores took all day to accomplish. And then there were days like this one, when she was finished by eight thirty a.m. and left with the day gaping ahead of her. She couldn't forget what Linda had said about being free to leave; and to prove that she could come and go as she pleased, she and Foo headed out behind the Great Dane and across the dry stream. A hundred yards up the side of the canyon through the rocks and chaparral there was a trail she had explored once before in the first week she and Willis had lived in the house on Red Rock Road, a time when she felt enthusiastic and hopeful about making a home there and wanted to know all the canyon's secrets.

Only wide enough for one person at a time, the trail scalloped the north-facing points and coves of the canyon, making its way in the direction of the county road. The first time Madora hiked it, she had been stopped by a six-foot rattlesnake as big around as her arm, lying stretched out across the trail sunning itself. She went no farther and hurried home. That evening she told Willis, and he forbade her to explore the canyon without him. His warning of rabid coyotes and cougars in the rough folds of the hills warmed her and proved how deeply he cared for her safety. She wondered now, as she made her way through the scrub with Foo bouncing ahead of her, if he had other motives for restricting her. She tried not to think about what those might be. Instead, she distracted herself with thoughts of Django, and when those were not enough, she worried about snakes and scorpions and mountain lions; but so little happened in her life that did not concern Willis or Linda that, in the end, every thought circled back to them.

Meanwhile, fearless with youthful energy, Foo dashed ahead of her on the slowly rising trail, scrambling in the gravel and rock, his muscular shoulders heaving as he made his way up the steep incline. Every few minutes, he ran breathlessly back to her, his small eyes almost crossed, his mouth pulled back, showing all his teeth. Smiling.

Sweat stung Madora's eyes as the path grew steeper, and she stopped to drink from her water bottle. The view of Evers Canyon lay wide before her. She saw the house and trailer and, marked by cottonwoods and sycamores, the curve of the dry streambed through the canyon bottom. There was a house against the opposite canyon side with a car parked out in front. Closer to the county road, a mobile home squatted in a clearing at the end of a long dirt track.

The trail grew steeper and Madora would have turned back except that in the steepest sections of the trail, someone had dug shallow steps out of the rock and spikes of rebar stuck up here and there for handholds.

At the top she puffed and bent double from the waist, her thighs quivering with strain. She drank more water, and when she recovered herself, she looked around and decided that the godlike view was worth the effort of the climb and explained the effort someone had gone to, to make the trail passable. The jagged terrain of the Cleveland National Forest stretched to the south and east, nothing but rocks and scrub, most of it too rough and unfriendly to explore. Far in the west she saw down the gentle seaward slope of the land to a line of blue that was just barely visible and which she knew to be the Pacific. North were more mountains and the six lanes of Interstate 8. If she could see far enough, she knew the ribbon of concrete stretched all the way to Tucson.

Not long before she met Willis, Madora and Kay-Kay had hitchhiked to Tucson to attend a concert for which Kay-Kay had won two tickets when she was the thirteenth person to call into the radio station managing the giveaway. The girls hitched in cutoff jeans and tank tops, carrying their concert clothes and makeup stuffed in backpacks: tiny, tight skirts and string-strapped T-shirts a size too small, high heels neither one of them could walk in comfortably.

Their first ride was with a middle-aged couple who took them a little beyond the Phoenix exit, the whole time telling them about the angel Moroni. The ride that deposited them in downtown Tucson was with a girl not much older than they were. She was heading to Austin, where she went to college. After she dropped them off, it had taken them two hours to find the house belonging to Kay-Kay's grandmother. Most of the long walk they had talked about the college girl and made fun of her, calling her boring and a loser.

Kay-Kay's grandmother was upset when she heard about the concert. When Kay-Kay called to make arrangements for them to sleep over, she had not understood that they would be spending most of their time away, listening to seven bands in a college arena, nothing but noise and bright lights until after midnight. She had made them a dinner with all the food groups and was irritable when they were too excited to eat any of it. After the concert, it was close to dawn when they got back to the house. All the doors were locked, and Kay-Kay's grandmother had put their things on the patio, where they slept on chaises until noon, rising only when the sun became too hot to bear. The house was empty, but the back door was unlocked. They took showers and ate cold cereal and drank beers from the refrigerator before making their way back to the highway to hitch home to Yuma.

Madora sat on a rock, remembering their adventure and how unafraid she had been.

In some ways, Madora's life was very simple and straightforward. Medical school for Willis was the first priority. And then, when he had his degree, they would marry and have children and settle down in a house not much different from the one Kay-Kay's grandmother lived in. But in order for any of this to happen, they needed money. They could earn it or borrow it, beg or steal, but without money they were headed nowhere.

Willis had an odd attitude toward money; even Madora could see that. Many months earlier, before Linda came into their lives, she had been putting away his folded laundry and found a blue plastic envelope crammed with papers she realized were bank statements. Knowing that Willis would be furious if he knew she had examined the contents, she put the folder back exactly where she had found it. But for days she thought about the statements and wished she had risked taking a good look at them. A few days later she opened his drawer again, but the plastic envelope was gone. She had spent most of that afternoon hunting through the bedroom for it but without success.

Sometimes Willis talked as if it would be a long financial struggle to save enough for medical school. At other times she got the feeling that he had enough put away already. She had once or twice been tempted to point out the contradictions but thought better of it.

In the casino a few steps from the diner where she had worked before her car broke down, the women were sometimes so eager to get back to the tables or the slots that they left their purses behind in the toilet stalls. It would be easy to steal from them, but Madora would be ashamed to take advantage of the poor fools. The only person she could think of who might have access to serious money was Django, but even if half of what he said about Huck was true, there was no way the guy would loan Django thousands of dollars so Willis could go to medical school. Besides, Django hated Willis and would never do anything to help him.

In Madora's thinking, her happiness and everything that mattered, her whole future, depended on getting money for medical school. Willis could call her stupid, but it wasn't true. There were things she understood without being told. He was a good man, but he was growing discouraged and had begun to see the world as bent against him. It was no wonder he was short with her and sometimes unkind. Money would change his outlook on life.

She might be able to overcome her pride enough to stand on a street corner with her hand out, but she could do that for twenty years and not take in enough money. She could go to work, but the only skill she had was waiting tables. Working in a diner for minimum wage plus tips was not the way to get rich quick. It wasn't fast money, but it was sure.

Back at the house she ignored the time. Linda would be fretting for her lunch, but Madora was in a so-what frame of mind where *she* was concerned. She tied Foo to the side of the carport, and when she had changed into her cleanest pair of jeans and a T-shirt out of the dryer, she walked fast down to the county road. Along the way, she looked neither right nor left to avoid seeing anything that might weaken her resolve.

After walking a couple of miles along the county road in the hot June sun, she reached the cluster of businesses near the on-ramp to Interstate 8. She stopped for a few minutes in the shade of a pepper tree, stuck out her lower lip, and blew breath up into her face. She was hot and sticky and wished she had money for a Coke. She was hungry too, and the smell of roasting chicken that emanated from the KFC a few yards away was hard to ignore. The cheesy smell of the pizza parlor across the parking lot was just as bad. She hurried to the on-ramp and stuck out her thumb before she could change her mind and go home.

Two women in a truck picked her up ten minutes later. Their names were Laurel and Candace and they were on their way to Phoenix to see Laurel's grandbaby who'd been born just two days earlier.

"Where you going?" Laurel asked. She was a pretty, fat woman wearing huge sunglasses.

"There's a casino up here about five miles," Madora said.

"You a gambler, then? Lord, I hope not," Candace fanned her face with her hand, and Madora admired her long shining fingernails. "I'm here to tell you, it's a curse and a vice."

Madora had never dropped a nickel in a slot machine and wasn't sure why anyone would ever want to. Her need for money was imperative, but it had never occurred to her to gamble. "I work at the diner. Least I hope I will. I used to."

Madora saw that the diner had a new sign. Eight feet high and thirty feet wide: *The All American Diner.* And on another sign just below it, a little smaller and flashing for attention: *Boys and Girls in Uniform Eat Free.* The signs were new and worrisome. She had never thought that the diner might have changed management. If she saw no one she knew serving or in the kitchen, she didn't know if she would have the courage to apply for work.

Candace drove off the freeway and right up to the front of the All American Diner.

"Good luck to you, now," she said.

Chapter 14

The diner was air-conditioned down to somewhere just over freezing. If Madora worked there, she'd tell Murray (the boss, as far as she knew) that he could save a lot of money if he raised the thermostat. She had goose bumps at the top of her arms.

Nerves maybe.

The waitress behind the counter looked up. It was Connie, who had been at the diner when Madora worked there. "Well, I'll be a monkey's uncle!" she said and enveloped her in a hug smelling of fried foods and Chantilly. "Girl, I was thinking of you just the other day. Wondering where you got to. How come you never came to see us? It must be, what? Almost two years?"

"Something like that," Madora said, flustered and pleased by the attention.

"Jorge!" Connie called out to the cook. "Look here what the cat dragged in."

The cook poked his head through the pass-through.

Under his handlebar moustache he was grinning. And still missing a front incisor lost in a fistfight. Madora wiggled her fingers at him and he laughed and wiggled his fingers back.

"You haven't changed a bit, Madora. Just got prettier's all. Sit down here and I'll get you something." Connie looked over her shoulder at a man sitting in the booth farthest from the door. He had a pile of papers laid out in front of him and his fingers flew over the keys of a calculator. "That's Vik; he's the new boss."

"What happened to Murray?" She had liked the fat old man who couldn't resist a milkshake. "Did he eat too much ice cream?"

"You could say so. He had a heart attack. Fell over one day and didn't get up again. We got the same owners, though. Vik's been managing for about a year."

"He's got the air-conditioning too cold."

"He says it makes people eat more."

Madora and Connie went on talking as if they had seen each other only a week before. Once or twice Madora heard her chatterboxing voice and it was hard to recognize herself as the same girl who got tongue-tied so easily. After about fifteen minutes her cheeks hurt from smiling.

A man came into the diner and sat down in a booth. His cowlicky hair was bright red.

"Lemme take his order." Madora had been away from the job for a little more than a year. "See if I can still do it."

"Honey, go ahead and be my guest. His name's Walt. He

comes in here a couple times a day. Works at the casino. Nice guy." She took an apron out from under the counter and tied it on Madora. "You've filled out, girl. You used to be skinny like a stick."

"Willis says I'm fat."

"Willis needs to get a pair of glasses." Connie patted her back. "Go on, now. We're running a business here."

Waitressing was like a pair of broken-in shoes Madora stepped right back into, feeling perfectly comfortable. She bantered and laughed with the customer named Walt, and when a couple of discouraged gamblers walked in, she cheered them up and said what they needed was some of Jorge's meatloaf.

"Comfort food," she told them.

The diner got busy for a while, and Madora enjoyed herself. First chance she got, she poured an iced tea flavored with lemon and pretend sugar and set it under the counter like she used to. At the top of her stomach, behind her ribs, butterflies fluttered the cha-cha-cha.

"I sure would like to work again," she told Connie. "Do you think Vik'd give me a job?"

"Go ask him. Tell him I'm your reference. I'll keep an eye on your customers."

Vik had been watching her at work, looking up from his calculator from time to time, chewing on his yellow pencil.

"What's your name?" he asked her.

"Madora Welles." If she had taken a minute to step outside herself, she would have been surprised by how relaxed she felt and how strong her voice sounded. She wished Willis could see her. She thought he would be proud of her. "Can I sit down?" It did not occur to her that Vik would say no.

He was a tall, narrow-faced man with blue-black hair combed straight back from a high forehead and skin the same golden-brown color as Foo's eyes. Madora had the feeling he was studying her, but she didn't mind this. It was his restaurant, after all, and she had stepped in and started working without even saying hello to him. He had a right to be curious about her.

"I'm not going to pay you for this last hour. You may be sure of that." He had an accent, sort of English. It was a nice voice, she decided. In charge but not mean. "You may keep your tips."

"I'll put them in the kitty; that's okay." Madora had been having so much fun, she would have paid for a chance to stay another hour; but time had passed quickly and if she didn't leave soon it would be a rush to make it home before Willis. "I used to work here."

"So I gathered."

"I'd like a job. Connie says some days she's beat off her feet, running around. She and I work good together."

"I also see that. But unfortunately, I have no money to pay another server for this shift." He put his hand on the pile of papers beside the calculator. "As you can see, there are many bills to pay. And never enough money."

"I'm good at waitressing," she said, surprised by her bravado. Right then, at that minute, she felt happier than she had in a long time. "And I'm a good worker."

"I have no doubt of that. But nothing changes the fact that I have no money for this shift."

She was uncommonly happy even as her hopes sank. It had been a good day no matter what happened, and her only regret was that she would not be able to tell Willis how much fun she'd had.

Vik patted the eraser end of his pencil against his lower lip. "There are such crowds. These gamblers never sleep. I will need an experienced server on the graveyard shift starting next month. Weekends only."

She felt like saying that gamblers were her specialty. She cheered up the losers and made them believe their losses would turn to wins the next time they threw the dice. The winners liked her too because she let them repeat their victory tales and never looked bored. But she could not work graveyard or weekends. Willis would be angry if she so much as brought up Vik's offer. She glanced at the big black-and-white clock over the pass-through.

"My boyfriend…"

"I understand, but I'm sorry. I believe you would have done a good job. Leave your phone number—"

"That's okay."

"Leave it here." He held out his pencil and a bit of paper. "Maybe next week things will change."

She backed away, shaking her head. "I don't have a phone."

"Madora, everyone has a phone."

"I'll come by again."

It was strange how quickly her confidence evaporated. She felt like someone caught naked in a public place. She looked at the clock and saw that five minutes had gone by since the last time she looked. *Willis, Willis, Willis,* she thought, and a tremor of fear went through her body. She tore off her apron and stuffed it under the counter beside her untouched tea.

"Madora, where you going?"

"I gotta get home, Connie. I don't know where the time went." She was making for the door, aware that in every booth, the customers had stopped eating and were watching her curiously. At the end of the diner, Vik had stood up as if he might need to rush forward and rescue her.

Maybe so. Maybe she would faint if she didn't get out of there fast.

"What about your tips?" Connie called after her.

Willis, Willis, Willis.

Madora was close to tears as she stood beside the on-ramp with her thumb out. Cars sped off the freeway, headed for the acres of parking around the casino, but it seemed that at that particular hour of the day—three, going on four—no one was leaving. Soon her arm and shoulder began to ache from thumbing. Behind her, a motor sounded close enough to mow her down.

She turned around. Walt, the customer from the diner, sat astride a motorcycle. She didn't know what kind it was; she didn't care. What she noticed was the size of it. In the diner he had been wearing Levi's and a sweatshirt and looked like an ordinary guy. Now he had on a leather jacket and helmet.

"Hey, you want a lift? I've got an extra helmet." He spoke over the noise of the bike's engine, and he did not sound like the man she had teased less than thirty minutes earlier. "I'm heading into town."

"I'll be okay," she said, though she knew she was dangerously close to tears. She looked at the motorcycle. "I don't like those things."

"It's safe. I've been ridin' for years." He took off his helmet, and the sight of his red hair reassured her a little. "Just hang on to me and you'll be fine."

"Someone'll give me a ride."

"Yeah. Me." He smiled. "Come on, I'll get you where you want to go. I won't let anything happen to you."

The situation felt familiar. In some way, at some time before, she had lived through something like this moment.

"Have you ever been on a motorcycle?"

She shook her head. "Do you know what time it is?"

He pushed up the ragged cuff of his leather jacket. "Quarter to four."

Her stomach sank. "How fast do you go?"

Speeding west on Interstate 8, her arms wrapped around Walt's midsection, Madora kept her eyes shut tight the whole time. It was frightening enough to feel the big bike under her, registering every bump in the road, throbbing with power, enough to feel the wind fluttering her eye-lashes and sometimes the sandpaper scrape of grit on her cheeks. And then, just as she had begun to relax and enjoy the ride, he exited the freeway and drove into the parking lot where the air smelled of pizza and chicken. Walt turned off the ignition and she sat with her cheek resting against his leather back, unable to move at first.

"You okay?" he asked and helped her off. Her knees were jellified. When he put his hands on either side of her head and lifted off the helmet, her hair fell around her shoulders but it didn't feel like hers. Nothing felt like her. She touched her cheek and chin and barely recognized the shape of her face.

Walt said, "I don't like to leave you here. You sure you don't want me to take you all the way home?"

"It's just up the way a little," she murmured in a voice that was strangely not what she expected to hear.

"It's awful hot and you don't have a hat."

His persistence had begun to alarm her. Every moment he stood talking to her was a moment she should have been walking toward home. She made herself look straight into his eyes. Willis was right; lying was a useful skill.

"I have to go in the market and get some stuff. Thanks a lot for helping me out." She took a few steps away, stopped, and looked back at him. He was a nice-looking man with cowlicky red hair and a sunburned nose, and even in his leather jacket he didn't look anything like the bikers at the house in Yuma. "Thank you," she said. "I feel so grateful. Really. I mean it."

She walked into the market and stood halfway up the soup aisle, where she could see beyond the check stand through the store's plate-glass windows. Walt stood a minute staring in her direction, then got back on his motorcycle and drove away. She felt a pang, seeing him go.

She waited inside the market for five minutes to make sure he wasn't coming back, then walked outside, across the parking lot, and up the county road with the sun beating at her back. When she got to Red Rock Road she started to run.

Chapter 15

Willis Brock's mother had been admitted to the hospital on the day he graduated from high school in Buffalo, New York. Willis's father was a general practitioner who had left town with his nurse years before, leaving his wife and son and a daughter named Daphne. Although Willis never had a good word to say for his father, he admired the medical profession and had taken all the Latin and science classes offered at his high school, intending to be a physician. On graduation day, his mother suffered the third or fourth of several heart spells that made her a semi-invalid, and instead of going to college, Willis was forced to remain at home seeing to her many needs as well as those of the anonymous men and women who rented rooms in the big mortgage-free house that was all Dr. Chasen Brock had left his family. He did not really mind; he could go to college later. The time he spent with his mother was precious, and as her health deteriorated he valued it more and more. Some nights they talked late and he fell asleep on the pillow beside her.

When his mother died, Willis kicked the tenants out, sold the house, and joined the Marine Corps.

He still had most of the money retained from the sale of the Buffalo house and all of the cash paid him in exchange for Linda's baby. Enough to get him into a med school in Antigua that he had read about on a client's computer. He remembered the counselor's condescension when she looked over his applications and the curl of her lipsticky mouth when she asked why he left the Corps. After the interview he sat in the Tahoe and thought about waiting for her to come out. He fantasized how good it would feel to beat her up. He pictured the look he would see on her face the moment before his fist broke her jaw. After a while he lost interest in the daydream and started to think about his career. He thought he would never be a doctor and the life went out of him like a lightbulb dying. Then he remembered the medical school in Antigua he had seen featured in a travel magazine at one of the houses where he worked. Although it wasn't prestigious, he knew it would suit him well enough. The nowhere location of the place might even be an advantage. It was doable, difficult but doable, he assured himself.

He could not afford another lapse like last night, however. Nothing ruined a doctor faster than booze, and it disgusted Willis to recall his drunkenness and the way he'd fallen through the kitchen door. Drinking to excess was a weakness and a shame, and if his mother were alive she would be scolding him, reminding him of the way his father had humiliated the family and brought it low.

In the long summer twilight, it calmed Willis's nerves and silenced his self-doubt to hide behind the big Tahoe's tinted windows and watch the girls. There was one he was particularly interested in.

He drove past Grossmont High School and a couple of junior high schools. So many girls, tattooed and pierced. Even the young ones still in their baby fat. The older girls, the skinnies, wore their jeans low on their narrow hips, flaunting butterfly tattoos and the Ts of their thong underwear. There were two or three he had followed home in the past to make sure they stayed safe. He wanted to throw coats and blankets over all of them, bundle them away, lock them up until they came to their senses and found some dignity, some self-respect.

Some weeks earlier, his attention had been taken by a pregnant girl in a pair of baggy-kneed stretch pants and an oversized pink T-shirt with *Sez who?* written on the back in glitter. Near a 7-Eleven, she was cadging hits off her friends' cigarettes and had a look Willis recognized. This was another one like Madora and Linda, thinking she was all grown-up when she was only a little girl who had gone too far and fast down the wrong road and lost herself along the way.

He had seen the pregnant girl another time when he stood in line at McDonald's. He had stopped in for a cup of orange juice, the best thing he knew for a quick energy boost. The previous two hours had been spent getting a client, Mrs. Waller, to eat a little oatmeal and then changing her diapers and bedsheets and running a load of wash. On his way home he would stop by again and shift the clothes from the washer to the dryer, and then tomorrow he'd fold them and put them away. She was a pretty-faced old woman with faded blue eyes in which Willis thought he saw a shadow of the devilish girl she had been. But she was addled now, in her eighties, and her only son was a barber in the Bay Area and rarely visited. Willis took good care of her. He imagined she was his mother; sometimes he even called her Mommy. Mrs. Waller was half out of the world, but when she heard that, her head snapped around and for a flash of a second her eyes focused. The poor old sweetie had never missed the ring he slipped off her hand and hocked for eighty dollars.

He liked having a bank account. Liked watching the balance grow. Every penny moved him closer to his dream.

In the McDonald's he had taken his orange juice to a table where he could watch the children in the tot lot. The girl was supervising a boy of eight or nine, and he was giving her trouble. Willis shoved open the door to the outside in time to hear the boy yell, "You're not my fucking mother."

"Hey, you! Kid!" Willis's shoulders had spasmed with the impulse to grab the brat and shake him until his brains rattled. He towered in front of him. "Clean up your language, son. You don't talk like that to a young lady."

"She's my sister."

"I never would have talked to my sister that way."

147

"Fuck you, old man. I can say what I want."

The girl must have felt Willis heating up. "It's okay," she said quickly. "I'm used to the way he talks. He doesn't mean nothing."

Up close Willis had seen her tormented complexion beneath layers of cheap makeup, the flecks of black mascara beneath her eyes, the scabby dandruff at her hairline. The raw vulnerability of the girl had touched Willis as Linda's had when he saw her panhandling in the rain.

"When's your baby due?"

"A few months." She didn't know exactly, which meant she hadn't been to a doctor.

"Are you taking care of yourself?"

She squinted at him, quick to be suspicious. "What do you care?"

"I'm a doctor," he said. "Babies are my specialty."

"How come you're here?"

He had talked to her about orange juice and blood sugar. "What's your name?"

"Shelley. What's yours?"

"Is your baby a boy or girl?"

"Don't know."

"You should see a doctor and get an ultrasound."

She watched her brother go down the slide backwards. "Where's your office?"

"I work at the hospital." The words had come to him as freely as the truth.

As if having a father who boozed and eloped with his

twenty-year-old nurse and pockets full of money embezzled from his medical practice wasn't scandal enough, Willis's sister, Daphne, had been foolishly taken in by a smooth-talking someone-or-other. Willis was twelve at the time, a bright and thoughtful boy with few friends, casting about for the direction he would take in life. He remembered the sound of a motorcycle idling in front of the house, the front door slamming and Daphne's high-pitched giggle followed by the gunning engine and the peel-out squeal of tires.

For days afterwards, Willis wanted to go find Daphne and bring her home. His mother doted on his honorable intentions. But there was nothing they could do, she told him. *"Your sister's ruined."*

The old-fashioned word—*ruined*—stayed with Willis and carried weight.

Sometime after this—he was inclined to conflate the two events, though they had occurred a year or so apart—his father's runaway nurse appeared at the front door when his mother was upstairs in her bed and the boarders had not yet come to the table for the evening meal. He had not recognized her, though he vaguely recalled his father once having a nurse in his office downtown in the Passway Building. She was pretty and flirty in those days, but the years since had been hard on her. She was roundly pregnant and told Willis that his father had run out on her, and her own family had turned her away as well. That was the first time Willis forged his mother's signature on a check, one hundred dollars made out to his father's ex-girlfriend.

Later he had to confess to his mother; he was that kind of son. He expected to be punished for his crime, but she surprised him, laughed tolerantly, almost with pleasure, and said he was a good boy, a gentleman—already a better man than his father. Willis was confused about sex and sexuality, shy and deeply confused by puberty. His mother told him, and he believed: *"Young women are vulnerable, and men like your father live to corrupt them. But not you, Willis. You're special."*

Buffalo was a small city, and from time to time he heard that Daphne had been spotted outside a club or speeding through downtown in a convertible late at night. He would never have learned of her death had not one of the boarders pointed out an article in the metro section of the city paper. His mother told him to put the paper in the incinerator at the bottom of the yard and come right back. *"Don't waste time reading it."*

Though normally an obedient boy, he read the item on the back page, third in a list of crimes committed in Buffalo that week. The paragraph said that not much was known about Daphne Brock except that she was the daughter of Chasen Brock, MD, who had been accused of embezzlement years earlier. Her assailant had done time for selling drugs. Cocaine and drug paraphernalia were found in the apartment they shared.

The world was crowded with girls as heedless of danger as he was sure his sister had been, and he wanted to rescue them all.

The day after his interview, he was in Grossmont again and saw Shelley up ahead outside the trolley station, wearing a scoop-necked T-shirt and the same stretchy pants and teetery platform sandals.

He stopped the Tahoe and lowered the passenger-side window, smiling in the way he knew would reassure her.

"Hey there, Shelley, you look like you just lost your best friend."

She leaned in the window, revealing deep cleavage. Embarrassed, Willis looked over her shoulder.

"I was supposed to meet my friends, but they're late or I messed up. They might be at the movie already."

"Can I give you a lift?"

He drove her to the mall entrance to the theater and stayed there, double-parked, watching her walk away. He thought of Linda lying on the bed in the trailer, crabbing for her freedom, and of Madora growing restless, asking questions. A girl like Shelley would be grateful for Willis's help.

He watched her walk away. *Next time,* he thought. It would be easy.

Chapter 16

He came home feeling good and found Madora frying up hamburger patties in a nervous state. The house smelled of onions. She began telling him how hard it was to get along with Linda.

"She squatted right there, in the middle of the trailer, and did her business. And I had to clean it up, Willis. Me. That's not fair." She was crying. "You have to do it, Willis. You have to let her go. You said the other night... that the decision was up to you. You said that and now I'm asking you please, please let her go."

He felt like a small, still pool in the middle of a whirling torrent.

"She was angry with you, Madora. What did you do to make her angry?"

"I was a little late giving her lunch."

"Well, do you blame her for being ticked off? I suppose you were taking a nap and slept through the noon hour. Is that what happened?"

"I guess."

"She doesn't have much to look forward to, Madora. Mealtimes are important."

"You have to let her go. Set her free, please."

He heard a troubling note of determination in her voice.

"And exactly how am I supposed to set her free?"

"Tie her up, gag her, drive her somewhere, and let her out. Far away, Idaho or Montana." She looked half crazy with the spatula in one hand like a club and her hair and face a mess. "She doesn't know who we are; she's never seen the house or the trailer. I just can't do this anymore. Don't make me, Willis."

Who would have guessed that Madora would develop a mind of her own?

He took her in his arms, let her sob against his shoulder. Her hair smelled of onions, and he thought of the many smells of women and wondered how they could stand to live with themselves.

"You've had a hard day. You're tired out and not thinking straight. I don't blame you."

She stopped crying but she clung to him, her body soft and pliant and like a stranger's bed pillow, faintly disgusting to him. After some moments he extricated himself and urged her to sit down. He pulled his own chair close to hers so they were sitting knee to knee.

"I thought we were together in this. I thought you wanted to help Linda as much as I do."

"I take care of her and—"

"And she's mean to you. I know she is. And you are so patient. I really admire that in you, Madora. Your patience."

A blush of pride brightened her cheeks.

She said, "But we can't keep her forever."

If Linda were gone, there would be a place for Shelley. And when Shelley had her baby he would demand more from the lawyer. Infertile couples were ravenous for Anglo-looking babies and would pay any amount of money.

"You're right. We can't keep her forever."

"But when you let her go—"

"When *we* let her go," he corrected.

"She'll go right to the police."

"Suppose she did? Didn't you just tell me she doesn't know anything for sure?" He laughed tolerantly. "Anyway, I wouldn't worry about Linda talking. You're not a student of human nature, Madora. But if you had a job like mine where you mix with all kinds of people, you'd get a feel for how they think. Linda will never go to the police. She's a rebel. She hates authority."

Madora appeared to be thinking about this. She stood up and he watched her absentmindedly begin to eat the onions she had fried, taking them out of the pan with her bare fingers.

Why not get rid of Madora? he wondered.

"Do I get any dinner?"

She looked at him and then down at her oily fingers. "Sorry, Willis. You know how I get when I'm worried."

"You eat. That's why I don't buy you sweets anymore."

There was nothing gross about Madora's figure, but she was plump and Willis preferred girls who looked a little starved. Their outsides and insides matched.

She watched him eat. "What if you're wrong, and Linda isn't like other girls and she does tell someone? What will I do if you go to jail, Willis? I couldn't bear it."

How had his life come to this? he wondered. How had he become the protector of these girls who fought him at every turn, who each in her own way sabotaged his kindness? He put down his fork and fixed Madora with an unblinking stare. He spoke with the confident leadership voice his drill instructor had used, a voice Willis had practiced alone in his apartment before he ever met Madora.

"I am not going to jail, and neither are you."

"Me?"

"I won't let anything bad happen to you."

"Me?"

"Madora, are you going to let this girl down? All her life everyone has let this girl down. Are you going to do it too?"

"What do you mean?" Her voice had ripples in it like wind across water.

"Is the government going to help her? What about her mom and dad? You think they can help her? They've already messed her up, Madora. A girl doesn't get messed up like Linda because she has a happy home."

"I'm afraid."

"You break my heart, Madora. After all we've been through together. I believed in you, and now you don't trust me."

She looked stricken.

"I saved you," he said. "Those men, those bikers, would have come looking for you. God knows what they would have done to you."

I know," she said. "I know."

"Well, then?"

"Linda isn't like me. I wanted to be saved. I was ready."

"Are you going to hold that against her?"

"But what are we going to do with her?"

"Don't let me down, Madora. I don't know what I'd do if you were to disappoint me."

Chapter 17

LA's vast freeway system was constantly undergoing repairs and expansion, which invariably required that some lanes be closed. Where there would eventually be six or even eight lanes in each direction, there might be only two or three for months on end. The same trip could take thirty minutes one week and ninety the next.

"There's no telling how long this'll take," Robin told Django as they drove up Interstate 5—as if he had not spent the whole of his life in Los Angeles and its environs.

Traffic slowed, even in the carpool lane. For fifteen minutes the cars inched along the asphalt, making scarcely discernible progress.

Django watched his aunt surreptitiously. His mother had a name for people who drove as she did, with their shoulders forward and tense, but he couldn't remember what it was. The memory lapse upset him. Though the sadness when he thought of her was almost unbearable, even worse was the fear that he would stop remembering. He wanted to remember everything she had ever said, the tone of her voice and the way she looked when she said it; but already he felt her going, losing substance, like a dream slipping away in the morning air. Or a symphony, its rich and complex orchestration dropping off, instrument by instrument. One day all that would remain of his mother would be a haunting one-finger melody, and eventually even that would vanish.

Tears burned the back of his eyes. He needed to ask someone how long the crying would last, how much was too much, too babyish. And then he wanted to throw something to get rid of the sadness, the memories, the reality of what was gone forever; but the only thing at hand was his iPhone, and pitching that through the window would only make things worse.

Robin had told him to put yellow tape on anything in the house he wanted to keep. Some they would bring back with them. Most of it was going to be shipped down to Arroyo. When Robin was occupied he would go into the music room and get the money his father kept hidden in a fake copy of a book called *The History of Early Pipes and Drums*. Jacky had told him that a man never knew when he might need a thousand dollars, cash.

Django was almost dying of boredom in Arroyo. He had been instant messaging and e-mailing Lenny and Roid since midnight and still neither of them had responded to his invitation to meet up at the house. It was summertime and they might be on a vacation, but that was no reason to ignore his messages.

He liked Madora but he didn't know why exactly, except that when he was with her he felt like he was helping in some way. She was mysterious without knowing it, full of secrets. Once he was thirsty and hot and asked if she could give him water with ice cubes. She didn't want to and it took some persuading. He had sensed her fear when she took him into the kitchen of the little old house. He had never been in such a dump, and it was hard not to let on. Maybe she was a little embarrassed to have him see the way she lived or maybe she didn't know any better. The grimy details of the place sort of fascinated him: the shadow of dirt around the doorknob, the closed-in dog and dust and people smell of the living room with a stained sectional couch so massive it took up almost all the space, no pictures or photographs on the walls, not even a calendar. No computer. No TV. No phone. Not even a radio. He knew not to ask her why she lived this way; he knew the answer she would say. Willis.

The more he knew Madora, the more he felt that there was loneliness and sadness in her that matched the same feelings in him and that when he could find a way to comfort her, it would make him feel better too. He didn't know how he would do it, but he was determined to come up with something eventually.

In about an hour he was going to be back in his old house, which was as different from the dump where Madora lived as any house could be. In Django's house there were a dozen or more television sets and a bunch of computers, plus a room for showing movies and a phone in every room including all the bathrooms. He had not told Madora this because he knew it would sound like he was bragging and she might feel bad. Maybe it was better that she thought he was the biggest liar in the world.

There were a few items in the house that Django wanted. But at the same time none of it was important to him anymore. Even the thousand dollars was just in case he needed it. He was stuck, caring and not caring: one desire canceled by its opposite, one feeling negated by its antonym. Like antimatter. The parts of him that were filled with life were disappearing, and all that was left was the longing for his mother and father. The void. He used to like that word, but now he knew what it meant.

Django had been talking to Madora about Jett Jones and she asked him to explain antimatter. He tried but she shook her head and said he lost her. She wasn't book smart or imaginative, but she was a good listener and asked questions, which his old teacher, Mr. Cody, said was a sign of basic intelligence. He hated it when she talked about Willis like he was some kind of wise and all-knowing saint. Only a bad guy would leave a girl like Madora out in the middle of the boonies in a run-down house with just a pit bull for company.

And there was something jacked about that trailer in the back. Madora said it was empty, but when he had wanted to look inside she wouldn't let him.

"It's locked," she said.

"How come you locked an empty trailer?"

"It was like that when we got here."

"You mean you never looked inside?"

She watered the plants under the carport, acting like Django was all of a sudden invisible.

"Did you?"

"I told you, I don't know what's inside it."

"How do you know it's empty if you never looked? It might be full of electronic equipment. It might be worth something. Money."

"You're crazy. There's no electronics in that truck."

But how could she know that for sure unless she had looked inside? Madora had been lying about the trailer; Django was sure of it; and he wondered why bother to lie about something so unimportant unless it *was* important?

The van was going seventy plus when an electric blue Lotus Elise passed it in the second carpool lane.

"Wow, did you see that?" Django cried, sitting forward. "I bet it was going ninety."

Robin looked at him.

"That car. It was a Lotus Elise. They can go from zero to a hundred in under five seconds."

"Sounds dangerous to me."

Django knew she was thinking about the accident on Interstate 395, and now he was too. He reached in the small cooler and took out a soda and a sandwich.

"You want something?"

She shook her head. "I'm fine."

He didn't believe that, not one bit.

She wasn't fine, Madora wasn't fine, and he wasn't fine. The whole world was fucked up. He checked his messages. Still nothing from those jerk-offs. And now he was crying again. *"Waterworks!"* That's what his mother said to him when he was five and fell off his new two-wheeler with training wheels, shaving the skin off his shin. He bawled, and she cried, *"Waterworks!"* and started him laughing and crying at the same time. And then she tickled him like she always did. His father said, *"Your mom's a tickling fool."*

Why did he have to keep remembering stuff about her? She was even in his dreams. In one he saw the hem of the skirt she bought when they went to India. She liked the little bells stitched at the hem. Later in the dream he saw the heel of her bare foot and her ankle with the thin chain around it as she disappeared through a doorway. He followed her into a room and knew that she was there, but he couldn't see her except as a twirling shadow at the corner of his eye. He woke up prickly all over and wondered if the dream was telling him something. He halfway didn't want go into his house today for fear her ghost would be there. Or that it wouldn't be.

Chapter 18

The house that Jacky and Caro Jones built in the Belfleur section of Beverly Hills was a distinctly western style that would suit a landscape in New Mexico or Seattle as well as this knoll in Southern California. Constructed of stone and Douglas fir, redwood, cedar, and glass, the design was long and low and followed the curve of the hill on which it was built, facing west toward the ocean and overlooking a deep, wild canyon. From some angles it seemed to disappear into the landscape. Mr. Guerin had told Robin on the phone a few days earlier that several offers had been made on the property already. Recession or not, there were still people willing to spend millions of dollars to live in a work of art.

Robin parked the van behind the house just as the back door opened and Mr. Guerin stepped out, his arms open. Django ran into his embrace. With a pinch of shame, Robin remembered that when Django came to Arroyo, she had stood with her hands at her sides, as rigid as a pole and just as ungiving.

Robin's friends would not call her cold. *Restrained* would be their word for her, or they might say that she was dignified, but never cold. *Restrained* and *dignified* would have pleased her and seemed accurate before Django came into her life. Now, as she watched her nephew and Mr. Guerin embrace, she had a flash of understanding. For a split second a light went on and she saw herself with stunning clarity. She had always envied Caro her uninhibited gift for life. Envied and resented and in reaction, she had gone to the other extreme, pulling a cool and dignified carapace about herself. She did not want to believe that her personality was little more than a reaction against her sister's, but she thought it might be the truth.

She heard the lawyer say, "Mrs. Hancock's upstairs, DJ. Go on up to her why don't you?"

Guerin turned to Robin and reached for her hands, holding them between his warm, dry palms. "My dear, I know this is difficult, but I so appreciate your coming." The shimmer in his blue eyes brought tears to her own.

He led her indoors, across a long enclosed porch crammed with shrouded outdoor furniture and into the kitchen. It was as if a maid had only moments before finished polishing the stainless steel, glass, and tile expanses. The hardwood floors gleamed in the sunlight pouring through the array of skylights. On the island counter someone had placed an arrangement of long-stemmed yellow roses—Caro's favorite since her teens—in a cut-glass vase.

Robin looked at Guerin, questioning.

"Mrs. Hancock," he said. "She's arranged them throughout the house. She was their housekeeper since before Django was born. You probably know that."

No, she had never heard of Mrs. Hancock.

"We had some great meals in this kitchen. Pasta, of course. It was the only thing Caro knew how to cook. We'd eat right at this counter. That's how you knew Caro liked you. She fed you in the kitchen." Guerin was garrulous in his grief. "She told me once that when Jacky got on her nerves she'd come down here and chop vegetables. Whatever was in the refrigerator. One of the women who came in to clean...afterwards...told me the big freezer was full of baggies of chopped onions and red pepper and celery."

"What did you do with them?" Robin didn't really care but she needed to keep Guerin talking while she struggled to compose herself into the pretense that visiting her dead sister's house for the first time was a business-as-usual kind of thing.

"I took everything downtown to the soup kitchen our church runs. I did the same with the contents of the pantry." He shook his head. "I still don't always believe they're gone. I used to talk to Jacky almost every day about something or other. His business affairs were huge, as you might imagine, and I tell you, I find myself with time on my hands these days. I'm thinking I might retire."

"And the will?" Robin wondered if the question was crass and decided she didn't care. She had not expected to be so emotional, and the important thing was to keep him

165

talking. Restrained. Dignified. Controlled. If Robin was not these things, what was she?

"Basically, the estate goes to Django. In trust until he's twenty-one. Of course, there'll be a generous allowance. You won't have to foot the bills yourself. We'll have a formal reading in another couple of weeks but I can tell you how it's going to go. Your mother will have an income, a nice one, so if she wants to travel or live in Tahiti, she can do it. Caro told me they didn't get along, but she was generous anyway. That was typical of your sister and Jacky. Huck gets a stock portfolio and some memorabilia, a lot of his dad's music stuff. God knows, he doesn't need more cash. Mrs. Hancock will be able to retire comfortably, and there are gifts for the rest of the help. They were generous people, Robin. The more they had, the more they were willing to give away. Jacky wanted Ira to have the house in Cabo. Jacky and Caro both wanted you to have the contents of this one."

"All of it?" She had expected a token, no more.

"Everything. Including the switch plates if you want them."

Robin folded her arms and pressed them hard and tense against her chest. "I had no idea. Everything about this has been such a surprise." She looked at the old man and he nodded. They both knew she meant Django too.

"I haven't handled this well, Robin. You deserved more preparation, but I must confess I wasn't thinking clearly for a while. It was such a monstrous shock." He kept talking,

talking. "I'm an early riser and I'd just made my coffee when the call came—a police chief up in the desert—and I literally dropped the cup. My wife came in and saw me just standing there, staring at the mess on the floor." He pressed the heels of his hands against his eyes. "Caro and Jacky were the most vital people I've ever known. I miss them all day, every day."

She wished she could comfort him, but she did not know how so she focused on practical matters.

"What about Jacky's studio? All the sound equipment and electronics?" In one of their rare telephone conversations Caro must have told her this.

"It goes to a high school music academy in Southeast. A charter high school, whatever that is. I've never been quite sure. He wanted Django to have his piano. And any CDs he wants. Jacky had thousands. Will you have room for it all?"

Robin stared over Guerin's shoulder at the digital clock on the stove. "They planned it all." The luminous numbers bored a hole between her eyes. "As if they knew..."

"Last year they tossed out the old will and I wrote a new one for them."

"That means she really wanted me to have Django."

"Oh, yes, my dear. They both did. They were very clear about that."

"But why?"

"She loved you, Robin. And obviously she trusted you. There's no money in the will for you, but you'll receive a stipend for acting as Django's guardian and everything else in the house, the furniture and the art, the rugs—all of it is yours, Robin. You'll be a wealthy woman."

If Caro trusted her enough to leave Django in her care, if she wanted her to have the contents of this beautiful house, why had she never reached out? What secret had Caro been hiding?

"There's one other thing." Guerin pulled a business card from his wallet and handed it to Robin. "Caro stipulated in the will that if anything happened to her, she wanted you to be the one to tell your father. She wrote his address and phone number on my card. He's not far away. Up the road in Temecula."

Robin escaped into Caro's home. Taking all afternoon, she walked through the rooms, down every hall, and looked into each closet and cabinet. As she walked she heard her sister's voice, a running commentary on the contents of the house.

Sell that painting. No one needs two hundred thousand dollars' worth of white on white.

Keep those baskets; they were made by an old Washoe Indian woman. No one else knows that pattern.

That bit of silk—it's nothing special, but I loved it.

Robin marked some of the items she wanted shipped to Arroyo with yellow tape; blue was for undecided and white for consignment. To do the job properly she would have to come back for at least another two or three days. Her mother might like some of the furniture, or perhaps she would move to Tahiti as Guerin had said, live in a hut, and take an island lover. At this point in Robin's life, almost anything seemed possible. She wondered if she would miss her mother if she left Southern California and added that question to the list she did not want to think about at present.

There were yellow roses throughout the house, and someone—probably Mrs. Hancock—had seen to it that the windows were open, filling the rooms with air and light. Robin imagined her sister's spirit, a sprite, dancing through the rooms ahead of her.

Django pulled out of Mrs. Hancock's comforting embrace. Turning his back to her, he wiped away his tears and fiddled with a line of vintage *Star Wars* figures his father had given him for his seventh birthday. He tore off strips of yellow tape.

"So how are you getting along down there in Arroyo?" Mrs. Hancock asked. "Do you have a nice room of your own, Django?"

"It's okay."

"Will it be big enough for your furnishings and all? Your father wanted you to have his piano. That's a Steinway grand. Will there be room for it at your aunt's house?"

"I guess."

"Well, I hope that means yes. Don't forget to put some tape on the bed and the dresser. And your PC."

"I've got my laptop already."

"You remembered that? With all you had on your mind?

That was smart, but you've always had a steady head on your shoulders, Django." He taped the furniture he wanted, the pictures and posters, the sports equipment, knowing that her eyes were on him the whole time. "There's not a bite of food in the house, but I could go down to Subway and get you a sandwich if you'd like. Or maybe one of those fancy coffee drinks from Mr. Locastro at Calabria? He was asking after you, Django. Up and down Sunset you've got friends sending their best wishes."

"Did Lenny or Roid call?" Maybe they had lost his cell phone number. "Did they come over?"

"I'm sorry to say, they did not."

"I've been texting and leaving messages."

Mrs. Hancock nodded and pursed her lips.

"Maybe they went on vacation. Roid was saying they might go to Hawaii." He felt foolish saying it. Even a digital dragon like Mrs. Hancock knew there were cell phones in Hawaii.

"You think maybe they got sick?"

Mrs. Hancock bent to pick up something on the floor, something so small he couldn't even see it from where he stood.

"Maybe there was an accident?" If there was anything Django had learned in the last weeks it was that with terrifying speed unspeakable things could happen to the people he loved.

"Try not to fret too much, dear boy."

She put her arm around him. Part of Django didn't

want to turn toward her and didn't want to cry again, but he couldn't stop himself. Sorrow was a time machine and he was a little boy again.

Mrs. Hancock said, "When a person suffers a great sadness, some of his friends can't help themselves; they just have to turn away. Roid and Lenny—they're just kids and they don't want to think about how this happened to you because it means it could happen to them likewise."

Mrs. Hancock smelled like roses, sweet and cinnamon.

"You know, I was married once, before I came to work for your dear mama and daddy. My good husband had cancer and died when he wasn't even forty. He never went to the hospital; I kept him at home and nursed him myself. At the end, the last weeks, his friends all stopped coming 'round. Our little house was so empty, Django. Empty as you feel right now."

He brushed his tears away with the back of his hand.

"I'd be lying if I told you I didn't care. To be sure I did, but in time I understood that the men he worked with, his poker club and all—they were afraid. They didn't want to think about death. They wanted to live their lives like they were immortal."

"Mr. Cody said we were a posse and that we were going to change the world."

"And, of course, you miss them. It's a dreadful time for you and don't I know that. Myself, I'm going soon to live with my daughter and her family up in Bakersfield, and everyone is telling me how I ought to be happy not to work anymore. But Django-boy, I'd stay with you if I could. If they'd let me, I'd raise you up myself."

"I could ask Mr. Guerin—"

"Your parents wanted you to go to your aunt. It's in the will."

"She doesn't know about kids. I don't think she likes me very much."

"What do you mean she doesn't like you? How can she not like a good, smart boy like you? I never knew a better boy. Are you minding your manners, Django? Do you remember to look around you or are you in your head all the time, dreaming up those Jett Jones stories so you miss half of what's going on?"

"I'm gonna live with Huck. It just takes a little while to arrange."

"Ah. I see. Well, it's a rotten situation all around, but give it time. That's all I know to tell you. In time the pain will fade a little." She stroked his cheek. "Learning that lesson is a part of growing up, my dear. It's a pity and a crime you had to learn it so young, but there you are."

"Will I forget them?"

"Those two? Your dear mother and that rascally wonderful father? Never, Django. No one ever forgets their kind. Especially not their son."

The garage had a side door. Django let himself in and turned on the lights. Each of his parents' cars was still in its place as if waiting for them to come back: a silver-blue Mercedes sedan, an old MG convertible with a wooden dashboard, a white Land Rover. But at the far end of the garage one space was unoccupied, and that was why he had come into the garage. In order to believe that they were really gone, he had to see the empty space where the gorgeous new Ferrari should have been. That empty space was more definitive than all the explanations given by Ira and Mr. Guerin and Mrs. Hancock.

He opened the door of the Mercedes and slipped in behind the wheel. The car was only a few months old and still smelled new, but his mother had left a scarf on the passenger seat, and when he wrapped it around his neck, the scent of her perfume was still in the fibers. Yesterday or that morning, an hour ago, he would have wept; but at that moment, alone and unobserved, his eyes were dry. Possibly he had used up his lifetime supply of tears.

The key was in the ignition where his mother always left it, and all Django had to do was open the garage door, turn the key, and drive out the gate and over to the 495, left on Highway 101, and then straight up the map to San Jose and then Los Gatos. It had been his mother's favorite car trip, and they made it almost every spring when everything was green. There were special places along the way where they always stopped for great hamburgers or to look at a spectacular view. Once she made Jacky detour into Morro Bay so they could look at the house on Estero Street where she had grown up. It was hard to imagine his mother living in such a plain little house, she who loved things beautiful and extraordinary.

The problem was, he didn't know how to drive.

Chapter 19

Foo woke Madora in the middle of the night, rattling the back door with his nose and whimpering. The warm wind blew up swirls of gritty dust that raked the side of the house and rattled the roof, putting the dog's nerves on edge, and hers as well. She let him in and together they snuggled under a comforter on the couch. Foo slept immediately but the noise in Madora's head kept her awake. Thinking back, she could not remember when she last enjoyed a good night's sleep.

During the months of Linda's pregnancy, as Madora fed and cared for her, she had made a fragile peace with her conscience by believing what Willis told her, that they were doing good. As Willis had once saved her, he wanted to do the same for Linda, and there was something almost holy in that. But now that it was time for Linda to start a new life, he resisted letting her go. Did he intend to keep her in the trailer for months longer or even years? It would mean that Madora and Willis would never leave Red Rock

Road; there would be no medical school, no marriage, no family.

As soon as she got back from the diner the day before, she had taken food to Linda, who had responded by making her mess in the middle of the little square of carpet beside her bed. Madora, her nerves already frayed from the rush to get home before Willis, stood in the door of the trailer and screamed at her until she wore herself out. And last night she had been so afraid Willis would find some clue that she had been away from the house, she had barely been able to talk sensibly.

Why had she ever thought he would let her work again?

One hundred questions and problems and doubts flew through her mind like the termites she saw swarming every spring. First one, then another and another and then a cloud of them. They chewed at the uprights that supported the roof of the carport. This year or next the carport would collapse, and the damage spread to the timbers of the old house, and it too would begin to crumble.

She listened to the wind and the scratch of grit on the window glass, and gradually, perhaps from exhaustion, the confusion began to clear. She saw not just the present but into the future as well. Even if there were a safe way to set Linda free, other girls would follow her, and probably they too would be pregnant. Recalling the night of the baby's birth, she remembered Willis's high color and excitement. He had been radiant with power that night. To feel that way again he would continue to imprison girls, calling it rescue, calling it a second chance, his mission. There were a thousand ways to hide the truth.

Willis said Linda would never go to the police because it was her nature to reject authority; but if he really believed this, why not set her free? Even if he was right and Linda never said a word, there would be no assurance that they could trust the other girls, the strays Madora was sure would follow Linda. One of them would tell her story to others like herself: girls and boys she met on the street, drunks and addicts and homeless. The story of her captivity would begin to move about like a living thing, gaining in detail and intensity. Inevitably, Willis would be found out and sent to prison. And what would happen to her?

Foo growled in his sleep, and his little tail wagged against Madora's thigh.

She did not want to go to prison.

"So," Willis said the next morning, "you've been after me to go to town. How 'bout this morning? Would you like that, Madora?"

"I guess." She moved slowly about the kitchen, groggy from lack of sleep. If Vik was in town, or Connie, they would want to talk about her visit to the diner. In town she might see Walt, and if he spoke to her there would be no way, afterwards, to explain the circumstances to Willis.

"What's the matter with you?"

"I didn't sleep much."

"You slept with the dog. On the couch. What do you expect?"

Willis had not taken Madora into town for months. She had lost count of the time. Of course she wanted to go with him. He seemed to have forgotten that Linda had not had breakfast, and Madora did not remind him.

"If you don't want to go—"

"No, I do, really. Can we stop at that bookstore where they have magazines? They're real cheap there, Willis."

He shook his head. "You'll want to stay all day, and I don't have time. I've got an appointment, plus we can't leave Linda alone for long. And the longer you put off cleaning up her mess, the tougher it'll be."

Madora wasn't going to do it. She wasn't even going to think about it.

"What kind of appointment? Is it about medical school?"

"What're you talking about?"

"You said you have an appointment."

He looked at her and slowly shook his head. "You ought to think about what you say, Madora. You really ought to try connecting your mouth to your brain for once."

"I didn't know—"

"You didn't know what? That when a man's got things on his mind, a good woman doesn't hammer him with questions?"

"I wasn't hammering."

He let out a long groan and rested his forehead on the tabletop. "You are so stupid, Madora."

She had no education, but that did not mean she was stupid. Willis was restless and discontented, mad at the world and taking it out on her. She tried to be understanding, but it was hard when she had her own reasons to grumble.

"I'm lonely," she said.

"Yeah?" He raised his eyebrows in mock surprise. "So's everyone else, Madora. There's nothing special about you."

By the time Willis parked the Tahoe in the lot behind the supermarket in Arroyo, he was in a playful mood. He pushed the shopping cart up and down the aisles of food, lobbing boxes of cereal and loaves of bread into the cart as if money was of no importance. He grabbed a giant-sized yellow packet of M&M'S off the shelf and tossed it at Madora like a beanbag. Luckily, she caught it. Twenty minutes later, standing in line for the only open cash register, she kept thinking what would have happened if she had missed it. She saw the package bursting and the candy-coated peanuts rolling underfoot. For half a minute she wondered if Willis might have thrown the bag at her in the expectation that she *would* miss the catch. To humiliate her. It was an odd thought and she was instantly ashamed of thinking it. Still, when she looked at the yellow bag on the conveyor belt, she did not want the candy.

Willis said something to the checker. The girl blinked and blushed and put her hand up to cover her mouth.

There will always be girls, Madora thought.

As they were putting the bags of groceries into the Tahoe's way-back, a woman called out from a few parking spaces away.

Beside Madora, Willis stiffened. "Hey, Ms. Howard, what's up?"

"Same as you, I guess. We got back from LA yesterday and there's nothing in the house to eat." She smiled at Madora like a woman in a magazine ad selling lipstick or toothpaste. Madora wanted to be introduced, but at the same time she longed to vanish from the scene. She felt conspicuous, as notorious as a woman with her face on a poster in the post office.

"I tried to call you, Willis, but the number you put on your application—"

"I know, I know. I thought about it after I left your house. I gave you an old one." Willis hit his palm against his head as if to knock some sense into it. "Most of the time, I forget I even own a cell phone. But it doesn't matter. I called your mother and I'm seeing her today."

This was the appointment Willis had spoken of at breakfast.

"That's great," Ms. Howard said. "And you'll give her the number where she can reach you?"

"Oh, sure."

He was lying, and so smoothly, without pausing or blinking. Madora knew he had no intention of giving anyone his phone number. Years ago, he had told her that knowing how to lie was a necessary skill, that people who couldn't lie convincingly were as handicapped as if they could not run.

"Honestly, Willis, if it were up to me, I'd hire you in a minute, but since you'll be working for her—"

"Not a problem. I'm going over to her place at two. I'm looking forward to the job."

Not a problem. Willis sounded different when he talked to this woman, casual and cheerful, as if nothing in the world mattered much. They were saying good-bye when a boy got out of the car. Django.

Ms. Howard said to Willis, "You remember my nephew, Django Jones?"

"I do. He made quite an impression."

Django looked at Madora, then at Willis. Willis stuck out his hand and Django shook it.

"How's your dog?"

"Healthy," Willis said.

Ms. Howard looked at Madora apologetically. "I'm afraid I can't introduce you. I don't know your name."

"Madora," she said softly.

"What a beautiful name."

Of all the things Robin Howard might have said, this was the least expected. Madora had never been spoken to so graciously by anyone that she could remember, and of course she was tongue-tied, couldn't think of anything to say. The glib, talkative girl she had been in the diner seemed like a mistake.

"It's a Greek name," Django said. "It means loving and levelheaded."

"Does it?" Ms. Howard looked at him, obviously surprised. "How do you know that?"

He shrugged. "I just do." Adding after an awkward moment, "I look stuff up. Online."

"Did you know that, Madora?" Ms. Howard asked.

She shook her head and tried to smile.

"Well, I'm sure the name suits you."

A few minutes later as they drove out of the parking lot, Willis said, "It was weird the way he knew that stuff about your name. A geeky kid like that? What're the odds, huh? You ever seen him before?"

"No," she said without blinking.

"And what was his name? Jangle?"

Madora could have told Willis that Django Reinhardt was the name of a Hungarian gypsy, a famous guitarist, and that Ms. Howard's nephew had been named for him.

"Maybe," she said. "Jangle. That sounds right."

Chapter 20

Madora put away groceries while Willis showered and changed ahead of his appointment with Ms. Howard's mother. She thought through the short conversation in the parking lot, going over it from every angle until she had exhausted all her impressions. It had been months since she had spoken even a few words to a female other than Linda and Connie. It was as if there were two planes of existence: the circumscribed one in which she lived and the wide world that belonged to everyone else. Her mother up in Sacramento lived in this greater world.

She wondered if her mother knew that her name meant loving and levelheaded.

Willis left for his appointment, and with her mind still hop-skipping, Madora went back to the trailer. She put a bucket of water, a bit of shingle, and a pile of rags next to the mess on the rug.

She told Linda, "You haven't eaten since yesterday. If you want food, you have to clean up after yourself."

"Fuck you, Madora."

"You can cuss all you want; I'm not going to do it."

"Willis'll make you."

"Why do you think I didn't bring you any breakfast? He said I didn't have to. Willis knows what you did and he thinks you're disgusting. But if you clean that up I'll fix you something good. This morning we went to the market and got lots of good stuff. No more bologna for a while."

"How do I know you're not trying to starve me to death?"

"Figure it out, Linda." She climbed out of the trailer. Looking back in, she said, "You've got fifteen minutes or no lunch."

She was trembling with nerves inside, her stomach flip-flopping fifteen minutes later when she went back to see if Linda had done the job. If the mess was still there, Madora did not know what she would do. If food wasn't enough to make her clean up, nothing else would work any better. Madora would not back down from her threat, though. She opened the curbside door and looked in. Linda had made an effort. Not much of one, but it was better.

"Okay," Madora said and dragged the rug toward the door. "I'll put this in the sun to dry, and then you'll get your lunch."

When she returned, Linda lay on the bed and Madora knew right away that she was more than usually upset. She lay facing the back of the trailer. In a skimpy tank top, her narrow, knobbed back filled Madora with sudden pity and a desire to make her happy.

"Come on and eat, Linda. I made you tuna fish with chopped onions and celery. A ton of mayonnaise." Silence. "And some cookies."

"I'm not hungry."

"But you need your strength." Rachel had said this to Madora when she kept her home from school with the flu. "My mom used to say food was like putting gas in the engine. Car can't go without gas, can it?"

She wanted to remember the sound of Rachel's voice, but it was like trying to capture a floating feather. Just when she thought she had it, it slipped away. Cautiously, she touched Linda's back. "Please. Sit up and eat. You'll never get to go home if you don't get strong."

At this, Linda turned over. Her small, teary eyes burned with a cold flame. "That's a load of shit and you know it. Stop lyin' to yourself. Just say it like it is. He's going to kill me, dump me in the desert. And you're going to help him."

Madora slapped her hands over her mouth.

"You'll do anything he asks, and don't pretend you won't." Linda swung her legs off the bed and stood up, holding a chair back to steady herself. "Killing me's the only thing he can do. And he's planning it. I know because I see it in his eyes when he looks at me. He knows I'll go to the police first thing I get free."

"Willis says you won't because you're a rebel and you don't trust people in authority."

"He's got that right, but if he thinks I'm going to let him get away with holding me prisoner for six months—"

"We kept you safe."

"He'll cut my throat and throw me in a hole. Or maybe he'll load me up with those pills he's got in his little black bag." She sneered. "*Dr. Willis Brock.* The great healer, Mr. Magic Hands."

"What do you mean?"

Linda's lips curved, making a smile. "What do you think I mean? You think he comes in here every night so we can talk about current events?"

"He's never touched you," Madora said. Whatever else, she knew this was true. "Willis isn't like that."

"I bet he doesn't touch you either." Linda's smile widened, revealing gaps where she had lost teeth. "Your precious Willis is a freak."

"Why? Because he doesn't treat you like the trash you are? You don't know anything about Willis. I've known him for five years and he would never... what you said."

"Fuck me?" Linda picked up the sandwich and looked at it. "Or kill me?" She put it down. "You're not a bad person, Madora. You're just sort of retarded."

"I am not!"

"You're one of those girls who never grows up. You just keep believing all the fairy-tale bullshit. Prince Charming and happily ever after. I know why you stay with him. You really believe it's gonna change. He leaves you alone all day and you daydream about a white wedding and a house and babies, but it's never going to happen. My baby's the only one you'll ever hold."

Madora's throat tightened like a fist.

"I bet sometimes you think about leaving, though. Am I right?" Linda laughed. "I am! You don't hide your feelings very well, Madora. A three-year-old could read you."

"He needs me."

"Oh, yeah, I bet he does. My old man needed me too. Needed me to go back in the woods with him."

"Willis isn't like that."

"My dear old dad said bad things would happen if I ever told anyone. He said he'd kill himself and it'd be like I'd murdered him. Well, I said good, shoot yourself in the head and go to hell. I took off and I'm never going back." Linda leaned forward. "You're scared of what'll happen to you if you walk away from him. I'll tell you what'll happen. You'll get free."

Linda reached out with her bound hands and picked up the tuna sandwich, her mouth twisted in disgust. Without warning, she threw it down and kicked it hard with her untethered foot. The slices of white bread fell apart and clots of mayonnaise and tuna smeared the floor. "Don't you ever get sick of this crap? Back and forth between me and your house or whatever you live in. You're his servant, Madora."

"He loves me."

"I bet he's got you thinking this is what you *want* to do."

Madora did not know what she thought anymore, but she would not be humiliated by this girl, this runaway, this street slut.

"Makes you mad, huh? The truth?"

"Clean up your mess." Madora stood at the curbside door with her hands knotted on her hips. "Starve yourself if you want."

"I'm not doing shit."

"Willis is going to be really mad when he sees—"

"So what? I could kiss his teeny-weeny and he's still gonna kill me. Can you get that into your dumb nut?"

"Stop saying that!"

Linda laughed. Madora couldn't get away from the trailer fast enough. She ran past the house and up the trail to her boulder. Dragging her knees up under her chin, she wrapped her arms around her legs and pressed her forehead into her knees so hard that her head began to ache. The more she wanted to cry, the harder she pressed. Foo sat on his haunches, facing her, panting and squeaking. At last she put her feet on the ground. She patted her thigh and he jumped up, settling into a seashell curl on her lap. He twisted his head, looked up at her, his sloppy tongue lolling.

"You're too big for this," she said, but if he had jumped down, she would have called him back.

For three summers during elementary school Madora had been enrolled in Methodist Bible camp. Monday through Friday, at eight sharp, a line of children, with Madora as close to the front as she could shove herself, climbed aboard a yellow school bus that took them an hour out of town to a camp where swimming was the reward for sitting still for Bible stories and lessons on hygiene and Christian behavior.

She anticipated the river before she saw it. Madora rolled down the bus window and through the dust she inhaled the river's green and wet-stone smell; and over the course of several summers and despite the Bible lessons taught by a team of earnest college students, Madora came to believe that God and flowing water were much the same. How Jesus fit into this, she never understood or really cared, for the river had captured her completely. It was as strong as God, with power to wear away the sandstone and make rocks smooth. It could be calm and soothing but had a temper too, so she knew she had better behave herself. Mostly the river was kind and good, though. It cooled her when she was hot, soothed her scraped knees, and gave her water to drink. Without it trees and bushes would not grow and there would be no small animals under rocks, no birds banking and drifting on the currents of air. No fish. At eight and nine and ten she had believed that God was all the creeks and rivers and streams flowing into lakes united in the greatness of the oceans and seas.

One day when she and Willis were living in a campground not far from Boise, they were caught in a roaring thunderstorm. As the rain drummed on the tent and they snuggled in sleeping bags side by side, she had told him her theory of God. He laughed at her. Willis talked about God and Jesus and heaven and hell with a derogatory conviction that it was all a story made up by a few powerful people to keep everyone else in line. He had many opinions and observations on the matter, and Madora listened mutely and knew that he assumed by her silence that she agreed. But in a rare act of rebellion, she told him he was wrong. There really was a God somewhere, in some form.

She had never wandered from her belief that at the root of all things there was something true and bigger than Willis, something almighty. That word thrilled her with hope that this Almighty Something had a plan for her life. In the plan, everything from her father's suicide to meeting Willis and not finishing school, even Linda, had happened for a reason.

She would not let herself believe that she had practiced mothering with stuffed animals and baby dolls, with dogs and cats, injured wild things and the neighbor kids, all for nothing, all so that she could spend her days waiting on girls like Linda.

That night she cooked a special dinner: chicken-fried steak and mashed potatoes and frozen green beans. For dessert she made chocolate pudding. Rachel used to sprinkle coconut on the top, but that was the kind of luxury item Willis would never let Madora buy, even on a shopping spree like the one they'd had that morning.

"This is nice," he said, looking at the table set with a cloth, two place settings laid out opposite each other. "You made a little effort. I appreciate that, Madora."

"I hope the meat's not too dry."

"That's why God made ketchup," he said, smiling and chewing.

After dinner she made coffee to accompany the pudding and again Willis commended her special efforts.

Normally she would bask in his praise, but this night was different from all others; and she feared that if she relaxed too much and felt too comfortable, if she allowed herself to be even a little lighthearted, she might use that as a reason to say nothing. She knew he had seen Ms. Howard's mother that afternoon and that the meeting must have gone well, because he was in a good mood. She almost asked him how it had gone, but first she had to talk about Linda again. To firm her resolve she remembered how Linda had spoken to her, the insult in her words and tone.

"She had another tantrum today. I made her a special sandwich and she threw it on the floor."

He smiled.

"It wasn't funny, Willis."

"I know, I know, but you gotta give the girl credit; she's got some spirit. I can't help liking her."

How could he say that when he loved *her*? She was the one he had chosen forever.

"The girl's got a tongue on her, I know; but then she's been through a lot, and living hard doesn't gentle a girl's spirit; that's for sure. But you'll do what you have to do. I'm counting on you."

"She says I'm a servant."

"Sticks and stones, Madora. Sticks and stones."

"If I didn't have to wait on her, you'd let me go to work."

"So you can be someone else's servant?"

"It's not the same thing. If I worked I could make money for medical school."

He sighed and stared at her for a long moment. "I don't have to listen to this." He pushed away the pudding half eaten, wiped a paper napkin across his mouth, and stood up. "Did you want to ruin dinner? Was that your plan? Well, you succeeded. I was having a good time—"

"When are you going to let her go?"

"This again? She'll go when I'm ready."

"She says it'll never happen. She says you're going to kill her."

The muscle along his jawline wormed. "That's what you think of me?"

"I told her it wasn't true."

"But you think it might be."

"She said awful things about you, Willis."

"You're just like your mother, Madora. You go along with a man until he trusts you—"

He smelled of sweat and dust.

"I do trust you."

"Words, Madora, just words. They can't hurt me, but they can't help me either. It's the way you act, what you're willing to do. That's what counts."

Fear pressured her bladder and her body tensed. Even her voice sounded tight. "I want us to have a real life and children and live in a house with neighbors. That'll never happen if—"

His right arm snapped back and forward, and the palm laid into the side of her head with enough power to knock her to the floor. Pain stabbed through her hip and up into her back as, gasping and whimpering, she scooted away from him, until she stopped against the refrigerator. She drew her knees up to her chest, protecting her head with her arms.

"Stand up."

She made herself as small as she could.

"Have some dignity, for godsake."

Already the left side of her face was swelling and her eye was closing. She began to cry.

"I told you to goddamn get up!"

She struggled to her knees and then her feet, leaned against the refrigerator for support. Her hip throbbed.

Willis poked his face forward, inches from hers. His breath was brown and bitter. "I don't want to hear you talk about Linda, about what's right for her. Do you understand? Can you put that in your stupid head and keep it there?"

"I'm not stupid," she cried.

"I said shut up!" He raised his hand again. She threw her arms up in front of her face.

But he didn't touch her. He stepped back and his chin dropped to his chest. For several minutes they remained as they were, facing each other. Outside under the carport, Foo was barking, and crows in the sycamores made a fearful racket. Dizzy, nauseous, Madora needed to sit down, but she was afraid to move. A voice in her head said she had done nothing to deserve being hit, another voice warned her to be careful, and a third told her it was her fault, she had pushed him too far. Her head spun with chatter.

Seeing stars, she fell forward. Willis caught her in his arms and helped her sit, and she wept with gratitude for the strength of his arms, the gentleness of his hands. He knelt before her, lifted her T-shirt, and laid his cheek against her stomach, wrapping his arms around her waist. She felt his lips move against her flesh as he spoke.

"God help me, Madora, what am I going to do with you?"

Chapter 21

Even asleep, Madora was aware of pain, and the night hours moved like a desert tortoise creeping between the whorls of tumbleweed. She got up after midnight and swallowed four aspirin, but they only gave her a headache to add to the tenderness in her back and hip and shoulder. She tried lying on the side that wasn't bruised, but that meant resting her beaten face on the pillow. She lay on her back and stared at the ceiling with a rolled towel jammed into the small of her back, holding a package of frozen broccoli against the side of her face. She dozed and woke to the sound of her own whimpers, her eyelids gummy with tears, stiff and sore from the nape of her neck to the base of her spine. The frozen vegetables had thawed and left a large wet spot on her pillow. She labored from bed to drink water and take more aspirin. In the kitchen she stood barefoot, watching the alabaster moths beat against the outside light. If she turned it off, some would still batter their frail wings in the fading warmth, lured to burning death by the memory of heat and light. Others would turn and fly toward the moon and stars.

She hated the little house now. It stank of her fear.

The next morning Willis behaved as if the violence of the night before had never happened. She waited for him to say he was sorry or just ask how she felt. He was going to be a doctor. At the least Madora expected him to tell her what to do about her damaged face. Instead, as she scrambled eggs and made toast, Willis brooded. He straddled a kitchen chair with his chin resting on the ladder-back, and his hair fell as straight and dark as a veil. He stared at the picture of the girl with an umbrella on the label of the blue salt box. Sometimes he toyed with the paper napkins, tearing them apart in long strips, twisting and braiding the pieces like a lariat. She sneaked a look at him. As handsome as ever. Or had something shifted at the center of his face, between his eyes?

Her swollen eye distorted her vision.

She moved tentatively, favoring her hip and lower back. Willis did not seem to notice any of this. He stared at the salt box, tearing strips of paper napkin, tension pricking out of every pore and filling the kitchen with its sour smell. Madora knew she did not exist for Willis just then, no more than did the stove and sink. They were fixtures, and so was she. She watched him eat the eggs she placed before him, stabbing his fork into them as if they deserved to be punished. Between mouthfuls he began to talk about his work and clients, their medication and oxygen tanks and squeaky wheelchairs.

"I clean 'em up, and they don't even say thank you. For what I do, a man like me, I'm just a pair of hands." He shoved his chair back and went to the sink, turned the water on hard, and lathered his hands and scrubbed under his nails.

His disgust surprised Madora. He always said he liked his clients and how much they appreciated him. Why else would they give him gifts? Cash bonuses, jewelry. One old gentleman had presented him with his wife's diamond engagement ring, and Willis sold it on eBay for five hundred dollars, which was the amount needed to fix the Tahoe's transmission.

His feelings were not much different from the way she felt about Linda, but she kept this thought to herself. Caution dug its claws in under her shoulder blades, and a snake of pain uncoiled across her lower back and down her hip. She opened the refrigerator and stared into the cold vault. Now she knew that she was breakable, and with this realization, the planet might as well have stopped and reversed its spin; the transformation of her world was that drastic. He had never hurt her before, but now that he had done it once, she had no doubt he would do it again if provoked.

He left an hour later without saying good-bye. Wearing pajama bottoms and a tank top, barefoot, she went outside. She thought about feeding Linda but decided not to. Later she would be even hungrier, and that would make her more compliant. Maybe.

She tied Foo to an upright supporting the carport, then

lifted the cage that held the coyote. Inside he snapped and growled and leaped against the chicken wire. She had constructed it from bits of wood and old nails she'd gathered around the property, the litter of previous owners' long-abandoned building projects. The coyote had grown heavy and she was not sure that the cage would stay together without the shelf beneath it. Holding it against her chest and supporting the bottom with her forearms, she crossed the road and went into the scrub. The rough ground hurt her feet, but she welcomed the distraction.

She walked several hundred feet beyond the road and behind a tumble of boulders many feet high and wide. Her right foot was bleeding when she stopped and put down the cage. She sat on a low rock and painfully brought her leg across her thigh so she could examine the sole of her foot, where a thorn had embedded in the soft-skinned arch. Pinching the protruding end between her thumb and forefinger, she drew it out slowly. A bubble of blood filled the tiny wound. She stared at it and then at the wilderness around her.

There were vultures in the sky that morning, drawn to something dead or nearly so. She watched them circle far off toward the county road. She had raised the coyote on a diet of scraps and dog food, and though he was small, he had grown strong. He had no experience in the wild, though, and she feared he had never developed the instincts to forage and protect himself. If a pack found him it might sense his vulnerability, kill him, and leave his bones for the vultures to pick over. As Willis always told her, it was the way of nature to prey on the weak. Nevertheless, Linda was right: it was better to be free.

She opened the door of the cage and stepped back and to the side. After a moment she saw the tip of the coyote's black nose and then his muzzle as he sniffed the opening, suspicious and prepared for something he would not like. When nothing jumped at him, he stretched his head and neck forward. A part of him quivered outside, free, while his shoulders and body were still caged. He retreated back to the farthest corner as if he had to think about the option newly opened to him. She imagined him summoning his courage. All at once, he darted out and stood in the open space between the cage and the wild, his whole body quivering. With excitement, Madora thought. And fear. And possibility. He lifted his nose and sniffed the air, and then, in an instant, vanished into the rough. A gusty wind whipped up the sand and gravel and erased his footprints.

Madora stayed as she was, watching the space where he had disappeared under a twisting manzanita with branches the color of blood. She let herself down onto the ground and leaned against the warm boulder. She hurt so much now. It was a struggle to believe that she would ever feel right again. The sun beat down and her eyelids drooped. Not fully conscious, she flicked away the ants that had discovered her ankles. Robin Howard came into her mind and then Django and the strangeness of that moment when, with Willis, they had stood in the parking lot, talking together like ordinary people. Django's aunt would never guess that Willis was a man who kept a girl prisoner in an old Great Dane trailer. Or that Madora was someone who would help him. She barely believed it herself, and for a few minutes she pondered the question of how she had become the girl she was, the path she had followed from the porch where Willis found her to this place of sand and rock.

Later, Madora limped out to the trailer and opened the curbside door. Without entering, she leaned inside and slid Linda's lunch tray across the floor, then closed and locked the door. In the house she lay on the sectional and dozed. The sound of rapping on the kitchen door awakened her. Barking, Foo leaped off the couch and ran into the kitchen.

"Go away," she shouted over the noise.

"It's me."

"I said go away." Foo had stopped barking. She heard the sound of his nails on the screen door. He would tear the screen, so happy was he to see Django. This would give Willis the perfect excuse to take him to the pound.

Once, in elementary school, she had visited the Yuma animal shelter on a field trip. The most common breed was pit bulls. The cages were full of them, two or three to an enclosure four feet by six or eight. They pressed their broad noses to the wire and looked up at Madora with doleful eyes, and their bodies wriggled with their eagerness to please. *Let me out, I'll be good, I won't bite. Let me out.* The children begged to pet and play with the dogs and would not listen to the shelter worker who tried to explain why the dogs could not be released. Some tenderhearted children had begun to cry, Madora one of them. The teacher had to take them outside and put them back on the bus.

"Foo! Stop it!"

She heard Django open the door and walk into the kitchen. "What's the matter with you?" he asked, standing at the foot of the sectional.

"Are you deaf or just stupid?"

"How come you're lyin' in the dark?"

"I have a headache and you're making it worse."

He leaned closer. "What happened?"

"Mind your own business."

"You look like you were in a fight."

"I fell out of bed."

Django said nothing.

"Go home."

"My aunt really liked your name."

"I don't care about your aunt."

"She's not so bad." Django sat on the floor. "So, how'd you fall out of bed?"

"I thought you wanted to get away from her."

"That doesn't mean I don't like her, okay? I'm not going to stay with her forever, but she's a good person. Only, listen to this, when I was at my old house, I went into the garage and—" His voice cut off. In the shadowed living room Madora saw him draw up his knees and begin to pick at the shag carpet.

"Don't do that," she told him. "You'll pull it apart."

200

He started over. "Me and Aunt Robin were at my old house and I went in the garage and all the cars were still there except, you know, the one."

Maybe this was a true story, not a Django fantasy. She could tell that it upset him to tell it.

"I was thinking how, if I knew how to drive, I could just get in one of them and take off for my brother's and nobody'd be able to stop me. Do you know how to drive, Madora?"

"Everyone in California knows how to drive."

"I don't."

"You're a kid."

"Dad was going to teach me."

For several moments neither of them spoke.

"I let the coyote go."

"Cool."

His quick and positive response angered her. "He's probably dead by now and it's my fault."

"You always think the bad stuff. But he'll be okay. He knows how to hunt. It's a survival instinct."

She hated when he used words like that, assuming that she knew what he meant. He went on about coyotes and wolves and she pretended to listen but did not.

He stopped talking and they were quiet again.

"I'm sorry you're hurt," he said.

"I'm okay."

"Did you go to the doctor?"

"Shut up, Django." She couldn't help crying. Foo put his face close to hers and licked her salty cheeks.

She said, "I'm going to see my mother."

"When?"

"Soon."

"Is Willis going with you?"

Madora was weary of carrying the truth alone. True, Django was only a boy, but such a boy might be able to help her. Immediately she realized it was too dangerous for him and for her.

He asked, "Where's your mother live?"

"Sacramento."

"Hey, that's great. Sacramento and Los Gatos aren't too far apart. You could live with your mother and I'd be at Huck's and we could visit. You'd really like my brother, Madora. And he's got this great house. It's kinda hard to get in. Willis'd never find you, honest to God. There's gates and codes and stuff, but once you're inside you'd be safe. You could even stay there if you wanted to."

He told her again about the many rooms in Huckleberry Jones's house, the helipad and garage big enough for six cars. He told her about Junior, the bodyguard he knew best, and Cassandra, the pot-smoking, bikini-clad girlfriend who had probably been replaced by now. He said there were video screens and games and PlayStations everywhere.

"It's so much fun up there, it's like a resort. You wouldn't believe it."

"I know."

*   *   *

At just after seven, Willis jumped out of the Tahoe carrying his medical bag and a bucket of Kentucky Fried Chicken. He smiled when he came through the kitchen door. "Hey, little girl, brought you some dinner." He put the red, white, and blue bucket on the table. "How you doing?" He tried to kiss her, but she winced and pulled out of his embrace.

"Still hurts, huh?" He said it as casually as if she had skinned her knee. "I'm sorry I had to do that, honey. But you'll feel better in no time. Remind me to give you some painkillers later. They'll help you sleep."

He began talking about the new job caring for Robin Howard's mother. "I meant to tell you about it last night, but then things got crazy, didn't they? I'm charging her full price and then some, 'cause, boy, can she afford it. You should see her condo. Nice stuff, nothing cheap. From all over the world. She started talking about all the trips she'd taken. She's been just about everywhere. Windows look out on the Sycuan golf course. She's not rich, but she's got some fine things."

He was cheerfully boyish, humming to himself as he set the table and laid pieces of chicken and scoops of mashed potatoes and slaw on the plates. Madora understood that this was the best apology he could manage: *I'm sorry, honey*, and a chicken dinner. In spite of her resolve, her heart softened a little.

"How's Linda? Did she eat?"

"I gave her food but I didn't hang around."

He wanted her to say more but it was part of his apology that he did not press her, not tonight.

"I want to change my clothes before we eat."

She followed him through the dark, airless living room and into the bedroom, where he stripped off the blue scrubs he wore to work. The light cotton scrub pants hung below his navel, resting on his hip bones. His smooth and almost hairless body had softened in the years since the Marine Corps. There was something feminine about it now, and when Madora tried to remember what it was like to want him sexually, her mind went blank. She looked away.

"I want to visit my mother," she said. "I can go on the bus."

In her thoughts she told him, *This is how you can say you're sorry and I will believe you.*

"Madora, no one in their right mind wants to go to Yuma in the middle of the summer."

He had forgotten that Rachel lived in Sacramento now. He had never cared much for the details of Madora's life, so the lapse of memory did not surprise her. She started to correct him but he interrupted her.

"Where do you think I'll get the money so you can have a vacation? And who's gonna take care of Linda? With this new client, I've got enough to do without adding that. For what I'm charging, she's gonna expect a lot of attention."

"I miss my mother."

"Since when?"

"I wouldn't stay long."

His lip curled derisively. "You think I don't know you, Madora? I know you better than you know yourself. You go up there, I know you'll stay. You won't come back to me."

Her cheeks felt warm. "I just want a couple of days."

Let me go, and I will forgive you everything. Always.

She watched his expression change from suspicion to irritation and half-humorous disbelief to a dawning hurt. She recognized this look and tried not to respond, but she had been conditioned to it.

"She's all the family I've got."

"I thought I was your family." Half dressed, he stepped toward her.

Madora's toes curled into the floor.

He cupped her face in his hands, gently so as not to hurt her. "I know this has been a bad few days and I was rough on you and I'm sorry. You know I never wanted to hurt you, little girl." He reached back and tugged the rubber band off his braid, combed his fingers through the thick, dark hair. "Now you want to leave me. Just when I need your support the most, you want to take off."

She remembered being small, laying her cheek against a velvet pillow on her parents' bed, the softness that made her want to fall asleep right there.

He said, "I'm going to do just what you said, baby. Take Linda up around Elko in Nevada, let her go. I'm just waiting for a few days off. If you'd given me a chance the other night, I would have explained."

He shook his hair back, over his shoulders. Often in

the evening, he would sit on the bed and she would kneel behind him and brush his hair until it lay flat and glossy on his back. He wanted her to do that now.

"You're right, she's a little bitch-kitty and the sooner she's gone, the better for us. And what happened last night? It wasn't just you, Madora. It wasn't all your fault. I've got to tell you, sweetheart, that med school interview at the college—it's still got me reeling."

One side of the pillow was velvet, the other silk. If she was very quiet, Rachel would let her sleep there in the afternoons. The sleep of childhood, deep and long and uninterrupted.

She whispered, "What about medical school? The island?"

"Oh, we're still going, but it's gonna take me a while to figure out how to swing it. Trust me, you'll see your mom before we go. Of course you will. Don't I know a girl needs to be with her mother sometimes?" His eyes were so dark, they seemed to have no pupils. "But right now, I need you more than she does. Okay?"

Madora looked into his eyes, and she knew she had been hoodwinked, lied to, and cheated. She had wasted her innocence and betrayed herself. But she had known no better. And as clearly as she saw this, she felt no anger. Here was the truth: as she was an unlucky girl, Willis was a boy with his own sad history. Thinking this, a mothering pity welled in her. For him and for herself.

Chapter 22

Willis stayed a while with Madora and allowed her to brush his hair, but it was as if a stranger's hands touched him. The girl he had rescued and with whom he had shared the most private yearnings of his heart would never—either now or in the future—beg to visit her *mother*, a woman she despised and rightly blamed for her father's suicide. But as Madora had grown fat and lazy, her vision of what was possible had been cut short and thickened like scar tissue. Now she limped through life on a stump, like most of the world.

She was nothing to him except a problem.

He left her in the bedroom and went back to the trailer, taking with him some of the chicken and two cans of orange soda. The trailer smelled of tuna and the unemptied toilet, and immediately Linda started in.

"I don't know where Madora is. She never came to see me. Not all day. I can't live like this, in this filth—"

"She'll clean it up tomorrow. I'll see to it, Linda." He left the door open, letting in fresh air.

"There's bugs," Linda complained. "They come to the lights."

Willis chuckled, feeling wise and tolerant. "Imagine we're having a picnic."

He let her sit in the open door with her legs dangling out of the trailer in the fresh night air, facing the cotton-woods and sycamores that crowded the sandy creek bed. He turned off all the lights but one.

"Isn't that better?" he asked her. "Go ahead and eat. You need to keep healthy."

She sneered. "What does it matter? I don't have to be healthy so you can kill me."

"Linda, no!"

"Don't give me that bullshit look. I know you can't just let me go, and you don't want to keep me locked up forever. You're weird, but I don't think you're that kind of crazy."

"You have no idea what I want." She started to speak and he put his finger on her lips. "Just listen for a change. Please?"

She shrugged elaborately and tore at a drumstick.

"I have a vision, Linda. A calling." He saw her greasy fingertips, her bitten nails, and felt a profound sorrow. He did not expect her to understand what he was talking about, not right away. A girl like Linda who had lived on the streets and knew the roughest kind of life might not even believe that there were men motivated by a desire to do good in the world.

"I know you better than you know yourself," he said. "I

know what you can be, the potential in you. I want to help you realize that potential; that's why I brought you here in the first place."

"You wanted my baby. To sell it."

A sigh shuddered through Willis.

Was it was too much to ask that girls like Linda and Madora stop thinking of themselves and consider the risks he had taken in order that they might have a second chance? If his mother were there, she would understand. For a moment, his mind left the trailer and went back to the days in Buffalo when he lay on his mother's bed and she stroked his forehead with her long white fingers and her sweet voice spoke about the wonderful future that lay ahead of him. *What should I do now, Mother?* The future had arrived and he was trapped in the company of girls who beat on his heart with their fists.

Linda tossed the chicken bone out the door into the dust. Madora had never been as coarse and raw as this girl. But given time Linda would learn, and with knowledge would come gratitude and appreciation. He must learn patience. He would look upon Linda as a means by which he would grow wiser, more tolerant, an even better man. He jumped to the ground and picked up the bone, brought it back, and dropped it on her plate. "You can't just leave garbage around. It brings raccoons and rats, and if the dog was to eat it—"

"Yeah, yeah, I get it." She spooned mashed potatoes and gravy into her mouth.

In the beginning Madora had been almost as feisty as Linda. He missed that now. And she had been so pretty, shy-wild, like a young doe in her first season. Until her eighteenth birthday he had been weak with longing for Madora and exhilarated by the willpower it took to restrain his desire. After he had given himself to her, his desire diminished. Now he still made love to her occasionally because she expected it, but he would have been happier to live without sex altogether. As for Linda, he felt no yearning at all for her. She was too shopworn for his taste, but perhaps after a year or two she would regain at least the illusion of purity.

"I know you're mad at me right now, but we can have a life, Linda. A good one."

"I wish you were dead. I want to see maggots crawling out your eyes."

Her bravado was a welcome change from Madora's whining.

"I'm gonna get out of here and I'll tell the police where you are. You and your fat girlfriend." Her eyes were pale blue with a spark of amber near the center. "They'll lock you up forever."

He chuckled.

"What's that mean?"

"It means you don't really know what's going on and you should stop talking and listen. You might learn something."

Her little mouth shone with a gloss of chicken fat.

He said, "I'm going to live on a tropical island for a while."

"Not if the cops get you first."

"Place called Antigua."

"Never heard of it."

"It's an island in the Caribbean Sea. You know where that is?"

"I guess."

"Antigua's way out in the middle of it, with beautiful beaches, like pearls and diamonds all ground up fine like sugar. It's near the equator, so the water's warm year-round and clear like glass." Linda probably didn't know what the equator was, but it didn't matter to Willis that she was ignorant. With time and training she would learn.

"You could go to school in Antigua."

"You're some kind of pervert."

The word stung, but he didn't blame her for using it. Girls her age had to be vigilant, and expecting the worst helped keep them safe. Linda had been too trusting in the past, and now she was making sure she didn't fall for another line. She was ignorant but not stupid. Willis respected this.

"You could lie on the beach and get a tan. You could sleep or go to the movies. You wouldn't have to do anything you didn't want to."

She curled her lip. "Except fuck you."

"Don't say that." He hated to hear that word on lips so young. "I'm not that kind of man." Mental pictures distracted him: this child-girl lying with boys and men for love or drugs or money or attention. Like Daphne, she had used her body as bartered goods.

He had never told Madora, or anyone, about Daphne. It made him sad enough to carry her face and story in his memory; speaking it aloud would add shame to his sorrow. But he wanted Linda to comprehend the danger she had been courting with her slutty ways so that she could better appreciate what he was offering her.

"My sister was murdered."

"So?" She tried to pick a bit of chicken out from between her molars, but she had no fingernails.

"She was like you."

"Oh, Jesus, get me out of here. I knew it. You're a loon."

She squirmed and pulled on her plastic wrist cuffs with her teeth.

"Daphne was young; she left home and got mixed up with bad people. I'm not going to let that happen to you."

"What do you care about me?" Her shoulders were up around her ears and fear had cinched her throat, breaking and cracking her voice so it hurt him to listen. "What do you do, just go around looking for girls to kidnap?"

"You were pregnant."

"That's it? You got a kink for pregnant girls?"

A kink? What did that mean?

The color in her cheeks had washed out, giving her blemished face a lunar pallor in contrast to the wild light in her eyes. "Oh, Jesusjesusjesus. I am so screwed, so totally screwed."

She was afraid, and why wouldn't she be? He imagined her pulse racing beneath his fingers, and he didn't blame her for lashing out at him. Still, it hurt to be misunderstood.

"Drink some of this." He poured orange soda into a paper cup and held it out to her. "It'll help you calm down." In medic training he had learned about panic attacks.

Despite her fear, she grabbed the cup and gulped the soda.

"Slow down." It would help her to see that he was levelheaded and in control. "You'll make yourself sick."

He listened to her ragged breath. He gave her more soda and eventually she leaned against the doorjamb, her shoulders dropped and relaxed. Willis did not press her and five minutes passed.

"Why are you going to Antigua?" She selected another drumstick from the bucket.

"I still need a few classes to get my MD. There's a great medical school in Antigua. One of the best."

Willis knew the school would be mediocre, his professors and classmates second-rate. But for a man such as himself this would not matter; degrees and certificates were a formality. Already he was a better doctor than most.

"What about Madora? I'm not goin' if she is."

"Madora has decided to visit her mother."

"How do I know I can trust you?"

"When I say I'll take care of you, I mean it. I'm an honorable man, Linda."

She looked at him for a long time, and he could almost see her mind at work as she decided whether to believe him or not. She had been close to flying off in all directions, but he'd helped her control herself, and probably done a better job of it than most doctors. And he had delivered her baby with skillful efficiency. On some level of understanding she recognized all this and felt safer with him because of it. Her eyes had opened wider; she wasn't squinting at the world anymore. She was seeing him and—maybe for the first time—noticing that he was a handsome man.

Good looks, his mother always said, were an advantage. Like being a good liar, they gave a man a leg up in the world. Right now Linda was thinking that maybe it wouldn't be so bad to live on an island with a handsome man who paid all the bills.

"Who did it?" she asked.

"What?"

"Who killed your sister?"

"Her boyfriend."

The man had beaten Daphne's face with his fists, shattering her jaw and cheekbones and even the sockets of her eyes, and with a bowie knife he slashed crisscrossing wounds across her chest and left her to bleed. Willis had searched out the metro section reporter, who was willing to describe the scene only when he told him he was her brother.

"It could happen to any girl. Alone like she was."

She pulled away from the door, her fear rekindled.

"I'd never hurt you, Linda, but there's guys... You must be careful."

He was too tired to make the pretty speech that would express the depth of his commitment to her safety. "Just trust me—you don't have to be afraid anymore."

Tired though he was, he could not go back into the house and lie beside Madora. Instead he sat with Linda and talked to her for hours. She asked about Antigua, and he described the kind of place he thought the island might be, remembering movies and television and ads in magazines. When she was asleep he dampened a cloth with water and wiped the chicken grease from around her lips. As he was leaving the trailer he picked the bits and pieces of the tuna sandwich off the floor and dropped them into the trash with the bones of their chicken dinner and the paper plates. He dumped the trash in the can behind the carport.

It was after midnight and the moon had gone, abandoning the empty landscape to the stars' surveillance. The air was bone-chillingly cold, as it often was in dry desert country in the deep night hours. Though he knew the chaparral was full of small life, he could not feel its presence. He seemed to be the only living creature under the indifferent stars.

He leaned against the hood of the Tahoe, and his mind, set free, circled back to the story of his sister, and he wished he had not told Linda about her. Who was Linda to him, really, that he should tell her the story closest to his heart? He knew what his mother would say. She would warn him to be cautious with girls. They were foolish and greedy and could not be trusted. That was probably why he liked the old ladies he cared for. Their minds rambled into parts unknown, but in their sweet withered expressions he saw their gratitude.

The longing for his mother came upon him again. He had believed in her in a way he doubted most boys and young men did these days. He wore his hair long because she liked it that way, and it soothed her mind to comb and braid it, sometimes working in bits of bright ribbon and beads from a broken necklace. She said he was beautiful. He laughed aloud now, remembering how upset that word, *beautiful*, had made him before he understood the power it gave him.

You can have the world, Willis. A few well-told lies and a beautiful face will get you anything you want.

After she died, Willis had not sold the house immediately. Instead, he chucked the boarders out, and after that it was a month before he settled on a plan for his life. Until then, he walked about the rooms mourning his mother and looking for her ghost in dark corners.

"I'll never leave you, Willis. I promise if you look, you'll find me."

Sometimes he saw her in old ladies' faces, but never for long enough. Eventually he realized what these passing glimpses meant. Even his mother could not be trusted, not completely. In the end, it was all up to Willis. The weight of responsibility weighed heavy upon him.

He had a long day ahead and much to do before he and Linda could leave Arroyo. He would be sorry to disappoint Mrs. Howard, who would be in considerable pain following her back surgery. And there were other clients who depended on him, but none of this could be helped. His time in Arroyo had come to an end. He leaned against the car and did his thinking and planning there, while somewhere in the rocks the feral cats yowled.

He had always been a frugal man, there was money in the bank from Linda's baby and the sale of the house in Buffalo, enough to cover expenses. And there would be a great many of those in the months ahead: identification papers, fake college documents and passports, tuition and books, transportation to Miami, airline tickets for two, plus meals, and Linda would need clothes. She would like to feel pretty and pampered. He had no idea what a house or apartment would cost on the island, but he suspected nothing would be cheap. He thought of Shelley and her unborn child and wished he had the time for her. The lawyer would pay top money for another baby, and she was so needy. But he was through in Arroyo. Done.

Madora was the only loose end, a worry, an irritant, a nasty bite that itched. She was angry with him for hitting her and, honestly, he did regret losing his temper that way, although she had needed to be chastised. She was angry with him for doing it and jealous of Linda. But she still loved him, underneath it all, and if he cared to, he could bring her around, cajole her and restore her trustfulness, her willingness to do as he asked, whatever that was. But it sounded like work to him, and he could not be bothered.

He would lock her in the trailer with food and water

and pay a couple of months' rent in advance to keep the landlord off the property. If Madora rationed what he left her, she would not starve. And it would not hurt her to suffer a little. She would be a kinder, more understanding person if she lived for a while as Linda had. She might one day thank him for helping her to grow spiritually. Eventually the landlord would come looking for more money. And when he did he would find her. By then he and Linda would be far away.

Chapter 23

Madora had once had a cell phone, but she forgot to keep it charged and lost track of where she'd put it. Generally it lived in a basket on the kitchen table, but it wasn't there one day when she wanted to call Willis, and when she told him he said she would lose her head if it were not attached. This was right after he brought Linda home, and all at once Madora was too busy to think about her phone. She didn't need one anyway; she had no friends, no one to call.

She wished she had been more careful.

The morning after Willis abandoned her to spend most of the night with Linda, Madora sat on her rock and waited for the sun. She closed her eyes and focused her attention, tried to remember the sound of her mother's voice on the telephone. Sometimes she caught a note of it but never for long enough to be comforted. Now that she had begun thinking about Rachel, she worried that she might have moved from the house in Sacramento and left no forwarding address. Maybe her new marriage had gone bust and she'd married someone else. If this were true, she could be anywhere with any name and Madora would never find her. This thought pressed within her skull like a solid thing with pointed corners.

It seemed weeks since she had slept the night through. Willis had not given her the pain pills he promised, and she had hurt all night, waking every hour or so, conscious that Willis was not in the bed beside her. He had left for work that morning without speaking to her.

Wherever her thoughts went, they came back to one thing. She needed a phone to call her mother and ask her to send bus fare. Rachel's response would be delivered to the mailbox, one of a dozen in a line at the corner of Red Rock and the county road. Mail was delivered around noon and Willis was always at work then. Every day until the money came, Madora would walk down early and wait for the delivery. Willis would never know. He would come home one day and see her empty closet.

The phone call was the first hurdle.

Madora had never spoken to anyone living in the houses and trailers along Red Rock Road. Willis liked his privacy, or so she had once believed. Now it was clear that what he liked was keeping a girl in the trailer with no one close about to hear her yelling for help.

The day was going to be a hot one. Already the air had ripples in it. Like curtains moving in the wind, she could step forward, part the air, and be somewhere else in the time it took to make a wish. On the other side of the rippling air, behind the curtains, there was a world she had abandoned when she gave her heart to Willis. Kay-Kay was out there and her mother and hundreds of people she might have met, places she would have gone, things she might have learned if she had not given her life to Willis.

She had to find a phone, and there was no time to waste. The courage to turn her back on Willis and call her mother was fragile and certain to shatter if she took time for chores or thought too much about it. She remembered hundreds of phone calls to Kay-Kay in high school, conversations that lasted half the night. They had talked about homework and boys mostly. And gossip. If they had heard of a girl living at the end of a road without a phone or a television, taking care of another girl kept locked in a trailer, Madora and Kay-Kay would have laughed and asked each other how anyone could be so cracked.

Madora had to walk down the road and knock on the door of the first house she came to, no matter who lived there. Willis said three men lived in the first house, cooking meth. He had told her that one night he saw someone walking down the middle of the road, dead drunk and staggering. Maybe this was true, but she knew it could just as likely be a story he'd invented to keep her homebound. Now she didn't care if there were drug dealers in the first house. She would go there anyway and take Foo with her. The dog was a softy, but a stranger would never know that.

There were many things she should do before she

started walking; but she dismissed all of them, ran back to the house and dug her mother's phone number out of the dresser drawer where she kept it, put on socks and tennis shoes, and slammed the kitchen door behind her. If her back and hip had not been hurting, she would have run down the road ahead of her fear.

One hundred yards beyond the house, Red Rock Road curved left around a boulder the size of a locomotive. To the right, the canyon bottom was half a mile wide and covered with rough chaparral, thickets of stiff, unfriendly bushes, interrupted occasionally by boulder piles and the white fountains of the yucca. The road went straight for a quarter mile and then turned, bordering the wall of Evers Canyon.

The first house was well off the road, a little distance up the side of the canyon in a grove of scrub oaks. Madora stopped at the tire tracks that marked the driveway. A run-nel of sweat ran down her forehead and into the corner of her eye. Foo sat on his haunches beside her, looking up as if in expectation of good times to come.

"We should go back," she said but moved forward.

The road to the house was not intended for walking and Madora's back and hip soon began to hurt her. In her experi-ence there had never been a fire in Evers Canyon, and the lemonade berry and deerweed bushes on either side of the driveway grew high enough to cast pools of welcome shade with their dense branches of leathery foliage. She stopped often to rest. An alligator lizard skittered out from a pile of rocks, startling her, and ran up the road ahead before darting into the litter of leaves beneath a chamise bush. Foo saw a rabbit and took off after it. The driveway dipped into a dry wash and then sloped up. Madora sat on a rock and rubbed her hip, wondering how much farther she had to go. At the top of the rise she saw the house again, and a few minutes later two or three dogs began yapping, small from the sound of them.

The house was trim and neatly kept, with a square of redwood deck out in front shaded by a bleached-out red-and-white-striped awning. A door and picture window faced the driveway, and a dusty Volvo station wagon parked in front bore a bumper sticker saying *Teachers Do It with Class*. A woman in Levi's and boots opened the front door and stood on the deck. She rested her hands on her hips.

"I don't like pit bulls," she said. Two small, white dogs with woolly faces charged out from behind her and leaped off the deck, going for Foo as if they meant to kill him.

"He won't hurt anyone." Madora crouched and Foo ran into her arms, trembling and wagging his stubby tail. The little dogs made their stand a foot away, barking and showing their teeth.

The woman called a name, something that sounded to Madora like *Shrek*, and both animals ran back to her.

"Who are you?"

"I live up the road." Madora felt fat and sweaty and ready to burst into tears. The little dogs had scared her. This woman scared her. The nervous hope vibrating through her body scared her most of all. "Can I use your phone?"

"How come I never saw you before?"

"I dunno."

"What happened to your face?"

Madora put her palm up to her cheek to hide the bruises. "I fell out of bed."

The woman harrumphed. "That's a new one. You drive the big SUV?"

Madora nodded, feeling confused and exposed by her questions.

"You drive too fast."

Madora pursed her lips together and nodded again.

"You can't bring that dog inside."

"I won't. He's good, though. He'll just stay here and wait for me."

The woman seemed to be thinking. "You drive that SUV too fast, you'll run someone down. There's dogs up and down this road."

"Not me. I don't drive it." Not for months. This woman would think Madora was a freak or a monster if she knew that all she did was care for a girl locked in a trailer.

"Must be a hermit."

Madora didn't know how to respond.

"Come on in, then." She held the screen door open with her foot. "It's cooler inside."

The air-conditioned house was a relief. After a couple of minutes in the house and a drink of water, Madora felt less stunned and took a moment to look around her. The room was sparsely furnished with a couch and chairs, but the walls were covered with framed photographs, groups and portraits, of children at all ages. There did not appear to be room for even one more.

"I used to teach school. They gave me a golden handshake because of budget cuts."

"I thought they were your children. And grandchildren."

"Never been married." The woman looked at the photos. "But I guess I had plenty of kids, huh?"

"My boyfriend says guys're cooking meth around here."

"Boyfriend." She harrumphed again. "What's he think of that face of yours?"

Madora wished she could hide from the sharp blue eyes.

"No meth on Red Rock. I'd call the cops if there were. There's just me and a retired sailor who lives in a trailer and drinks too much, gets to wandering sometimes. A guy way back off the road raises emus. The big birds, you know? For their meat."

Madora would have liked to see an emu up close.

"What happened to your phone?" the woman asked.

"I lost it."

"They make them too little. I can't even see the keys without my specs." She patted the pocket of her plaid camp shirt and pulled out a pair of metal half-frames that she positioned near the tip of her nose. They magnified the size of her eyes, making her scrutiny even harder for Madora to bear. "I asked what your name was."

"Madora."

"I'm Ellie Dutton." She stuck out her hand.

Madora rubbed her palm on the back of her shorts. She regretted not taking the time to comb her hair and brush her teeth. "Nice to meet you."

Ellie handed her a small cell phone. Madora didn't know which key to press first.

"You want me to dial for you?"

"Yes, ma'am." Madora handed her the slip of paper with her mother's number.

"Where is this? I don't know this area code."

She also should have brought some money to pay for the long-distance call.

"Sacramento?" Madora said.

Ellie pursed her lips and made a clicking sound with her tongue against her palate.

"Okay," she said, adjusting her glasses. "Shoot."

Madora's hands were slippery as she took the phone from Ellie and held it, her whole arm shaking as she listened to the sound of ringing in a room far away. She sat on the nearest chair, not waiting for an invitation.

"Hello." It was the voice Madora had been trying to remember. Not sweet but not hard either, a mellow, husky voice. "Hello? Who is this?"

Me, Mommy. Me.

"Madora?" Rachel made a choking sound. "It is you, isn't it? Madora? Oh, I know it's you, honey. Talk to me, baby. Talk to me."

Madora held the phone away from her ear and looked

at the display. A dozen thoughts ran through her mind, but the one that ran fastest, the one that wheeled and turned and screamed, was the one that said if her mother knew about Linda and the trailer, she would turn her back on Madora and never speak her name again.

She pressed the red button.

Ellie Dutton looked at her curiously.

"No answer."

Chapter 24

Coyotes woke Robin a little before dawn. They often came at that hour, when the rabbits were in the garden feasting on chard and parsley. She put on slippers and went downstairs. She stepped outside armed with a saucepan and a big metal spoon and went up the path toward the vegetable garden. In the moonlight the rabbits skittered for cover. Yellow eyes of the wild dogs gleamed from the bushes. For an instant, she felt a primal fear, the residue of time beyond memory; and then a flood of something more than courage washed it all away, and she dashed at the pack, banging on the pan, yelling at the top of her lungs.

Did she dream this?

She woke feeling pinched and achy, as if she had not done more than skim the surface of sleep for seven hours. Overnight every doubt and worry and question that had arisen since Django's arrival seemed to have taken up residence in her back and joints.

Across the room on her dresser there was a business

card with Mr. Guerin's name on the front. On the back Caro had written their father's address and phone number in her swooping forehand.

Django wondered if his aunt was sick. She stayed in her room until the middle of the morning and when she left the house she didn't pause on her way out the door to list a dozen things he couldn't do or should be careful of. She just left, wagging her hand over her shoulder, saying she would be back.

Alone, he spent the morning wandering around the house, opening drawers and closets, poking his nose into cupboards. His snooping failed to uncover anything of interest, just sheets and towels, and plastic bins of junk he couldn't imagine anyone wanting: heating pads and a hot-water bottle, a Water Pik and lots of sample-sized tubes and bottles of hand cream and mouthwash. The tidy ordinariness depressed him.

Mr. Guerin had said he would arrange to have the piano sent to Arroyo. Django wished it were in the house now.

His father had promised that when he completed five years of piano lessons, he would teach him to play the guitar. For a long time his twice weekly piano lessons were just a means to that end, but now he missed the piano in a way that was almost a physical need. He wished that he had asked Mr. Guerin to send it right away, the next day. When it came it would be both a link to his father and an escape, a way to pass time and lose time.

He sat on the couch and texted Lenny and Roid. He did not think they would answer him. They had their lives and he had his, a boring new life in Arroyo until he moved up to Los Gatos. That morning he had wanted to ask his aunt if she had called Huck, but she was so weirded out since they went to LA, he didn't think she would know what he was talking about. After he moved north, Lenny and Roid would start paying attention to his texts. They would go crazy when they found out he had a helipad in the backyard and be begging him to send the chopper down to pick them up. Django might get Huck to do it, but no hurry. First he'd make his so-called friends wish they had been nicer to him.

He was in the kitchen thinking about lunch when the phone rang. He looked at the retro white instrument hanging on the wall and waited for the answering machine to click on. In school he had learned about an old-time scientist who trained dogs to respond when they heard a bell ring. He was like those dogs. The phone rang, and he automatically thought it was his mother. Automatically. She was dead—he finally believed that; but he was still like one of those stupid dogs. As soon as he heard the phone, her voice clicked on in his head. *Django, darling boy, it's Momma.* There was nothing he could do to stop his response and he feared that when he was an old man he'd still hear *Django, darling boy, it's Momma* whenever the phone rang.

"Django, you there?" It was his aunt. "Django, pick up the phone."

She sounded even more tense than usual, and out of nowhere Django thought about the piano again, remembering the German piano tuner who came to the house several times a year. If he wasn't in school, Django hung out with him the whole time, watching how he fingered the strings inside the big instrument, listening to the different tones they made as he loosened and tightened them, fascinated by his trade that was at once an art and a craft and yet neither of those really. Some of the sounds made Django wince, they were so off-key.

Aunt Robin said, "Okay, here's the thing, Django. I've got to meet with Mr. Conway—the lawyer, you know? There's some stuff I've got to settle with him." She rushed from one sentence to the next, not stopping for breath. "And then, I'm not sure, but I think I'm going up to Temecula. Do you know where that is? It's in Riverside County. I don't know for sure if I'll go but I didn't want you to worry if I'm late getting home." She stopped talking. Then, "This is too weird—I know you're listening... Okay, so here's the deal. I might go, I might not, and I'm not sure when I'll get home. Or if I'll go. It's just something I might do. Spur of the moment. So, I don't know how long I'll be. You can fix your own dinner, right? There's pizza in the freezer." Another long pause. "Use the microwave, not the oven. And, Django, don't go off on your bike. Stay home. The boxes of stuff we brought from the house... you should empty those, okay? You might find something to play with. Just don't go off on your damn bike. Stay put, Django."

231

Something to play with. His aunt didn't have a clue how funny she was.

He made two peanut butter and jelly sandwiches. He liked iceberg lettuce with PB and J, but the crisper was empty except for a few limp carrots. In Django's home the refrigerator had been twice as big and always full of good stuff. Aunt Robin never had time to go to Whole Foods and no matter how often she went to the regular supermarket, there was never anything to eat. No cold cuts, no iceberg or good tomatoes, no juice boxes, no cookies. He made another sandwich and stuck all three in a plastic bag and put it in his backpack.

In his bedroom he found the money he'd taken from his father's study and stuck the roll down deep in his jeans pocket. He didn't care what Aunt Robin said; he was going to buy Foo. Madora might not want to do it at first, but when she saw a thousand dollars in cash, she would change her mind. He would tell her to use it to leave that freakazoid, Willis.

He ditched his bike behind a boulder and approached the house from the back, crossing the dried creek bed and pushing through a thicket of cottonwoods. His shoes scrunched on the sandy ground where the grains were as big as BBs; and gnats and no-see-ums swarmed around his head, exploring his ears and going for the moisture in his nose and at the corners of his eyes. From the treetops, the crows announced his arrival. He took off his baseball cap and flapped the bugs away, but they returned as soon as he stopped.

The trailer's curbside door was open and Foo lay in the dirt near the steps, his bony head resting on his paws. Inside, Madora was talking to someone. Django heard only a few words every now and then, but it was her tone that interested him. It slunk down like a dog caught creeping up on a butter dish. It upset Django to hear her speak that way. She was his friend and he did not believe she could ever do something so bad she would sound that ashamed of herself.

The bugs were making Django crazy; plus he was curious, and he wanted to defend Madora, though he wasn't sure against what.

He stepped out of the cottonwoods and into the clearing. Foo whirled and began barking. In a few steps Django stood at the trailer's curbside door. Foo charged, barking and looking lethal, but when he realized it was his friend Django, he stopped barking, wagged his tail, and wriggled his back end.

With a quick glance Django took in everything of importance.

In the trailer, a stringy-haired girl lay on a cot, her hands cuffed in front of her and one leg dangling off the side with something around it and attached to a wire rope that ran across the floor and up the wall to an eye hook screwed into the skin of the trailer near the roof. Madora stood on a chair with a hammer in her hand, trying to pull out the hook.

"Hey." He put one foot on the brick-and-board step up

to the door, but Foo stopped wagging his tail, growled, and wouldn't let him go any farther. Django knew the dog and the dog knew him, but Foo was a pit bull and he decided not to push their friendship.

"Get out of here." Madora waved her arms and almost fell off the chair.

Foo began barking again and the girl on the cot saw Django and started screaming for help. High in the trees, the crows announced trouble to the length of Evers Canyon. Madora jumped off the chair and ran to the door and tried to pull it shut. She stopped, listening. Django heard the sound of a big car coming up the road fast. He wished he'd stayed where he was in the cottonwoods, but he could not run away now and leave Madora. He wished Lenny and Roid were with him.

"This isn't your business," Madora said. "Go while you can."

The way she leaned against the door, Django knew that she was still in pain. From her fall out of bed. He knew Willis had hurt her. A righteous rage flared up in him and burned away his fear.

The girl lunged off the cot toward the door, dragging her tether. Her screams were like nails down an old-fashioned chalkboard. A car door slammed and Foo shot off around the trailer, more barking. A man's voice yelled for him to shut up.

"Go!" Madora cried.

"I'm not scared of him."

"You should be!"

Willis wheeled around the corner of the trailer, looking twice as big as he had standing in the supermarket parking lot. Django felt the temperature spike ten degrees.

"What the fuck?" Willis gawked at Django and then at Madora. "You bitch! You stupid bitch!"

Django started to protest but no sound came out of his mouth. The temperature went up another ten degrees.

Willis looked up at Madora, standing three feet above him in the open door. He saw the hammer in her hand and the chair against the opposite wall. As the scene came together in Willis's mind, it did the same in Django's. Madora had been trying to pull out the eye hook to free the girl who was standing up beside the bed now, the slack of the wire rope gripped between her hands. She was lifting it, banging it down hard on the trailer's wooden floor. Banging and banging and screaming.

Willis shoved Django aside and leaped up the steps into the trailer. The girl kept swinging the wire rope and banging it on the trailer floor like a maniacal fourth grader playing jump rope. Willis grabbed Madora by her hair and wrenched her backwards onto the floor at the same moment the wire rope caught him across the shin. He yelled and released Madora as he fell, clutching his leg where the wire rope had hit it. He staggered toward the girl, his hair loose and wild about his face. She banged and snaked the rope between them, screaming obscenities as Willis tried to dodge it. He glimpsed the hammer Madora had dropped, and lunged for it at the same moment she did. Foo jumped from the ground into the trailer and dug his teeth into Willis's ankle. Willis swung around, cursing, and drove his fist into the dog's ribs, knocking the wind out of him, sending him tumbling out the door and onto the ground.

Madora screamed, "Foo!"

It happened so fast. Django saw her arm go up, and as Willis turned his head away from Foo and back to her, she slammed the hammer into the side of his head. Django watched Willis's face. One moment he was raging, the next he was like a man who'd lost his glasses, squinting. He sobbed and fell over.

Nobody moved; nobody said anything. Foo jumped back into the trailer and lay down beside Madora and put his bull head on his paws, looking up at her.

Django returned to his senses before Madora and the girl. His thinking was like a man sending and receiving code at light speed and understanding it all, multiple messages simultaneously, making sense of it all in a way he never could on an ordinary day, under ordinary circumstances. He looked at the girl and the way the furniture was arranged in the trailer, the hook and the tether and the handcuffs, the hammer still in Madora's hands. The plots of books and movies and countless television dramas sped through his mind. He recalled the stories he'd heard about abductions and kidnappings and young women held as captives in basements and closets and sheds. Good ideas and bad: he had no filter. In his mind he was the victims and the perps and the police at the same time, and he was seeing a pattern. His thoughts combined and recombined and fell into place.

"We're getting out of here."

He stepped up into the trailer and grabbed Madora's shoulders. He shook her and she stared at him, not blinking as her head bobbled. If her eyeballs had started spinning, Django would not have been surprised. "Pay attention."

"I killed him."

"You didn't; he's breathing."

Madora and Willis had been keeping the tethered girl prisoner. The evidence of a terrible crime was right in front of Django but he didn't care. In contrast to his cool and distant aunt, Madora had been warmth to him, a lonely girl who wanted his company and thought he was funny, as his mother had. With Madora he could show off and talk about his old life, about his mom and dad and Huck and his friends at school. So what if she didn't believe him; she listened anyway.

The girl begged him to release her but he tuned her out.

His thoughts were everywhere at once, remembering, seeing, anticipating, leapfrogging and slipping sideways, kaleidoscoping too fast for close attention, and in the process creating brand-new thoughts.

Madora had been Willis's accomplice.

No. He would never believe that. It could not have been that simple.

"I've got an idea," he said. Half an idea, but the rest would come.

"He's gonna die," Madora wailed.

Django thought *concussion* but kept the word to himself. "No, but he'll have a headache. That's all."

The girl on the bed started screaming again.

"Make her be quiet," he told Madora. "I have to figure this out."

But Madora was crying and helpless in her own way. She dropped to her knees and wrapped her arms around Foo.

By an act of will, Django shut out the noise and confusion and let his mind open like an old-fashioned blueprint unscrolling across a table. It was all there, the light-speed messages, the code, the media memories and news stories coming together and making sense like the plot of a Jett Jones adventure.

Chapter 25

Willis lay on his side with his head twisted at an awkward angle. In the fall he had driven his teeth into his lower lip, and blood had collected under his tongue and dribbled onto the trailer floor. Django held the back of his hand an inch from his mouth and felt a strong brush of air.

"I never meant to kill him."

"I told you already. He'll be okay. But we have to get out of here before he wakes up."

"The police'll catch us." Madora covered her mouth. "I'll go to jail."

Django, now that he was thinking clearly, took a minute to look at the sepia stain of a bruise around Madora's eye and cheekbone. He turned around and kicked Willis hard in the ribs because a man who would beat a woman was the lowest form of life in Django's universe. He stood up straight, feeling tall for the first time in his life.

"I'm going to get you out of this. You won't go to jail."

He did not know what laws he was going to break, but

he was pretty sure there were some. It was equally clear that whatever arrangement Madora and Willis had, when Django saw her on the chair with the hammer she wanted out of it. He would help her and in the process help himself; and if it all went south and he got arrested, Huck would help him. And Mr. Guerin. He was sick of being sad all the time and he did not want to think about death and the grave and car crashes anymore. He did not want to sit in Aunt Robin's house and wait for his life to start again. He was ready to *do* something.

"Take that girl out to the Tahoe and put her in the backseat. And fix the seat belts so her hands can't reach—"

"I know how," Madora said.

Like the crows flying up, cawing a racket, and then finally coming to rest, silent and evenly spaced among the branches of the trees, his mind had settled too.

"What's her name?"

"Linda."

He stood over her. "Do you want to get out of here, Linda?" She stopped screaming. Her blank expression told him nothing. She was a zero unit. He leaned closer. Inches from her face he yelled, "Do you want to get out of here?"

Linda's eyes and nose and mouth wrinkled together, and she burst into pitiful infantile crying that was almost worse than her screams. He looked over at Madora hunkered at the table now, her eyes as big around as fishbowls.

He was twelve years old but at that instant he was pretty sure he was the oldest person in the trailer. Except for Willis.

240

Jett Jones, Boy of the Future, versus the Dark Entity. He told Madora, "Use that dish towel to make a blindfold."

Django thought he saw Willis's fingers move.

"And hurry up." There was definitely some twitching going on. "There's gonna be a shit storm in about five minutes."

He was nervous, but not afraid. And stronger than he had ever realized. He held Linda still while Madora tied the blindfold. She tried to raise her hands to pull it off, but they were still cuffed. She started screaming again. Not scared, just mad. The loop around her ankle was held together with a padlock.

"Do you know the combination, Madora?"

She shook her head.

"Shit."

On the ground Willis groaned.

"Okay, here's what I want." He handed Madora the hammer. At first she shrank from taking it. Django pointed up at the eye hook on the wall. "Just get up there and finish what you were doing. Then loop the rope or whatever it is. She'll have to carry it. Or you can. We have to get her to the car." He looked at Linda, wishing she were not blindfolded. If she saw his face she would know that he meant every word.

"Girl," he said, "if you don't cooperate, we'll just leave you here with him."

When Linda was in the car, Django ran back to the trailer. He left the lights and air-conditioning on.

The generator would run until the fuel ran out. The cops would find Willis long before that. He nudged Willis's foot with the toe of his Nike. His eyelids fluttered and he groaned. *A bad concussion*, Django thought, and for the first time he felt afraid of what he had gotten into. Willis needed a doctor and Django would make sure he got one. But he and Madora needed time first. Eventually Willis would regain his senses and remember seeing Django in the trailer and connect him to Aunt Robin. When that happened, Django wasn't sure what would happen to him except that he would be in trouble. The biggest kind of trouble. For a second he thought about not following through with his full plan, but he knew that if he backed out now, he would always regret it. This was his opportunity and Madora's too. He had to take it.

He dug in the pocket of Willis's scrub pants and withdrew his wallet. He did not need money, which was lucky because the guy had only a couple of dollars. Django removed his identification. For a little while after the sheriff's department found him, Willis would be a John Doe. He eased his hand into the shirt pocket and pulled out a cell phone. *Cheapo*, Django thought. *A throwaway.*

And just what he needed.

He left Willis where he lay, locking him in the trailer. Madora stood at the Tahoe's passenger-side door, her arms wrapped around herself. The midafternoon sun poured down on her, but she looked like she was knee-deep in winter.

"You're driving," Django said.

Her eyes opened wide. "I can't. My license isn't good."

"You have to do it. I don't even know where the gears are."

"But, Dja—"

"Don't say my name!"

"We can't just leave him."

"He's a bad man. Keep telling yourself."

Django knew the word that described a man like Willis. He was a sociopath. He had kept Linda captive, handcuffed and tethered her and made Madora live alone at the end of a road going nowhere, using her as a servant and almost as much a prisoner as the girl in the trailer. But what had convinced Django that Willis was a bad man and put in motion the risks he was taking now was what he'd seen when Willis charged into the trailer: the raw terror on Madora's battered face. She hadn't been confused or panicked or angry when she hit Willis with the hammer. She feared for her life.

He held up Willis's throwaway phone. "When we get out of the county, I'll call the sheriff." And then he would toss the phone, keeping his own to use in an emergency.

He would tell the police there was a girl named Linda cuffed and blindfolded behind Arroyo Elementary School and a man in a trailer at the end of a gravel road. He would give them no details, just enough to get them to the trailer eventually. Though Django had taken Willis's driver's license and car registration, the police would figure it all out eventually and be able to track the Tahoe. Django hoped all this would take long enough for him and Madora to get onto the crowded LA freeways.

But if something went wrong and the police caught them going north, he had his own phone, programmed with Mr. Guerin's number. Home and office.

Madora persisted. "Where are we going?"

Django leaned in close and whispered. "To my brother. To Huck."

Chapter 26

R obin's father lived in unit number three of a single-story condominium complex called Oak Creek Haven: pale peach-colored stucco and a fake tile roof festooned with hoops of pink and red bougainvillea but no oaks or creeks that Robin could see. Nor did it seem like much of a haven, surrounded by four- and six-lane surface streets and big-box stores.

She sat in her car, staring at the traffic. In the cup holder next to her she could see her sister's handwriting on the back of Mr. Guerin's business card. Robin had programmed the address into her GPS and followed its directions, so precise and impersonal that they demanded obedience. She had driven to Temecula without thinking what she would do when she got there.

A double horse trailer paused at the corner and turned right on red. Robin could see a horse's head looking out. It probably had no more idea why it was where it was at that moment than she fully understood why she was parked outside her father's condo in Temecula.

Her last clear memory came from a time not long before he left home. It was cold in Morro Bay and a gusty wet wind chased the rag ends of a rainstorm across the sky, creating patterns of shadow and light across the lawn, where her father stood with his back to the house. Robin was in the living room, looking out the picture window. Behind her, Caro had spread the contents of her paper-doll box across the carpet in scenes: the prom, the vacation, the slumber party. Down the short hall connecting the front of the house and two bedrooms, their mother was cleaning the bathroom, filling the little house with the smell of ammonia.

"Can I go outside and help Daddy?" Robin yelled to her mother.

"It's wet and cold and you've already got the sniffles."

"But it stinks in here."

"You heard me."

Robin's father was a slight and pale-skinned man who spent his weekdays under fluorescent lights at a desk in a bank in San Luis Obispo, his weekends in the garden. Sitting in the parking lot outside his condo, Robin remembered how narrow his back was as he stood beside the Eugenia bush that separated their house from the one next door. In her memory, the houses on both sides of Estero Street were similarly small and unremarkable, their facades and floor plans all the same.

All at once she saw her father's back grow rigid, and she heard a sound, a scream loud enough to make Caro look up from her paper dolls.

"What was that?"

Robin did not answer; she was transfixed, watching him. His upper body torqued and his arm went back and up and she saw the hedge clippers leave his hands and go flying—blades over handles over blades—through the air and into the street, their sharp mouth open wide, as if they, and not her father, had screamed.

Two days later he left his family and Robin never saw him again.

She rested her forehead on the center of the steering wheel and counted backwards from one hundred. She reached zero and got out of the car. In the late afternoon, with a wall of rugged mountains blocking the ocean breeze, the air in Temecula was still and fumy and blazing hot. From somewhere on the other side of Oak Creek Haven she heard the plonk of a tennis ball and children's voices making the kind of happy noise that meant a swimming pool in the summertime.

She had not called ahead to prepare her father. She wanted to see the look on his face when he opened the door, wanted to see if he recognized her immediately or if there was a moment—even a fraction of a moment—of confusion.

She entered the complex and followed a cement path between unimaginatively landscaped borders of succulents and salvia and more bougainvillea. Unit three had a tiny walled patio in front and a door with a decorative cage around the peephole. A pagoda-shaped hummingbird feeder hanging

247

from the eaves swung slightly as an iridescent bird whirred away, startled by her appearance. Moisture pimpled at the back of Robin's neck. She rang the bell and then exhaled.

No going back.

The man who answered the door was even smaller than she remembered, maybe five feet eight on a confident day. What remained of his hair was still dark brown, cut militarily short. Behind a pair of glasses with shiny metallic rims, his eyes widened.

"Well," he said. "Well."

"You recognize me." Embarrassed, she laughed. Of course he did. He was her father.

He opened the door wider, and she felt a breath of cool air and smelled spices as she stepped inside.

"You're cooking chili," she said and laughed again. Chagrined, self-conscious: these feelings should have been his. He was the one who had done the leaving; he was the one with something to be embarrassed about. "I remember your chili."

But until that second, she had not.

"I didn't like it," she said, recalling that she and Caro had once fed theirs to the neighbor's dog. "You seasoned it with vinegar."

He nodded as if she had said something wise.

"You're like your mother. Pretty."

A splash of light flashed through a window and stung Robin's eyes.

The condominium was nicer than she had anticipated,

spacious and full of light, furnished with a few simple pieces. Off the kitchen, a set of French doors opened onto what Robin saw was a second and larger patio. Above the table, a ceiling fan paddled lazily.

Frank Howard went into the kitchen, an area divided from the living room by a granite-topped bar and pony wall, and took a pitcher of iced tea from the refrigerator. Without asking if she wanted any, he poured a tall glassful over a pile of ice cubes and a sprig of fresh mint.

"Sugar?"

"I don't like iced tea."

"Pomegranate sun tea." He put a teaspoon of sugar in the glass and stirred it. "Refreshing."

"I won't like it."

He smiled. "You're more like your mom than just your looks."

This was a dig, and to prove him wrong, Robin sipped the iced tea. She did like it and managed a smile.

"I have something to tell you. Maybe you know already. It was in all the papers—"

His cheeks and jaw seemed to lose tone, adding years to his face. "I read it in *USA Today.*"

"You shouldn't have found out that way."

"Death is death. No matter how you hear about it, it's never easy. There was a picture of Jacky in the entertainment section. With Keith Richards." His face brightened. "He knew them all, didn't he, Robin? It was like Caro married into rock-and-roll royalty."

"Did you go to the funeral?" At the time she had been too stunned and confused to stand still for obits and homilies. "Apparently it was quite a show."

"What about the boy?"

"He's living with me now. He's a sweetheart, actually. I like him." *But I'm not sure he likes me.*

"I saw him from time to time when he was little. Smart. And so confident. Just a tyke and he could carry on a conversation."

"He's miserable with me."

"Under the circumstances, he'd be miserable no matter where he was."

"I'm going to call Huck and persuade him to take him."

"You're sure you want to do that?"

"I'm old, I'm boring. At least with his brother he'd be entertained." Put this way, it did not seem like a very good reason.

They sat, looking over each other's shoulders to where their ghosts of Caro stood observing their strange reunion.

"Is there anything of hers you want? She left me most of the contents of the house."

"No. I was only in it a couple of times. Too big. I never felt comfortable in Beverly Hills."

This surprised Robin. She had thought her father and Caro were as close as he and she were distant. "I thought you were..." Now that she wanted to be specific, she wasn't really sure what she had thought. "Tight?"

He laughed and Robin remembered her mother once

saying to him: *Not everything is a joke; not everything is amusing.*

"Ask me what you want to know, Robin. You came and I'm glad. But there's no easy way."

"I wanted you to know about Caro."

"Yes, but for that you could have called."

"Even I'm not that cold."

"I never called you cold."

"You said I'm like Mam."

"You have some of her ways, Robin. But that's to be expected. And I wouldn't even say she was cold." He leaned toward her. "Now that you're here, you should ask your questions."

"I shouldn't have to," she said, affronted. "You owe me an explanation, Daddy."

"Give me a question. A place to begin."

She had expected him to defend himself. She wanted to hear him try.

He said, "You don't know how many times I thought I'd just call you and make a date." He lifted his hands and stared at them as if by doing so he could understand why they had failed him in this simple task. "In the end, I couldn't, you see."

"What? You don't drive? You didn't know my address?" She sounded like her mother, and she suspected her father was thinking the same thing. He kept his thoughts to himself, which made it worse somehow. "I was eleven when you left. I'm forty-three almost." Tears caught in her throat.

251

Drusilla Campbell

"Why didn't you love me? Did you leave because of me? What did I do wrong?"

"Nothing, you did nothing wrong."

"You just left and Mam never said why. You just left me."

She had never meant to pour out her feelings this way. But now that she had exposed herself, she could feel her inhibitions falling away.

"I loved you, Daddy." And for some mad reason, she loved him still. "You just left me. How could you do that?"

Frank slouched in his chair, avoiding her eyes, saying nothing, patting his lips with his fingertips. *He's paralyzed,* she thought. He wanted her to go; he wanted her to stay. He wanted honesty but he had lived decades with lies and omissions and made himself comfortable with them. She saw it all clearly because she too was well acquainted with the mind's ability to hold equal but contradictory thoughts at the same time and to move through life precariously balanced.

She wanted Django to stay; she wanted him to go.

She wanted to go to Tampa; she wanted to stay.

She wanted an explanation from her father and she was afraid of what he would tell her.

He said, "I guess it's time to show you something." As he walked across the living room to a maple chest of drawers on which were arranged several framed photographs, Robin noticed that he limped.

"Are you injured?"

"A skiing accident, years ago."

It tested her imagination to see her father on skis.

"The ankle never mended properly."

"Are you in pain?"

"A little."

She did not want to care so much when genes alone connected them, bits of human matter so small she would not believe they existed except that scientists told her they did. What pain or rage had prompted him to scream and throw the lethal clippers that day? After such a long time he might not even remember doing it.

He brought a photo back to the table and handed it to Robin.

"The pain in my leg reminds me of a happy time."

It was a photograph of a good-looking middle-aged man in steel gray ski pants and parka, a blue tasseled watch cap pulled down to his eyebrows.

Her father asked, "Do you remember him?"

She didn't.

"You don't remember Boyd Glover?"

"Should I?"

"He and his wife lived across the street in Morro Bay. On Estero. They had no children. I doubt if you ever set foot in their house." A sigh rose from deep within him, almost a moan. "I had to divorce your mother, Robin. It was either that or I'd kill myself, and I was pretty sure divorce was the lesser sin."

She could not make sense of what he was saying.

"I know your mother told you we were legally separated,

Drusilla Campbell

but that's her private version of reality. I've got the divorce papers in the next room if you doubt me. I swore I'd never tell you. She thought it would warp you girls somehow if you came from a 'broken' home. I guess she was afraid she would turn you and Caro into the kind of girls who hung out with rock stars." He smiled at the irony. "Marriage, the Catholic Church, sleeping under a picture of the Sacred Heart of Jesus, and loving Boyd, knowing how deep in sin I was and not caring..." His expression hardened even as his voice broke. "I didn't care what Nola told you so long as I was set free. But she made me pay."

Robin had come in search of answers and truth, but it was too much and now she wanted none of it.

"Boyd suffered an aneurism in 2002. I fell apart. Caro and Jacky kept me going for the first year." Her father put the photo back on the maple chest. With his back to her, he said, "The deal I made with your mother, the bargain was...she would only give me a divorce if..." He paused as if he had been running for years and could only now pause for breath. "She would only give me a divorce if I relinquished all my rights as your father." He stood looking down at the framed photos, his hand pressed to his forehead. "All the times I thought of how I'd say this and now..." He took another breath and expelled a deep sigh.

"Robin, I promised never to see you or try to get in touch. Your mother needed a pound of flesh and I gave it to her. For my freedom."

254

"Are you saying you gave me up in exchange for a divorce?"

"I'm ashamed, Robin, but try to understand the way it was back then."

"Why not Caro? Why did you choose me? What was wrong with me?"

"Oh, God, Robin, nothing was wrong with you. You were a wonderful little girl. It was your mother who chose. She knew how much I loved you and she wanted to hurt me as much as she could. You were the pound of flesh, the price I had to pay."

Nola had been a good and responsible mother, hadn't she? And Robin loved her, didn't she? How could she take this new information in and arrange it to make sense not only of yesterday, all the yesterdays, but of now, this moment?

Robin said, "I've always thought—"

"What she wanted you to think."

"You didn't have to accept the deal." *You didn't have to trade me for your freedom.* "You used me."

"I did, Robin. I used you, yes. But I never looked at it that way. I believe, I have always believed, that you saved my life, my sanity. You gave me my freedom. A chance to live. I loved Boyd more than I'd ever loved anyone. If I stayed with your mother, I'd have killed myself. I was that close to doing it."

"And Mam knew you were gay?"

He nodded.

"All these years, that's what this has been about? Did Caro know?"

"Not the details, of course. When she was little and came to visit in the summer, Boyd and I were very careful. But she figured it out as she got older."

"Before, when we were kids, she must have wondered why I never saw you."

"Oh, she did. And she didn't like it. Early on, she begged me to invite you to come with her when she visited. She said it was no fun visiting me without you. I couldn't tell her the truth, of course. I just kept saying it was impossible and eventually she stopped asking. I came out to her when she and Jacky got married."

"After that, she could have told me. We were all adults by then."

She felt a growing anger. "You both chose to shut me out. Did you think I couldn't take it? That I'd be shocked or horrified . . . ? Did you think I'm so backward—?"

"Robin, what I'm going to say to you will be very hard to understand. I made a promise, an oath, to your mother. And I made Caro honor my promise."

By the force of her rage and unbridled will, Nola had drawn them all into the conspiracy to keep Robin ignorant of the truth.

"And the longer we kept the oath, the harder it was to break it."

The truth was more awful than Robin had imagined. She felt it in her stomach like a poison she had been forced to swallow. She wanted to go into the bathroom and stick her finger down her throat, except that she knew nothing would come up. The poison was inside her forever.

"If your mother had chosen to make public what she knew about Boyd and me, she would have ruined not just my life but his as well. He was a public-school teacher. At that time in history, he would have been blacklisted. And no bank would have hired me, a known homosexual."

"Mam never needed to know. You could have come to me—"

"I would have known, Robin. Nola hauled out the Bible and made me swear on it, made me kiss the page where the commandments are written down." His cheeks flushed. "And then I kept my word. And I made sure Caro kept it too. I know that must sound old-fashioned or crazy, backwards, but I couldn't break it. Then a year or so ago, I found a way to keep my word and still open the door. I told Caro that if you ever came to her and talked about me or asked questions about what happened, she could give you my address. That's probably why you're here today. In the end, I think she wasn't willing to keep my secret and I'm grateful to her. You wouldn't be sitting with me now if she had." He sagged in the chair. "Maybe this is all horse pucky. Maybe I was just a coward. It's been a long time and I don't trust my memory anymore. The way you're looking at me right now? I just know I never wanted to see that expression on your face."

He went into the kitchen and began to wipe down the

granite counters. "I still go to church, you know. I went back after Boyd died. I can't say if anyone knows I'm gay; I don't make a big deal of it, and so far the priest hasn't barred me from the sacraments." Her father stared at the floor and he seemed to be speaking to himself. "Sometimes I wonder what God thinks of me. Nothing good, I'd guess."

"Daddy, there's no sin in being gay."

"I know that. My sins are the small, mean kind, Robin. Cowardice and selfishness."

Robin wanted to believe that her father loved her, that he was telling the truth when he said he felt he had no choice but to make the bargain with Nola. And certainly she felt sympathy for him. His life had been difficult. But she did not know if sympathy and *wanting* to believe and forgive were enough to get the job done.

"The only brave thing I ever did in my life was those twenty-plus years with Boyd, and that took it out of me; every bit of courage and determination I had went into that." He stopped wiping circles on the counter. "Mostly I'm just an ordinary man, Robin, a retired banker who wanted a quiet, orderly life with someone who loved me and I loved back. Sometimes Boyd called me a stick-in-the-mud because I never wanted to go anywhere. He liked adventures. I actually walked up to Machu Picchu because of him. Trained for a year to do it."

Finding nothing to say and without waiting for an invitation, Robin refilled her iced tea and walked out onto the back patio and sat on a bright blue cushioned chaise.

The sun had tipped behind the mountains but the air was still hot. She closed her eyes. Somewhere in the complex children still laughed and splashed, and a radio played what might have been an old Jacky Jones hit. After a few moments, she felt tears behind her eyes and for once she didn't fight them, let them slip onto her cheeks, let them fall.

Sounds through the screen door told her that her father was working in the kitchen, making a meal. In a little while he would bring a tray and put it beside her chaise. He would pull up a chair and sit, not too far from her. Eventually, she would take a chance, reach out, and he would take her hand and hold it and not let go.

Chapter 27

Django told Madora where to drive and she did as she was told. Not because she believed in his fantasy but because she knew that without his confidence to guide her, she would still be standing in the trailer staring down at Willis's body while Linda yelled and Foo barked and the crows in the trees screamed their story. Now, more than three hours after leaving Arroyo, she was driving the Tahoe in the middle of Los Angeles traffic while Django fiddled with the car radio. He couldn't find a station that satisfied him. When he wasn't doing that, he talked and talked and talked.

"Lucky we're not on 15. There's a mega pileup near Escondido." He switched the radio from FM to AM and back to FM, found an oldies station, and relaxed a moment. "We might hear my dad."

Madora tried not to think.

Once she'd been driving thirty minutes or so, she felt comfortable behind the wheel of the Tahoe and remembered Willis telling her that once you learned to drive, you never forgot how. On the 405, the big half-circle freeway around downtown LA, they traveled in the carpool lane and she felt safe and literally above it all in the SUV's high cab. Django kept saying that they were "making good time," as if he had driven on this highway fifty times before. And maybe he had. Madora wondered if she would ever discover the nugget of truth that lay at the heart of his fantasies about Beverly Hills and Huck and flying in private planes. Occasionally she saw a cop car and a tide of nausea rose in her. Django said it was too soon for them to be looking for the Tahoe. He had called the sheriff as they crossed through Camp Pendleton, north of San Diego County. He told them where Linda was, behind the Arroyo Elementary School, and then threw Willis's cell phone into a muddy ditch at the side of the road. He said it would take them a few hours to find Willis and get enough details to be on the lookout for the Tahoe. How he came up with that time frame, she had no idea.

Madora wished she could figure out if leaving Willis in the trailer was the smartest, or stupidest, thing she'd ever done.

"Django, stop playing with the radio. You're making me nervous." Foo tried to snuggle onto her lap and she shoved him off.

North of Sunset, she maneuvered her way across six lanes of traffic and took the 101 exit to Ventura. Now they were heading north along the ocean.

"It'd be faster if we took the 5," Django said, "but that's the way they'll expect us to go. We'll take our time this way and just look ordinary, like a family."

Some family: a girl and a kid and a dog in a dirty black SUV with a bent-up rear license plate. Madora didn't know if she should laugh or cry.

They stopped to use the bathrooms at a Denny's restaurant, and Madora spent a dollar on a Snickers bar, leaving her with a total of seventy cents in her wallet. She had seen Django shove an apple-sized wad of bills in the glove compartment. She did not ask him where he'd gotten the money, knowing he would tell one of his whoppers. She thought he had probably stolen it from his aunt, which made her sorry. She had seemed like a nice woman. They were past Santa Barbara, well out of LA, when the sun began to set; and the shield of brilliance reflected on the water gave her a headache.

"I've gotta stop for a while," she said and turned off the road around Gaviota. She drove under the freeway and along a narrow road to where half a dozen vehicles were parked.

"Surfers," Django said. "Let's go down on the beach. Foo needs to run around."

At the edge of the sand they removed their shoes and tucked them out of the way behind a tussock. The breeze off the water, stiff and chilly, blew Madora's hair back from her face, and she faced directly into it. She almost believed that if she stayed that way long enough, the wind would blow all the confusion and contradiction out of her head, and she would be able to take charge of her life instead of trusting Django.

It didn't happen. They got back in the car and drove on and she was no more sure of herself than before the wind blew. She began to talk because it was easier than thinking.

"Willis took me to the beach once. If you go way down near the border there's a long, wide beach, a couple of miles, I guess. We walked almost to Mexico, I think." Behind them, the tide had come in and filled up their footprints so that when they walked back, there was no sign that they had ever walked that way before. "We only went that one time. Willis didn't like the sand. He said it was just another kind of dirt and why would anyone want to walk barefoot in the dirt."

That afternoon was one of the few occasions when Willis ever told her anything about his family. His mother. She had been a fastidious housekeeper and scrupulous about such things as clean clothes and frequent baths. In the heat of the summer Willis had been told to shower twice and sometimes three times a day. It seemed ridiculous to Madora. She laughed and Willis took offense as if she had insulted his family or his mother.

Thinking about it as she drove through the gently rolling coastal mountains, she was struck by how little she knew for sure about Willis's life before the night they met. She had never thought of him as particularly secretive, but now she realized he must have consciously hidden things from her. She would never know. Whatever happened in the future, she and Willis were no longer a couple. The waves were coming across the sand, washing away their footprints.

If Madora had been alone, she would have pulled the car off the road and sobbed into her hands. Instead, she asked Django a question, knowing he would tell her more than she wanted to know and that when he stopped talking the moment of tears would be behind her.

"How much farther is this place?" *Los Gatos.*

"Are you sleepy? Maybe we should stop for coffee in Santa Maria."

"I'm just asking."

"I don't know. Maybe five hours." He described the route they were taking up 101 through San Luis Obispo and Paso Robles to San Jose.

"Are the cops looking for us yet?"

For once Django admitted that he did not know. "It depends on how long it takes them to find the trailer."

He said that by now his aunt would have reported him missing, and sooner or later the cops would link her to Willis. Linda must be in custody by now and would waste no time blurting out the story of her captivity and the baby, and she would say that Willis had stolen him.

Madora thought about the baby boy and his proud parents. She thought of the clothes they had bought him. The car seat and the crib and the stroller. If Linda decided she wanted the baby back, they would have no legal right to him. More than anything else, even her own safety, Madora wanted him to have a happy life.

Django figured that eventually the sheriff's people would find the trailer and Willis and see the unmade bed and the other rough furnishings. They would know that everything Linda said was true.

"Do you think Willis will confess right off, tell them everything?" Django asked.

"No." At first he would refuse to speak. Madora knew how proudly stubborn he could be when he was convinced that he was right. But once he began to talk he would explain over and over that he had been helping Linda, giving her a second chance. He would want the police to admire what he had done.

"Your aunt'll figure out we're together," she said. "By now she's probably scared blue, calling the police and all. Linda will say I was with you. A boy. Your aunt'll remember my name." It would all come together, like the center of a bull's-eye.

Django slumped down in the passenger seat and for a while he was quiet. Madora knew he was thinking about what they had done.

He said, "We've got to get to Huck's. Once we're there, we'll be okay. He'll take care of things."

Madora looked at him with a mix of wonderment and disgust. "When're you going to give up? When are you going to stop lying?"

"It's true; you'll see. My brother'll tell you—"

"You said he was your stepbrother!"

"My *half* brother. Huck. Me and him have the same dad. Had. And he's rich, way richer than anyone. He'll get a lawyer and I'll call Mr. Guerin…"

Madora leaned forward and gently banged her forehead against the steering wheel.

"Hey! Watch the road. What're you doing?"

"I'm trying to knock some sense into my head."

"Just trust me."

When this was over, she would never trust anyone again, but now…she did not see that she had any alternative.

After another long period of silence, she asked, "Are you sure I didn't kill him?"

"He's got a concussion; that's all."

"Like brain damage?"

"If we're lucky he won't remember his own name, but he's okay. I told you, Madora. He was starting to wake up when I locked the door. He's just going to have a headache."

"I'm going to jail. I know it."

"Huck and Mr. Guerin'll get you a lawyer, the best."

"Oh, great, I only go to jail for ten years, not twenty? Not life?"

"You didn't do anything wrong. Not much anyway. You were, like, brainwashed."

"What's that mean?"

"It means Willis said he was helping Linda. He said it

over and over and over and you got so you believed him. That's brainwashing. Have you ever heard of Patty Hearst?"

Did Django ever get sick of being the smartest kid on the planet?

"She was this really rich girl who got kidnapped by the Symbionese Liberation Army. My friend Roid did a report on her."

"She got kidnapped by a whole army? How do you know that?"

"Not a real army. Just a bunch of people who wanted to overthrow the government."

Madora decided to believe him. The alternative, that everything out of his mouth was a lie, was too much to endure and made her want to drive the Tahoe into the side of a hill.

"I fed her and washed her." She thought of the many days she had looked straight at Linda's tethered ankle and swept around it. The mornings when she had hauled in warm water and made sure Linda washed herself. All the meals she had carried from the kitchen to the trailer. Detail by detail and day by day, she remembered it all and was awash in guilt and remorse.

She kept her eyes fixed on the busy highway but she felt Django looking at her. She did not have to see his expression to know that he agreed. She had done something terrible.

"Why did you do it?" he asked.

"You said I was brainwashed."

"But when it was happening, why did you think you were doing it?"

She had loved Willis and believed in him and that without him, she would be lost. And he needed her too.

"I thought he'd kill himself if I gave up on him. Like my dad did."

In Santa Maria they stopped for gas and Madora bought coffee and a package of white powdered doughnuts. They stayed off the highway and drove west on a narrow road that cut through the middle of hundreds of acres of deep green vegetable fields. Foo whimpered for attention, and Django let him lie on his lap. Madora gave the dog one of the doughnuts. They listened to the radio and Django told a circuitous story of Jett Jones and the Dark Entity.

"Can you just shut up?" Madora couldn't take anymore. "Can't you for a few hours stop making up stories? Jett Jones and all that shit; none of it's real. Get it? It's just stories. And your brother? He's not rich; he's some ordinary guy. Stop pretending. He's probably a drunk or a needle freak. We'll get up there and he'll be living in a trailer and the only lawyer he'll know is the one got him off a DUI."

Django gave her a dirty look, which Madora took to mean that her criticism had struck home; and after that, for many miles, he stared straight ahead. Foo snored with his head tucked under one end of the seat belt. In the quiet dark they passed through towns Madora had never heard of, and on either side of the two-lane road fields of vegetables stretched by. Back on 101, the Tahoe's headlights illuminated the name of a winery or tourist attraction. A motel sign made her yawn but she guessed that if she went to bed she would stare at the ceiling, thinking and worrying and stabbing herself with guilt, so she might as well be driving.

It was midnight and she had a buzzing headache behind her eyes. She did not want to think about Willis, about the mess left behind and the emptiness ahead. The quiet was full of too many possibilities.

"Okayokay," she said, "I'm sorry I was mean."

Django made a noncommittal sound.

"Just so you know, it's hard driving on a road like this. It's way tense with all the cars coming at us."

"So? You oughta be glad we're not on the 5."

He fiddled with the radio again, picking up the voice of a man, reading from the Bible, and two other men arguing politics. He turned it off.

"Do you wish you were still back there with him?" he asked. "Is that what you want?"

She wanted the baby to stay with the couple who paid for him. For herself, she wanted not to be afraid that she had killed Willis or brain damaged him or that the police would find and arrest her and send her to jail. She never wanted her mother to know what she had done. And she did not want to be scared of what could happen in the next five minutes on this road that seemed in the pitch blackness to become both faster and narrower. The hours passed and her nerve threads stretched until they were like the

269

vibrating strings of a musical instrument. She could not stand another minute of it and pulled off the highway in King City. In the parking lot of a Quality Inn, she opened the car and Foo bounded out and immediately relieved himself. Madora began walking the perimeter. Django hurried with her and had the good sense not to talk. Overhead the sky was clear and full of stars. Foo nosed around in the bushes at the edge of the parking lot but never wandered too far off.

Although Linda would be found by the police eventually, unharmed and obviously healthy, the newspapers and television would surely say that Willis was a demon and a monster. Madora's name would be part of the story and people would say the same about her, adding *stupid* as well. Her mother would hang her head in shame. Madora tried to remember why she had let Willis bring Linda into their lives in the first place. He kept saying that they were giving her a second chance, rescuing her the way Madora had once been lifted from the unlucky downward spiral that was her life and set on a new path. Willis said it over and over, and she had believed him. Hearing an assertion repeated was not, by itself, reason to believe, and yet she had done so and even helped him. She wondered if *brainwashing* was a word Django had made up.

They drove through miles of rolling empty land, the night sky dotted with plane lights and occasional stars and off in the distance the glow of a town.

Was it possible to go from being one kind of person to a

completely different person in the space of just a few days? That's what seemed to have happened to Madora. She had loved Willis and wanted to be with him for the rest of her life. Now the thought of him and of what they had done together filled her with horror. It seemed like Django must have gotten the brainwashing thing backwards. To Madora it meant clearing out and cleansing. That was what seemed to be happening to her now. When had it begun? Holding the baby? The night Willis killed the rabbit? After those experiences, her thinking had begun to change. And then Willis had hurt her, and after that she saw him the way he was.

But like an old-fashioned vinyl record that jumped back and repeated the same word or phrase, she kept trying to understand why it had happened in the first place. Why had she made Willis the center of her life, her guide and support? The question rankled, and no matter how intently she worked to distract herself—counting backwards by threes, making words from the names of towns like Guadalupe and Atascadero—*why, why, why* interrupted her concentration. She realized she might never know the answer completely. What she had done was unforgivable; that much was as plain as daylight.

The Santa Cruz Mountains lay to the left and the sun was coming up through the tinted window on the passenger side, warming the Tahoe's interior with the smells of stale coffee and panting dog. In San Jose they were caught in morning rush hour but Highway 17 going west toward the mountains was easy driving. They took the Saratoga Avenue exit into Los Gatos. It was bordered in pink oleander bushes and the plants in the landscaped center strip had been carefully clipped and mulched. A *rich-looking town*, Madora thought. So maybe Huckleberry Jones wasn't dead broke.

Django consulted the GPS on his cell phone and told her where to turn, right and left along streets without sidewalks, streets with tall, thick trees and houses behind gates and walls. At a narrow road he said, "Turn here! Turn now!"

Gum Tree Lane curved up and around a hill for almost a mile. Near the top, the clear, crisp view was of Los Gatos and the whole Santa Clara Valley from the Santa Cruz Mountains across to the foothills in the east. Madora had never seen so many streets and buildings and wanted to turn the Tahoe around and drive down into the crowded valley and get lost there.

"Don't stop." Django was out of his seat belt, bouncing. "We're almost there."

In the backseat Foo picked up on his excitement and began barking.

At the top of the hill there was a turnaround in front of a tall cream-colored stone wall with a wide oaken double gate. Madora put the car in park and dragged on the emergency brake.

"Now what?"

"Wait here." Django leaped from the car and Foo

bounded after him. He ran to where a metal box was set into the wall and pressed several keys and after a moment the gate swung open.

With Foo beside him, Django ran through the gate, gesturing for Madora to follow. Between fearsome cactus gardens, lethal with thorns, and mounds of scarlet bougainvillea, the road narrowed, becoming wide enough for only one vehicle, and there were traffic bumps every few yards. Slowly it was dawning on Madora that all the stories Django had told her were true.

Ahead another wall loomed and another gate, this one constructed of metal bars and ornate curlicues. Through it Madora could see the shape of a house and cars behind banks of shrubs and trees. A man was coming toward them.

"Hey, Junior," Django called, waving. "It's me!"

He ran back to Madora and stuck his head in the car window.

"That's Junior. He's one of Huck's bodyguards. Remember? I told you about him?"

Junior was the biggest man she had ever seen. He wore a T-shirt that fit close to his skin, and his forearms were covered with tattoos. She remembered Jammer sitting cross-legged on the floor of the party house, his gold tooth and the scar like a notch cut into his hairline. Reflected in the rearview mirror, the first gate was far behind her, the driveway narrower and the gardens on either side, barbed and thorned and deadly. All someone had to do was push a button and the first gate would close, trapping her, locking her in.

"Hey, kid," Junior said. "How'd you get here?"

"My friend brought me. Where's Huck?"

As Madora watched, Junior put his hand in his pocket. "China, Djang."

Junior raised his arm and pointed something the size of a phone. Madora waited for the iron gate ahead to open.

It's true. Everything. All of it's true.

But the second gate would not open until the first closed. It was a security thing. Madora thought of police and guns and prison, and she knew without seeing it that police cars were parked around behind the bank of trees and shrubs.

She jammed the Tahoe into reverse. Django yelled and ran toward the car but she didn't stop and made it through the closing gate with only a second to spare, into the turn-around and down the hill.

Chapter 28

Two Years Later

On the day Robin had returned from visiting her father she had been irritated to discover that though it was almost dark, Django was not at home and his bike was gone. He was off riding somewhere, she supposed, and had lost track of time, but he would be home before nine. She had known she would have to tear into him then for disobeying her. He would say that he was safe in the dark because his bike had front and back lights and reflectors on every surface where they would stick. She would have to ground him; she supposed that was what a good guardian would do.

Later, when she realized he was not coming back, she had felt guilty for taking his tardiness so casually. She had been happy to have time alone to think. It would take her the rest of her life to absorb what she had learned from her father.

She made a large gin and tonic and took it out onto the patio behind the house. The drip hoses had been on that afternoon and the soil in the planters near the house where she grew marigolds and petunias every summer smelled sweet and damp. It was a smell she associated with summer as much as the scent of the flowers themselves.

She needed the time alone and had actually thought, *Thank God Django's not here. I couldn't deal with him now.*

The summer after their father left them, their mother had enlisted Robin and Caro in the huge task of tearing out the front lawn, digging up the sod and working in yards of new soil purchased from Reiner's Nursery. Her mother had painted the house herself, a bright yellow with blindingly white trim, as if she wanted to announce to the neighbors that despite what they might think, she did not need their sympathy. That summer and every summer until she sold the house and moved south to be near Robin, she had planted a vast cottage garden in the front, clusters of common annuals like black-eyed Susan and coneflower, cupflower and nasturtiums and cosmos and rudbeckia. At the height of summer, passersby sometimes stopped their cars to take photos of the yard. Robin remembered her mother standing at the picture window, watching the cars slow as they drove by, a look of stubborn satisfaction on her face.

If the people in the neighborhood and driving by had known how she lied and connived, how she had carved her pound of flesh from Robin's heart, the house with the flowers would have been notorious.

Caro, Nola, Frank. They had all conspired to keep the secret from Robin. She had gone through her life blaming herself for her father's abandonment, believing she had done something wrong or not been good enough, while Caro, Nola, and Frank knew the truth. Any one of them could have told her the truth, but each had what seemed to them a *good reason* not to. Even Caro had been drawn into the cruel compact Nola had forced on their father in exchange for his freedom. Robin did not know what to think now, what to feel except empty. Cavernous.

At nine thirty, she had finally called the sheriff's office, and in the early hours of the morning, the pieces of the story began to come together. Linda had been found staggering out from behind the Arroyo Elementary School dragging thirty feet of wire rope. She told a story of abduction and a long captivity. She talked about Madora and a boy who seemed to know a lot about everything. He had a name she could not remember. Linda did not know what kind of car they were driving but it seemed to be an SUV and she thought it was black. That was enough for an Amber Alert. Many hours later sheriff's deputies found the house on Red Rock Road and Willis locked inside the trailer. He connected Django to the case and then Robin.

Early the next morning she had told the officers where she thought Django and Madora were going and they contacted the police department in Los Gatos.

In August Robin and Django began a seven-month stay in Tampa, Florida. It was odd, Robin thought, looking back, that what neither of them had really wanted turned out to be a good move after all, the best thing they could have done. In a new environment where neither of them felt at home, they kept each other company and had become friends. His spirit of adventure spurred (and sometimes shamed) Robin to try new things. Scuba diving scared her half to death but she liked rock climbing and bicycling. In Florida, where almost everyone seemed to be in transit between one life and another, there was nothing to remind either of them of Caro or the past. Django began to heal, and Robin, without really trying, began to reinvent herself, peeling off the layers of protection one by one. In the Tampa office of Conway, Carroll, and Hyde she made friends and was encouraged to attend law school.

They returned to Arroyo after seven months away and the house she had once loved felt fussy and dull. One morning she picked up the phone, called a Realtor, and put it on the market. She took the LSAT and, as the attorneys at Conway, Carroll, and Hyde had known would happen, she scored high. She enrolled in a local law school and she and Django moved to a condominium in the urban center of San Diego, only three blocks from Petco Park, where on summer evenings they could sit on the balcony and watch baseball through binoculars. She surprised herself by becoming quite a Padres fan.

Django was a serious piano student and attended a private school where he had a small, tight circle of friends who envied him for living downtown and often used the condo

278

as home base. Robin had stopped being surprised when stray teenagers appeared at the breakfast table. Sometimes she visited her mother, who, since her successful back surgery, had become a world traveler, taking off for the South Pole or Ulan Bator and returning to her town house only long enough to wash her clothes and repack her bag. Seeing her once or twice a year was all Robin could manage.

She had never told her mother that she knew about the bargain struck long ago, the separation that was really a divorce. She had many reasons for her silence, but the basement truth was that Robin knew if she once started, the eruption of anger and hurt might never stop. She didn't want that. Instead of taking it out on her mother, she vented to Dr. Rose, a skillful therapist who seemed willing to stand in for Nola when necessary.

Conversations with her father were almost always stilted and artificial, as each tried to act as if theirs was an ordinary father-daughter relationship. Though she understood why he had turned his back on her, from time to time the memory of rejection flared up, a laceration that never healed completely. Perhaps, if she could discover the courage to confront her mother, the wound might close forever; but the truth was, as she had discovered in therapy, she was a little afraid of Nola. Confrontation with a woman who could build a life based on a lie and use her daughter's happiness as a bargaining chip would be an ugly thing.

In her bedroom Robin kept several framed photos of Caro she'd brought back from the house in Beverly Hills.

She often looked at the one taken the day she and Caro went horseback riding. They had been chosen for an excursion sponsored by Holy Rosary Academy to a ranch off Highway 1, in the hills near San Simeon. Eighteen girls wearing trousers under their blue and red academy tunics milled around the ranch, standing and sitting on the fence rails. It came time to ride, and Robin was afraid of her horse, a soft-eyed, sway-backed mare named Chloe. Her confusion about how to place her foot in the stirrup and hold the reins, her fear of being up high and the discomfort of sitting on the hard leather saddle with her legs stretched wide around the old mare's midsection, the heat of the afternoon, and the dust all conspired to make her unhappy. She turned to Caro for understanding and was just in time to see her sister swing into the saddle and take off around the turnout ring, cantering a figure eight.

For years their father had been taking Caro to riding lessons in Griffith Park. It was a very Caro moment and Robin did not blame her sister for it. She didn't blame her for any of it.

Chapter 29

Sometimes Django still had a Pavlovian reaction to the ringing telephone. Say he was in the kitchen pouring a bowl of cereal and his cell phone rang. He'd think: *Mom.*

For the last year he had been seeing a psychologist, Dr. Belknap. She and Dr. Rose shared an office but Dr. Bee specialized in teenagers. Half the kids Django knew had shrinks. Dr. Bee said Django was depressed—like this was a flash from outer space. A bunch of his friends were on meds for ADD or they were bipolar or whatever. It seemed to Django that it just went along with being alive. He could take meds too if he wanted, but he preferred to go without. He told Dr. Bee that after everything he had been through, he would probably be depressed for the rest of his life; he might as well get used to it. He wasn't suicidal or anything close. Just flatline.

Probably music kept him from going crazy. It set him free.

Lately he'd begun composing—trying to, anyway. He

thought of his father spending hours in his music room playing the same few bars over and over, changing the bass line, the beat, the key. Ira said when Django wrote something good enough he would help him get it recorded. Alone in the condo, fiddling on the piano, he talked to his father as if he were sitting somewhere just out of sight, listening. Maybe he was.

Dr. Bee said he wasn't crazy. Nowhere near.

Django also talked to Foo.

His aunt hadn't been so hot on the idea of a dog, especially a pit bull with a head like a boulder; but then Foo wagged his tail and panted dog breath in her face and she gave in. He was the best friend Django had.

If it weren't for the piano and Foo, he'd wig out.

During one of his sessions with Dr. Bee he had talked about how Foo seemed to understand him, how he felt safer and not so depressed when Foo was around. This led to explaining where the dog came from. Dr. Bee was the only person Django had ever told the whole story of Madora. Her and Mr. Guerin. The police knew a lot of what happened because they practically gave him the third degree to get it out of him, but Mr. Guerin stayed with him the whole time so it wasn't so bad.

He wondered where Madora had gone that day she backed out of the driveway and roared down Gum Tree Lane. To Sacramento probably, but he never let on to the cops. Eventually they had found her mother on their own. Django had watched her interviewed on television, and from the way she was crying, he didn't need to be an empath to know she was scared and worried about her daughter and telling the truth when she said she had never seen or heard from her. It was like Madora had dropped off the edge of the world. Django hoped she was safe and not hooked up with another pervo. No one had ever mentioned the roll of cash in the Tahoe's glove compartment, so he hoped that meant Madora had taken it when she dumped the car. For a few months the sheriff made a big deal about finding her, but eventually they lost interest. They had Willis, and he was the sleazebag they wanted.

Django had never regretted driving up to Huck's that day, leaving Willis locked in the trailer and Linda back behind the elementary school. For a while he was in a world of trouble, but once he and Aunt Robin got to Tampa, it was like they had moved to another planet. He just wished he knew if Madora was safe. He had asked Mr. Guerin to spend some of his trust money looking for her and he said he would when Django graduated from high school. Dr. Bee said Madora had been as much a prisoner as Linda. She got that right. He wished his mother were around to talk to. She liked philosophical conversations. Aunt Robin preferred facts and was going to make a great lawyer.

Basically, Django's life was turning out okay. His new school was okay and he got along with Aunt Robin okay. Okay-okay-okay, but nothing great, except the piano and Foo. They were stellar. Huck too. Django spent vacation time with him. They went up to Canada to a private lake and fished every day, which got sort of boring after a week. But Huck listened when Django talked about music, and his friends were cool. They treated Django like one of the guys and let him drink beer. Another time they went for a cruise in the Caribbean on a big sailboat. More fishing, but he got to scuba, which was awesome. Otherwise, sailing was boring, but okay.

Dr. Bee said he should be patient; he wouldn't always feel flatline. He didn't believe her but he didn't disbelieve her either. He was just blah about the future and she said that was fine, take it one day at a time.

His idea was that he was a prisoner. Like Linda in the trailer he was locked into missing his mother and father and he was never going to be happy until he found the key and got out. Dr. Bee said there wasn't a key. She told him grief was a process, like learning to play the piano and practicing scales a million times a week, and he just had to trust the process. It sounded like shrink bullcrap to him, but he didn't have any better answer so he pretended to believe she knew what she was talking about. Sometimes he would go along and start to feel better and then the phone would ring and he would wait to hear his mother's voice. Instead he would hear the doors slam shut and the locks click and everything would start all over.

Chapter 30

Two years later, all Madora had to do was close her eyes, think about her escape from between the double gates, and her whole body remembered how it felt to speed down Gum Tree Lane, careening around corners so fast she scared herself. But what had scared her even more that day was the big man Django called Junior, and the cop cars she was sure lay in wait for her behind the bushes and trees. Her leg shook and jerked as she braked to avoid a ground squirrel's dash across the road; she overcompensated on the next curve and heard the tattoo of gravel hitting the Tahoe's hubcaps. At the bottom of the hill she turned right because it was faster than waiting for a green light; and at the next light, a mile farther on, she turned right again. A city block later, a sign had told her she was on Bascom Avenue, eleven miles from San Jose.

She could not tell where the actual city began. She drove through blocks of houses and apartment buildings, office complexes surrounded by grass and gardens, more houses, and then strip malls and vast parking lots. The surface street expanded to three lanes each way with a wide green and floral center strip, narrowed again, and then widened once more. Almost every intersection had a bank of lights and an array of confusing signs.

Madora's chest ached from holding her breath. Her shoulders burned with tension.

She had ditched the Tahoe in a mall parking lot and waited forty minutes for a city bus that stopped not far from the Greyhound station. In her purse she carried the eight hundred and seventy-two dollars Django had left in the glove compartment. She had not had much experience with money, and at first she felt rich with so much cash in her pocket, enough to last for weeks, she thought. But a one-way ticket to Sacramento cost more than twenty-five dollars, and lunch—a hamburger with stale fries and gluey cheddar cheese—cost five. She had seen right away that her nest egg would not last long.

Madora sat on a bench outside the bus depot, and for a little while her thoughts had drifted as she watched the busy street; but gradually they focused, and she began to assess the facts of her situation. By now the sheriff's department was looking for her and maybe cops too. Tomorrow or next week uniformed officers would knock on Rachel's door and pepper her with questions. If she was still married, her husband might say she had to choose between Madora and him. Madora did not want her to have to make that choice, and she knew that the most loving thing she could do was stay away from Sacramento.

Without giving it great thought, Madora adapted her plans from those of a girl going home to her mother to those of a girl on the run.

Two blocks from the bus station, the manager of a modest hotel catering to low-budget travelers was glad to hire Madora for cash at slightly less than minimum wage, no questions asked. No social security number, no driver's license. She told him her name was Marilyn and he believed her. The hotel company owned a motel about three miles away where she could afford to rent a room by the week.

For the next two years she had walked to and from work every day in all kinds of weather, setting out before sunup, getting home after dark. As she walked west in the morning, the sun rose and warmed her back as it had when she sat on her boulder at the end of Red Rock Road.

One day she met a Vietnam vet called Sarge by the people on the block. He and his dog, a bowlegged brindle pit bull named Pokey, lived behind a car repair shop and were the unofficial night watchmen for the area. On her way to work, Madora stopped at a Jack in the Box most mornings and bought the dog a hamburger. She was making a deal with God. If she took care of Pokey, Django would take care of Foo.

She lived alone and so quietly that after two years none

of her neighbors knew her last name, and though she was often too tired at the end of the day to do more than strip to her bra and panties and climb into bed, she did not pine for her old life. But she did miss Foo. If she had time in the morning she sometimes sat beside Pokey on the curb and laid her arm across his muscled shoulders, and he turned his head and licked her ear. Sarge kept a long-running conversation going with himself. It did not seem odd to him that Madora talked to Pokey like a friend.

Once she had lived in Rachel's house, following Rachel's rules. Then she lived in Willis's house, and he had another set of rules. Living alone, she made her own rules. She started work on time and, when she could, earned extra money staying late or helping in the kitchen of the all-day breakfast joint next door. She ate three meals a day and never watched television after nine p.m. because to do her job, she needed a good night's sleep. Her life in San Jose was a wide spot in the road, not a dead end. A resting place. A time-out.

She kept her room at the motel spotless, and despite the worn carpet and burn marks on the dresser, it had the advantage of being her own, with a key and a dead bolt that locked on the inside. Her work at the hotel was physically exhausting, but she was young and strong and smart enough to watch and learn the tricks of the older women who had been cleaning all their lives. She wore a mask and gloves and covered her hair with a plastic shower cap. The hotel was a pass-through for students and underfunded tourists, not an affluent clientele that tossed around hundred-dollar bills; but coins and small-denomination bills were ordinary finds on the closet floor and between the chair cushions. The other maids told her she could keep found money; no one expected her to give it back. She received occasional tips and put away all she could, hidden in an envelope taped flat to the underside of the table next to her bed.

Cleaning rooms, walking to and from the hotel, standing in line at the corner market, and talking to Pokey: her life had taken shape, and the pattern of the weeks became months and then years. On her day off she liked to go to the movies and sit near the back. Sometimes she moved around the theater, changing her seat three or four times during the feature, just because she could. She visited the library and read the paper. For a while, Willis was front-page news.

Months after he was sentenced to fifteen years in prison, she did not quite believe that bars would hold him. She remembered how easily he had seduced and conned her and she was sure he would scheme a way to escape punishment. She had an uneasy sense that he might suddenly leap at her from behind a Dumpster or break into her room. Occasionally she worked for tips only at a bar a few blocks from the hotel. One Saturday night when the place was packed and rowdy, a man approached her who was so like Willis that she dashed for the back room, crashing into another server with a tray of beers balanced on her palm.

A librarian taught Madora how to use the Internet and she read the transcript of the trial. The press and government attorneys called Willis the word Django had taught her: *sociopath*. Every online article had pages of comments from readers, and no one seemed to believe that he had not raped Linda though she swore he had never touched her that way. Regardless, they all thought he was a monster.

In a long feature article Madora learned about Willis's sister, Daphne. After reading it she had put her head down and cried until the librarian came over and asked if she was feeling ill. She had never heard of Daphne, never even knew he had a sister; and it was a betrayal that Willis talked about her to a reporter, someone he barely knew. But the story helped her make sense of him and his compulsion to save girls who lived marginal lives. Madora knew that he had taken advantage of her youth and innocence, but she never thought of him as a monster.

She had been alone and frightened when he found her, teetering on the edge of a precipice. He never said he was her guardian angel. He just held out his hand and she took it.

Two years passed in this way and she was not unhappy. Gradually and without realizing it, she prepared for the next and necessary stage of her life.

Clarity came to her one morning as she was cleaning an unpleasant mess left behind by a group of backpackers: beer cans and spilled wine, food wrappers, vomit in the bathroom. It was not the worst she had seen, but it amazed her that people could make such a wreck of their rooms and then walk away, leaving it for her to clean up. As she stood in the doorway wondering where to begin her work, she realized that she had done the same thing when she fled San Diego with Django, and then again, when she abandoned the Tahoe, called herself Marilyn, and walked into another life, leaving the mess of the old one for others to deal with. Now all her nights were restless and filled with troubled dreams that she knew would not end until she cleaned up after herself.

For the first time that she could ever remember, Madora made a plan for her life.

First, she would see her mother and tell her everything so that when the detectives and investigators came to question her again—as they were sure to do—Rachel would know the truth. She might not want to see her. Madora tried to prepare herself for that chance. She would beg for just five minutes to say that she had been very wrong to leave Yuma with Willis and foolish not to heed her mother's warnings. She wanted her to know that she loved her. An apology would just be words, but she wanted to say she was sorry for all the pain she knew she had brought into her life.

That conversation would be the hardest, and afterwards, Madora thought she could face anything.

In San Diego the police station was only a few blocks

from the bus depot; Madora had checked the address. She did not know what the police would say or do when she walked in off the street and confessed that she had been Willis Brock's accomplice. She had not taken Linda off the street herself, nor had she bought the generator and the padlock and devised the tether. But she was as guilty as Willis because she cooperated and supported him. Worse than any specific act was her silence through it all. She had not spoken up until after the baby was born. That was the mess she had made and wanted to clean up.

A little more than two years after coming to San Jose, Madora gave notice to her employer, who offered her a raise if she would stay, packed her belongings, and walked to the bus station. On the way she stopped to say good-bye to Pokey and Sarge, and the old guy's bleary eyes teared up when she kissed his cheek. They were the only friends she said good-bye to.

It was a dry, hot day in Sacramento, not a day to be walking on a sidewalk that fried through the soles of her sandals, but Madora had a swing in her step anyway. She turned right off Sixteenth Street onto D and spontane-ously sighed, grateful for the massive sycamores whose wide-leafed canopies stretched and met in the middle of the street, creating a tunnel of dappled shade. On a lawn a sprinkler circled, raining over the sidewalk in flagrant disregard for city water restrictions. She walked right into it and stood a minute, feeling as she had when she was a child, that God was in the blessing of water. A small girl watched her from the window and grinned, showing two gaping spaces in her teeth.

Be lucky, Madora thought and waved and walked on.

Making beds, cleaning tubs and toilets, and pushing an old commercial Hoover six days a week: for two years Madora had done hard physical labor and lost the weight she had gained living with Willis. Her legs were strong from walking to and from the hotel, and despite the heat she moved quickly down D Street, faster than she wanted to. She almost did not want to find her mother's house.

Looking over his fence, a man admired the pretty girl in a turquoise T-shirt, wet and clinging, striding along with purpose. He did not see when, two blocks on, her pace slowed. She had brought her courage with her to Sacramento, but like a pond in July, it had shrunk to a puddle.

She had learned that lives change, turn around, go up one hill and down another; they ended in a cul-de-sac or staring down a long highway. Some disappeared over a cliff. The compulsion to make amends had brought her to Sacramento and would send her south to San Diego in a few hours. She had already bought her ticket. Whatever happened there would mark the end of one life and the beginning of a new one. She would finally be free.

The houses on D Street were old and each was unique. A few had additions and fancy landscaping, but for the most part the tidy homey residences showed their years. It was garbage pickup day. Black and blue and green barrels butted up against the curb in front of every house. The black and blue gaped open and empty, but the green barrels crammed with yard clippings awaited the automated truck Madora heard groaning and clanking a few blocks away.

A special sense keyed to her mother told Madora that Rachel and Peter Brooks had been happy on this street.

She scanned the house numbers and realized that she was on the wrong side of the street. She could cross; there was no traffic; but the street seemed more like a moat than a strip of asphalt. Behind her a curtain moved; a blind cracked half an inch. A round Chinese woman stepped onto her porch and stood snapping the rubber band around yesterday's rolled shopping news as her gaze followed Madora, who walked more slowly now. In one of the houses a phone rang and Madora had a crazy thought that up and down the street neighbors were calling each other, talking about her.

She felt sure that her mother had been happy on this street where the neighbors knew each other's histories, their griefs and disappointments as well as their triumphs. In the gutter a six-foot strip of red, white, and blue crepe paper was the last reminder of an Independence Day celebration. Madora saw in her imagination a long table set up on the sidewalk, laden with chili beans and fried chicken and potato salad, festooned with flags and patriotic bunting. A band comprised of neighborhood boys and girls gathered on a lawn and made happy noise until after dark. Madora knew all this without knowing it. She stopped, closed her eyes, and saw Rachel and Peter dancing in a driveway.

A trio of pugs barked at Madora and jumped against a chain-link fence.

She smiled at their ferocity.

Madora's plan for the future went beyond Sacramento and the police station in San Diego. When she could, she would get her high school diploma and then take a course in junior college that Django had told her about, one of the five hundred subjects he had yakked about as they drove north up Highway 101. Trained as a veterinary assistant, she would be around animals all day and good at that. The last step would come when her life was completely settled. Then she would try to find Django and thank him for what he had given her. He was only a boy, a kid. But what a boy, what a kid. And the last person who would ever have to rescue her.

Rachel's house had no fancy room addition, but the lawn was mowed, and under a window, bright-headed zinnias grew up from mounds of sweet alyssum. The house was freshly painted and a small porch finished off with a rail stretched across the front. The door was painted violet. Madora smiled because violet had always been her mother's favorite color. She imagined her laying on one coat after another until she got the perfect shade.

The door opened and a woman stepped off the porch and down the path, tossing her hair—gray!—back from her eyes. She was thin, barefoot, tanned. She grabbed the black trash bin with a hint of familiar fierceness, tilted it back onto its wheels, rolled it off the street, up the driveway, and behind a fence. A moment later she strode back onto the street and reached for the blue bin. The pugs yapped to get her attention. Rachel looked across the street.

"Quiet down," she said. "You know me."

Madora whispered, "Mommy," too softly to be heard.

But Rachel stared across the street at her. "Madora?" She stepped off the curb and Madora went to meet her.

Along D Street, in every front yard and at the same precise moment, the sprinklers—every one—clicked on and filled the air with light and sparkle. From every house Madora seemed to hear the voices of men and women and children, the sound of news on the radio and announcements on television; dogs barked and cats jumped up to a dozen windowsills; children ran down the hall and up the yard, calling for their parents to *come quick, come see.* Birds in their cages sang and crows in the tops of the sycamores sent the message up and down the street and over the hedges and fences.

"Rachel's girl is here. Madora has come home."

Questions for Discussion

- In the opening pages of *Little Girl Gone* we are introduced to Madora and we learn that her father committed suicide when she was a young adolescent. How did this affect Madora's emotional development? No one talked to her about his death; no one helped her to understand what happened. In what ways could she have been helped through the experience?

- Both Madora and Robin grew up without fathers. Why is a father important in a girl's life?

- Neither Madora nor Robin fully understood the circumstances of their fatherlessness. How much should children be told about what goes on in their family? Are secrets an unavoidable part of family life? Has there been a time in your life when a secret caused a family crisis?

- Django is a highly imaginative boy. What were the circumstances of his growing up that led to the development of his creative thinking? Does it empower or endanger him? Is there a point where imagination becomes a hindrance more than a help?

- Why does Madora love Willis? Does he love her? Can you understand her love for him?

- Why is Linda's baby important in Madora's maturation? What does the reader know about Madora because of her scene with the baby? And later the same day with Linda?

- At first glance the friendship between Madora and Django seems an unlikely match. What factors contributed to their strong bond? Have you ever had an unusual friend, someone who came to mean a lot to you?

- The theme of *Little Girl Gone* is captivity and all the different ways people can feel imprisoned. Linda is a literal captive, but what about Robin and her father?

- For Django, freedom is his half-brother's walled and gated home. Is there somewhere you have visited or lived that seemed to free you to be more completely self-expressed?

- When we read in headlines about girls held captive, it's natural to wonder about the people who cooperated in the crime. Can you understand why Madora lived as she did, helping Willis to keep Linda locked in the trailer? Was there any excuse for her behavior?

- Willis didn't physically hurt Linda. She wasn't sexually abused. According to Robin he was well liked by the old people at the retirement home. Was he actually a bad man? It might be an interesting exercise to try arguing both the yes and no position.

- Why was Foo an important character in the book?
- How did the setting—the house at the end of Red Rock Road, arid countryside—contribute to your experience of the story?
- How will Robin be changed by what she learned when she visited her father in Temecula?
- At the end of the book we learn that Madora intends to turn herself in to the San Diego police. Why does she choose to do this? What do you think will happen to her?
- What is the mood at the end of the book? Did you find it uplifting, confusing, or depressing? Or some other feeling?

Drusilla Campbell presents a

gripping story of three generations

of women who must overcome

a legacy of violence, secrecy,

and lies . . .

Please turn this page for
a preview of

THE GOOD SISTER

Chapter 1

San Diego, California
The State of California v. Simone Duran
March 2010

On the first day of Simone Duran's trial for the attempted murder of her children, the elements conspired to throw their worst at Southern California. Arctic storms that had all winter stalled or washed out north of Los Angeles chose the second week of March to break for the south and were now lined up, a phalanx of wind and rain stretching north into Alaska. In San Diego a timid sprinkle began after midnight, gathered force around dawn, and now, with a hard northwest wind behind it, deluged the city with a driving rain. Roxanne Callahan had lived in San Diego all her life and she'd never seen weather like this.

In the stuffy courtroom a draft found the nape of her neck, driving a shudder down her spine to the small of her back: she feared that if the temperature dropped just one degree she'd start shaking and wouldn't be able to stop. Behind her, someone in the gallery had a persistent, bronchial cough. Roxanne had a vision of germs floating like pollen on the air. She wondered if hostile people— the gawkers and jackals, the ghoulishly curious, the home-grown experts and lurid trial junkies—carried germs more virulent than those of friends and allies. Not that there were many well-wishers in the crowd. Most of the men and women in the courtroom represented the millions of people who hated Simone Duran; and if their germs were half as lethal as their thinking, Simone would be dead by dinnertime.

Roxanne and her brother-in-law, Johnny Duran, sat in the first row of the gallery, directly behind the defense table. As always Johnny was impeccably groomed and sleekly handsome; but new gray rimed his black hair, and there were lines engraved around his eyes and mouth that had not been there six months earlier. He was the owner and president of a multimillion-dollar construction company specializing in hotels and office complexes, a man with many friends, including the mayor and chief of police; but since the attempted murder of his children he had become reclusive, spending all his free time with his daughters. He and Roxanne had everything to say to each other and at the same time nothing. She knew the same question filled his mind as hers and each knew it was pointless to ask: what could or should they have done differently?

Following her arraignment on multiple counts of attempted murder, Simone had been sent to St. Anne's Psychiatric Hospital for ninety days' observation. Bail was set at a million dollars, and Johnny put the lake house up as collateral. He leased a condo on a canyon where Simone and their mother, Ellen Vadis, lived after her release from St. Anne's. Her bail had come with heavy restrictions. She was forbidden contact with her daughters and confined to the condo, tethered by an electronic ankle bracelet and permitted to leave only with her attorney on matters pertaining to the case and with her mother for meetings with her doctor.

Like Johnny, Roxanne visited Simone several times a week. These tense interludes did nothing to lift anyone's spirits as far as she could tell. They spent hours on the couch watching television, sometimes holding hands; and while Roxanne often talked about her life, her work, her friends, any subject that might help the illusion that they were sisters like other sisters, Simone rarely spoke. Sometimes she asked Roxanne to read to her from a book of fairy tales she'd had since childhood. Stories of dancing princesses and enchanted swans soothed Simone much as a lullaby might a baby; and more than once Roxanne had left her, covered by a cashmere throw, asleep on the couch with the book beside her. Lately she had begun to suck her thumb as she had when she was a child. Roxanne faced the truth: the old Simone, the silly girl with her secrets and demands, her narcissism, the manic highs and the

304

black holes where the meany-men lived, even her love, might be gone forever.

A medicine chest of pharmaceuticals taken morning and night kept her awake and put her to sleep, eased her down from mania toward catatonia and then half up again to something like normal balance. She took drugs that elevated her mood, focused her attention, flattened her enthusiasm, stifled her anxiety, curbed her imagination, cut back her paranoia, and put a plug in her curiosity. The atmosphere in the condo was almost unbearably artificial.

Across the nation newspapers, magazines, and blogs were filled with Simone stories passing as truth. Her picture was often on television screens, usually behind an outraged talking head. Sometimes it was the mug shot taken the day she was booked, occasionally one of the posed photos from the Judge Roy Price Dinner when she looked so beautiful but was dying inside. The radio blabmeisters could not stop ranting about her, about what a monster she was. Spinning know-it-alls jammed the call-in lines. Weekly articles in the supermarket tabloids claimed to know and tell the whole story.

The whole story! If Roxanne had had any sense of humor left she would have cackled at such a preposterous claim. Simone's story was also Roxanne's. And Ellen's and Johnny's. They were all of them responsible for what happened that September afternoon.

*   *   *

Roxanne's husband, Ty Callahan, had offered to put his work at the Salk Institute on hold so he could attend the trial with her, but she didn't want him there. He and her friend Elizabeth were links to the world of hopeful, optimistic, ordinary people. The courtroom would taint that.

The night before, Roxanne and Ty had eaten Chinese takeout; and afterward, while he read, she lay with her head on his lap searching for the blank space in her mind where repose hid. They went to bed early and made love with surprising urgency, as if time pressed in upon them, and before it was too late they had to establish their connection in the most basic way. Roxanne should have slept afterward; instead she got up and watched late-night infomercials for computer careers and miraculous skin products, finally falling asleep on the couch, where Ty found her in the morning with Chowder, their yellow Labrador, snoring on the floor beside her, a ball between his front paws.

"Don't look at me," she said, sitting up. "I'm a mess."

"You are." Ty handed her a mug of coffee, his smile breaking over her like sunlight. "The worst-looking woman I've seen this morning."

She rested her forehead against his chest and closed her eyes. "Tell me I don't have to do this today."

He drew her to him. "We'll get through it, Rox."

"But who'll we be? When it's over?"

"I guess we just have to wait and see."

"And you'll be here?"

"If I think about leaving, I'll come get you first."

In the courtroom she closed her eyes and pictured Ty with his postdocs gathered around him, the earnest young men and women who looked up to him in a way that Roxanne had found sweet and faintly amusing back when she could still laugh. She knew how her husband worked, the care he took and the careful notations he made in his lab notebooks in his precise draftsman's hand. With life falling apart and nothing certain from one day to the next, it was calming—a meditation of sorts—to think of Ty at work across the city in a lab overlooking the Pacific.

Attorney David Cabot and Simone entered the courtroom and took their places at the defense table. Cabot had been Johnny's first choice to defend Simone. Once the quarterback for the San Diego Chargers, he had not won many games but was widely admired for qualities of leadership and character. His win-loss statistics were much better in law than in football. He had made his name trying controversial cases, and Simone's was definitely that.

Simone, small and thin, her back as narrow as a child's, sat beside Cabot, conservatively dressed in a black-and-white wool dress with a matching jacket and serious shoes in which she could have hiked Cowles Mountain. In her ears she wore the silver-and-turquoise studs Johnny had given her when they became engaged. As intended, she looked mild and calm, too sweet to commit a crime worse than jaywalking.

Conversation in the gallery hushed as the jurors entered and took their seats. One, a college student, looked sideways at Simone; but the others directed their gazes across the courtroom to the wall of rain-beaten windows. Among the twelve there were two Hispanic women in their mid-twenties, one of them a college student; three men and a woman, all retired professionals; a Vietnamese manicurist; and one middle-aged black woman, the co-owner of a copy shop. Roxanne tried to see intelligence and tolerance and wisdom in their faces, but all she saw was an ordinary sampling of San Diego residents. For them to be a true jury of Simone's peers at least one should be a deep depressive, one extravagantly rich, and another pathologically helpless.

Just let them be good people, Roxanne prayed. Good and sensitive and clear-thinking. Let them be honest. Let them see into my sister and know that she is not a monster.